THE QUEEN'S TREASURE

John James Pitcairn

R. Austin Freeman

THE QUEEN'S TREASURE

By R. Austin Freeman & John J. Pitcairn
writing as
CLIFFORD ASHDOWN

*Edited & Introduced
by Norman Donaldson*

Frontispiece by William Dixon

OSWALD TRAIN: PUBLISHER
Philadelphia
1975

Copyright © 1975 by Winifred Mary Johns

All Rights Reserved

FIRST EDITION

Printed in the United States of America

CONTENTS

INTRODUCTION ix
1. A STRANGE LEGACY 15
2. IMPERSONATION 30
3. THE RUINED CHAPEL 41
4. AN UNWELCOME MEETING 55
5. QUESTIONS OF IDENTITY 68
6. A NEW ALLY 81
7. A TUDOR INTRIGUE 92
8. A WOMAN'S HEART 107
9. THE OLD MANOR HOUSE 115
10. SOME MIDNIGHT ADVENTURES 125
11. A FOOTPRINT 134
12. THE AMBUSCADE 142
13. A PLAN OF CAMPAIGN 151
14. A PIECE OF PARCHMENT 160
15. A MYSTERIOUS LETTER 172
16. A HARBOUR OF REFUGE 185
17. THE SECRET PASSAGE 195
18. THE QUEEN'S TREASURE 207
19. THE TRAP 219
20. THE RIVER ROAD 231

THE QUEEN'S TREASURE

THE QUEEN'S TREASURE

INTRODUCTION

FOR seventy years the manuscript of this adventure story has lain unpublished among the Pitcairn family papers. The title page bears the pseudonym "Clifford Ashdown," the disguise adopted jointly by R. Austin Freeman, who was presently to create the great scientific investigator Dr. Thorndyke, and John James Pitcairn, a lifelong prison medical officer. The collaboration was born around 1900, when Pitcairn found the semi-invalid Freeman (who had been discharged from the colonial service several years earlier after a bout with the deadly blackwater fever) a position as his assistant at Holloway Prison in north London.

Pitcairn's only child, Winifred Mary (Mrs. T. H. Johns), to whom Freeman is now but a dimly remembered nursery visitor, was told by her parents that Freeman disliked the mechanics of writing, while the creation of plots caused him no difficulty. Pitcairn, on the other hand, loved to scribble but could never think of anything to write about. The procedure therefore adopted was for Freeman to lay out the story's skeleton and for his colleague to develop it and write it out, after which Freeman would edit it for publication. In this way three series of short tales were created, all of which first appeared in *Cassell's Magazine* between 1902 and 1905: *The Adventures of Romney Pringle* (published in volume form by Ward, Lock in 1902); *The Further Adventures of Romney Pringle;* and *From a Surgeon's Diary*. The first of these was introduced to American readers in 1968 by Oswald Train; *The Further Adventures,* never issued as a book in England, was published by Train in 1969; and *From a Surgeon's Diary* is forthcoming.

The precise date of conception of *The Queen's Treasure* is unknown. Probably it was the last work of the partnership around 1905. By that time, Freeman was settled in Gravesend, thirty miles east of London on the south bank of the Thames, living rent-free in return for tutoring four children, and Pitcairn was medical officer at the newly founded institution for teenage offenders at Borstal, a few miles further east.[1] It was easy enough for the two friends to meet regularly and plan their stories, though Freeman by that time had already written at least one Thorndyke story, publication of which was delayed for several years.

Why the collaboration foundered is unclear. The break when it came was total; the two men seem never to have met again. Freeman avoided all reference to the Pitcairn partnership in later years—indeed, seemed unduly secretive about this and other details of his pre-Thorndyke years. The Pitcairn family's version of the break is that the partners fell out over a point in the editing. "J. J.," it seems, had obtained advice on a French phrase from a Madame Broquet, a friend of Mrs. Pitcairn whose

[1] For further details of the collaboration, see my *In Search of Dr. Thorndyke* (Bowling Green University Popular Press, Bowling Green, Ohio, 1971), especially Chapter III: "The Other Half of Clifford Ashdown." See also "Clifford Ashdown: A Retrospect" in *The Further Adventures of Romney Pringle* (Oswald Train, Philadelphia, 1969).

INTRODUCTION

name, incidentally, will be found attached to a male character in the present novel. Freeman saw fit to "correct" the phrase on the authority of a French lady acquaintance not further identified. That this alone could shipwreck a sound relationship seems doubtful. Divergent interests were already separating them; while Pitcairn labored over *The Queen's Treasure,* Freeman worked alone on his long Gold Coast romance, *The Golden Pool* (1905), and was of course distracted also by dreams of Thorndyke.

The Queen's Treasure reveals many Freemanian touches in its choice of subject and general outline. Like *The Golden Pool* it is about a treasure hunt, and, although set in London and Kent, the principals are but lately returned from the Gold Coast, which Pitcairn never visited. Deceptive variations in compass readings caused by long-term oscillations in the positions of the magnetic poles were undoubtedly suggested by Freeman. Indeed he was to use them himself much later as the basis of his tale "The Blue Scarab," which first appeared in *Pearson's Magazine* in January, 1923. He may also have helped with the history of Sir Francis Drake's supposed treasure. On the other hand, the style is Pitcairn's own; the prose bears no trace of Freeman's hand. The local allusions in Kent belong to Pitcairn and Borstal, not to Freeman and Gravesend. Mrs. Johns remembers a local farmer called Johnny Stapleton—"a rough diamond who was fond of the bottle," as she puts it—on whom Siton in the novel is evidently based. Indeed, the original name in the manuscript is "Staple," changed for reasons of prudence to "Siton" only after the novel had been typed. Other people and places from the Borstal area have been similarly introduced.

Not only did Freeman not edit the manuscript (he probably never even saw it) but it received no final polishing by Pitcairn either. Much editing and some pruning have been necessary to make it acceptable to the modern reader. In particular, Amy's character, excessively clinging and more than a shade hysterical in the original version, has been stiffened, and one or two of the mushier love scenes moderated and shortened.

The story has many attractions. The historical rationale for the treasure's existence and particular location is well established, and when found it is surely more vividly depicted than any fictional treasure before or since. One can almost see the dazzling golden monstrance, hear the chink of the jewelled rings, feel the crushing weight of the bullion. The secret passages, with the well-preserved trap above ground contrasted with the fungoid horrors and rotten woodwork of the subterranean sections, are especially noteworthy, and all the details are expertly dovetailed by Pitcairn into a story that displays many unexpected twists and turns.

For the specialist, *The Queen's Treasure* plays an important role in the Ashdown saga. In reading the Pringle stories one may wonder how much the prose owes to Freeman, how much to Pitcairn. Freeman's writing at this date is on record in *The Golden Pool* and some shorter pieces, but until now we have had no example of Pitcairn's unalloyed prose. *The Queen's Treasure* provides it.

Freeman, of course, went on to write many books and stories, the great majority of them chronicling the affairs of Thorndyke and the other denizens of 5A, King's Bench Walk. He died in Gravesend in 1943. Dr. John James Pitcairn, who was born in 1860, two years before Freeman, left Borstal in 1907 for service at Birmingham, Portland and Wandsworth. He retired at the age of sixty to live with his wife and his married daughter's family near Truro in Cornwall. He wrote a column of medical news for a professional journal, collected books, dabbled in photography, and indulged his lifelong interest in architecture and natural history, traces of which are evident in the pages that follow. He died in 1936.

I am happy to thank my friend, N. E. S. Norris, F. S. A., for his interest in Freeman and Pitcairn. It was his enthusiasm more than any other factor that led to the present publication. It was he who, by copying the manuscript and making the copy available, enabled *The Queen's Treasure* to appear at last.

—*Norman Donaldson*

Columbus, Ohio
January, 1974

CHAPTER 1

A STRANGE LEGACY

"AS you say, Sanders, the world *is* very small nowadays. Who on earth would have expected to make a discovery about his own family on the Gold Coast, of all places?"

"And did you?"

The other stopped in his walk. "Haven't I told you of my queer legacy?" he asked.

"I don't think so, Gardiner; indeed, I'm sure you haven't. May I congratulate you?"

"Ah, that's rather a question. Got a light? Thanks." Gardiner paused in the act of lighting his pipe and gazed at the moving shoreline. He was a man above middle height, with a lean but straight and well-knit figure that gave promise of considerable strength and agility. A pair of keen blue eyes shone on either side of a hawk-like nose, and high cheekbones accentuated the sharpness of a rather hollow-cheeked face, which was clothed with a grizzled iron-grey beard cut to a point. With his alert, almost commanding air, his facial characteristics were strongly reminiscent of an earlier type of adventurer, a companion of Drake or Howard. Naturally grave and sedate, he was now gay and animated, his eye sparkling with the excitement of a homecoming long delayed. His companion, Sanders, was of similar height but of fuller habit and a less masculine cast of feature. Clean-shaven, his delicately aquiline features were displayed to their best advantage. In spite of a trace of sensuality about the mouth, his was a handsome face; not so austerely Anglo-Saxon, perhaps, as that of Gardiner, its dark complexion suggested a sunnier cradle. For the rest there was a hesitation in the carriage, a furtive expression in the eyes, a restless anxiety which no assumption of gaiety was able to conceal, all in marked contrast to the easy, confident air of Gardiner.

The latter pointed with his still unlighted pipe. "I say, we've passed Southend, so that must be Canvey Island over there. We should soon be in now."

The *Black Prince,* thirty days out from the Gold Coast, had already slowed down to the speed necessary for safety in the rapidly narrowing channel. The deep-laden barges tacked incessantly across her bows and every now and then a tug in quest of a sailing vessel dodged in and out among the majestic outward-bound steamers.

The level marshy banks were cheerless and desolate in the misty evening, but to Gardiner they seemed to open welcoming arms. His eye had long been wearied by horizons of mangroves rising from poisonous swamps, perpetual dense green backdrops to the unceasing surf of the inhospitable West African shore. Now he looked with pleasure on the twilight scene. For this was home. Home—the ever-present thought amid the sordid huckstering of trade, the clash and barter of rattling cowries, the jangle of Hausa and Ochi and Fanti. Home—dreamed of in the siesta of the torrid noonday, during dark nights, silent but for the humming of the mosquitoes, through the delirium and parching sweats of deadly malaria. Yes, this was home. As he stood in grateful contemplation of the scene, the match flickered uselessly in his hand. He was roused by the voice of his companion.

"You were speaking of the legacy," Sanders prompted.

"Ah, yes, I was forgetting. Well, there was an awfully decent French trader called Broquet who thought I had been of some service to him. One day when I called at his store in Sekondi I found it closed. As I wanted to see him particularly, I went up to his place and found him there very bad with fever. As he lived alone I had him carried to my place, called in the doctor, and generally looked after him. Poor chap, he made a poor fight of it; indeed, he never properly recovered. In a few weeks he was able to get up and go home, but he could only potter around a bit—too weak to do any work to speak of. He said he should never see France again and events proved him right."

"Whisky?" asked Sanders.

"Not a bit of it—nearly a teetotaller. But he must have been living very badly, hard up and generally down on his luck. He had speculated and lost all his savings and was owing a good deal into the bargain. His salary was mortgaged six months ahead. At the last he hadn't got much more than the clothes he stood up in."

"So he hadn't much to leave?"

"Not a sou. And he never said a word about it till the end. Well, after he left my place I thought he was going to pull round a bit, but I suppose he was broken-hearted. When he came to see me about a week before he died he said he knew he was done for. I tried to cheer him up a bit but it was no good. He wept and talked a lot about what I had done for him and all the rest of it. I had noticed he had a book with him and wondered if he was leading up to something. Sure enough, presently he handed it to me and asked me to look at it. It was an old book of Vespers bound in parchment, very nicely printed, elaborately illuminated and altogether quite a handsome affair. He told me to look inside the front cover and—you'll scarcely believe this—what did I see there but my own name!"

"Good heavens!"

"Yes, Christian name and surname in full, written in faded ink; Medway Gardiner. It wasn't easy to make out at first, but as soon as I got accustomed to the queer way the letters were formed it was quite plain. Now, my father's name was Medway, and his father's before him, and so on for centuries back, for it's an old family name. It's only the modern fashion of giving people two names that is responsible for my own 'John Medway' so I was rather in doubt at first about which member of my family it might have belonged to. Then I made out the date and saw it concerned a very remote one indeed."

"And what was the date?"

"Fifteen eighty-three. Broquet told me it had been in his family for ever so long—just how long he couldn't say. His father had told him it was a family treasure and must be carefully preserved. The Broquets came originally from Douai, where the Vespers book had been given to them by the English owner."

"And he was your ancestor?"

"That's the curious part of it. My own people have always regarded themselves as the only branch of the family. I have heard my father speak of an ancestor, the first Medway Gardiner of all, who lived in the days of Elizabeth and had an estate near Maidstone. Like most country gentlemen of the period he was a Catholic. He got mixed up in some plot or conspiracy against the government, a dangerous thing in those days for anyone who had possessions to forfeit. Being on the losing side he had to bolt and so it came about that the estates were lost."

"Whereabouts are they?"

"At a place called Embrook. Thinking it over recently I remembered my father telling me the family tradition was that this Medway Gardiner was tried in his absence and sentenced to be hanged or beheaded. Having no other resource he turned soldier of fortune and was believed to have fought with the Spanish Armada."

"And killed in it, I suppose?"

"No, his must have been one of the ships that survived. He died somewhere on the continent—Douai as likely as not, for that was the headquarters of the English Catholics. Anyway, Broquet said he should never get better, and as he hadn't a soul belonging to him and had little else to leave me, he wanted to give me the book of Vespers now. At the least it seemed to have some family interest for me and if it should turn out to have any other value attaching to it, all the better. He would have been able to make me some return for what I had done for him."

"And is it of any intrinsic value?"

"Well, that I can't say. Probably not. Broquet showed me a lot of figures at the end of the book which I couldn't make head or tail of, and he suggested that if it meant anything at all it must be a cipher."

"What did it read like?"

"Just a lot of figures and crosses with a text from the Bible, all mixed up without rhyme or reason. I don't suppose for a moment there's anything in it, but just to please the poor chap I fell in with his ideas and accepted the book."

"But haven't you ever tried to thrash it out and see if it has any meaning?"

"Oh, yes; over and over again. In the evenings, when I had made up my books and had nothing else to do, I used to pull the thing out and read it backwards and forwards and upside down and try to get some sense out of it."

"I should say, from what you tell me, that the name must be more than a coincidence."

"Exactly. And that's the only thing which keeps my curiosity aroused, the possibility that it may be a family secret of some kind."

"Maybe a valuable secret."

"Hardly, after all these years. There are plenty of vague stories of Spanish galleons wrecked off the coast of Scotland with treasure aboard, but I'm not likely to risk any money trying to fish it up, even if I came to know where some of it lay. Now I've made my little pile I mean to invest it judiciously. I've worked too hard for sixteen years to lose it in any wildcat speculation."

"Still, it might be worth investigating."

"Perhaps. But even if it meant certain money I don't know that I'm keen on making more. I haven't a relation in the world; they're all dead now. I don't mean to let it drop, but there's no hurry. I've no head for puzzles myself, but I've been thinking . . ." Gardiner put his pipe in the pocket and gripped the ship's rail. "There's a man I was at school with at Gattenwood who might help me. He was a bit older than I was, so we weren't very chummy, but our fathers were old friends. He works in the Record Office and he's what you might call an expert at reading old documents. I did think of writing to him about this affair, but I put it off and off, and as there's really no hurry I shall wait till I see him in town."

"What's his name?" enquired Sanders, with some show of interest.

"Blakemore. No doubt you've heard of him, he's often mentioned in the papers."

"Yes, the name sounds familiar. But were you at Gattenwood?"

"Yes—what about it?"

"Why, so was I. I don't remember you there, but now I come to think of it I seem to remember a Blakemore."

"Short thick-set fellow, very good at football."

"That's the one! But who was this Broquet?"

"Price and Vernon's agent. When he died they sent out Browning to take over the show."

"Oh, yes. I knew Browning. In fact I bought a little concession at Futenta from him."

"Did you though?" Gardiner's voice showed real interest. "I remember his telling me about the Futenta business. He said he didn't think there was much in it, but he meant to stick to it till he could meet with some speculator who would trade. I suppose you were the man he waited for?"

"Yes. We settled it all in full form just before he died."

"Died! What are you talking about?"

"Why, he died only a few weeks before I left."

"Nonsense! I had a wire from him at Madeira. He took over my business on behalf of his firm when I cleared out."

"Browning?"

"Certainly." Gardiner frowned. "Look here, which Browning do you mean?"

"Why, James, of course. I never heard of more than one."

"Oh, yes. There were two. I remember now hearing of a Browning who died at Axim, but I mean John Browning. Everyone at Sekondi knew Jack. He's the man who owned the Futenta concession. Here, hold on. What's the matter?"

A mist floated before Sanders' eyes. He staggered to a bench, Gardiner's voice reaching him as through cotton-wool.

"Nothing; it's nothing," he murmured, trying to regain control of himself. "I felt a little bilious, that's all."

"I suppose the change of motion," said Gardiner sympathetically, and began to speak of mines and concessions and minerals. Sanders' thoughts wandered dismally to the salient events of his shattered life: to his expulsion from Cambridge, his small patrimony eaten up by the restitution that had barely saved him from a felon's cell; to the opening, so eagerly seized, of employment at Sekondi; to his struggles to rise from the lowly clerkship in the miserable store; to his futile efforts to wrest wealth from the hands of Fortune—those niggard hands forever closed to him—one gamble succeeding another, each plunging him deeper in the slough of debt; to the ledgers, elaborately garbled to hide his defalcations; to Browning, the owner of the concession, the dead man who would never repudiate his signature forged to the deed of transfer; last of all to Lewis, the prospector eager for the fortune offered to him by Sanders at a tithe of its market value, the Shylock who had lopped another hundred from the poor thousand when Sanders had held out for half cash and notes instead of all bills with their risks and enquiries and delays. And now, all this—the theft, the forgery, the false pretences—all this had been useless. Good heavens, at this very moment perhaps the police awaited him! Fortune was as inexorable as ever. Surely, it would be better to end it once and for all by a swift plunge into the muddy waters around. But—how sweet life was. Was there no other way? What was Gardiner saying?

"—so, you see, I'm afraid the man who sold you that concession must have been a swindler. Have you parted with it?"

Sanders hesitated. A second more and he would have blurted out the truth, but in that second his hand, with an action recently grown mechanical with him, gripped the little packet of notes and gold he wore sewn in an inner pocket. The contact nerved him to struggle on. His plight was not yet absolutely desperate, and it was almost cheerfully that he answered, "No, fortunately."

"Ah! Well, it might have been worse. If you had sold it you might have found yourself facing a charge of false pretences."

Sanders winced. "Why couldn't I have heard of it before now?" he murmured.

"Well, it's pretty clear no one at Axim knew there were two

Brownings on the coast—no one that you knew, anyhow. But, cheer up, where are you going off?"

"I don't know," Sanders answered rather wearily. Long before this, he realised, Lewis must have discovered the fraud and applied for a warrant. The authorities in London would have been warned by telegraph and the vessel might be boarded by police at the first port of call. True, his appearance had altered since he left the Coast: the sea air, the indolent life, the good living, and above all the pleasurable sense of at last winning in the desperate game he had played for so long, had contributed to a smoothing of wrinkles, an increase of girth. These, a new confidence in his bearing, and the shaving of his beard as they entered the Channel had altered him greatly from the nervous furtive gambler he had been seven or eight weeks ago. But there remained his name. There was no repudiating that; Gardiner's presence eliminated the idea.

"Well," said Gardiner cheerily, "I'm thinking of landing at Tilbury and going straight to a hotel. I want to feel as soon as possible that I've really come home. I want to sleep in an English bed, and eat an English dinner. You come and dine with me, and I'll soon see if I can't make you feel as happy as I do. I don't like to part with a man when he's down on his luck. Things will look brighter in the morning. And if we can't think of any way to get your money back for you, why then, you shall help me in my affair. Look, there are the lights of Gravesend. We shall soon be in now. Let's collect our traps so we may get them all cleared and ready to go ashore. By Jove, here comes the customs launch. Hurry up!"

By the time, some half-hour later, they stood side by side on the tender as it plunged into the silvery shimmer cast by the huge arc-lamps at the entrance to the dock, Sanders had caught some of Gardiner's contagious cheerfulness. So far, all had gone smoothly. Their luggage, which now surrounded them in a miniature rampart, had been cleared ahead of the other passengers' by subornation of a steward, and they alone were thus able to land at Tilbury. The customs launch had borne no one more formidable than the examining officers, and the cold glare which flooded the landing stage revealed not a single uniformed figure. So eager was Gardiner to disembark that, when a rail was unshipped to make way for the pier gangway, he stood forward as if about to spring ashore without its assistance as the watery gap narrowed.

Just as the man at the bows with a final swing sent the hawser loop flying through the air to the waiting dock-hand, a hail from the water turned all eyes aft where a steam launch, apparently in pursuit, had just entered the lighted area. It was in charge of a customs officer, and a couple of passengers sat in the stern.

"What is the matter?" asked Gardiner, craning on tiptoe the better to see. "Have we forgotten anything?"

With a heavy thud the tender struck her bow full on the stage and rebounded into the stream. There was a cry, followed by a loud splash, and Sanders was thrown to the deck amid a tumble of boxes and trunks. When he scrambled to his feet again Gardiner was nowhere to be seen. As soon as he grasped the fact that his companion had fallen into the river, Sanders sprang to a life-buoy and, tugging at its lashings, shouted "Man overboard!"

There was a brief scamper towards him and, with a flash of his knife, the nearest hand released the buoy. As it swirled off, the man commented, "He won't have much chance unless he's a good swimmer."

"Who is it?" shouted the captain.

"Passenger, sir."

The captain hailed the launch: "Man overboard! Can you see him? There—there!" pointing to the fast-disappearing buoy.

There was a heated conference between the officer in charge

of the launch and the two passengers. Then the little craft, porting her helm, swung impetuously around and started downstream in pursuit. Helped by the rapid tide and her efficient engine, the launch skimmed over the shimmering water and in a second or two was lost to sight and hearing.

"Shall we lower the boat, sir?" asked one of the hands as the captain, having watched the launch out of sight, came down from the bridge.

"No good now," was the reply. "If *they* can't find him no one can." He walked to Sanders. "Relation of yours, sir?"

"No, no. Only a friend I travelled with," murmured Sanders faintly. The sudden tragedy had followed so closely on the earlier shock that now he felt sick.

" 'W. S.,' " said the captain, reading the initials on the nearest trunk of the fallen pile. "Does that stand for his name or yours?"

Sanders opened his mouth to reply. "Mine" trembled on his lips, but even as the word framed itself, with a mighty effort he kept silent. "His name or yours?" Could this be his last chance of escape? A vista of freedom opened suddenly before him. Was Fortune, at the eleventh hour, repenting of her sorry treatment of him? The fatal admission remained unuttered. He stood there without a name, as free to take that of the prosperous trader as that of the pursued felon. The one man who alone might betray him was gone, perhaps forever.

The rapid thudding of a screw arose, and the customs launch shot once more into the light and slowed up just ahead of the tender.

"Got him?" asked the captain, as the launch's boat-hook rattled along the chain that festooned the landing stage.

"This is all we could find so far. Stand by there!" The lifebuoy came spinning onto the deck.

"So your time was too valuable to let you look for him?

Why the devil didn't you say so? I'd have sent my own boat after him." And the captain gave the life-buoy a vicious kick across the deck.

"I've come back to land these two gentlemen who want to come aboard of you," was the reply.

"But what about my passenger?"

"We're going back, right enough. They know about him right up at Northfleet by this time—I left half a dozen boats looking for him."

As the two passengers scrambled onto the landing stage the launch steamed off again in quest of the missing man.

"What's up now? Smuggling?" murmured the captain, and, turning to Sanders, "What name did you say, sir?"

Sanders, who had been clenching his teeth to prevent their chattering, stammered: "It was his—Mr. Sanders—William Sanders. My name is G—Gardiner!" Swaying, he reeled against a trunk and slid fainting to the deck.

"You have some passengers from the *Black Prince*, haven't you, captain?" said the shorter and smarter of the two men as they stepped on board the tender.

The captain hesitated. Like the majority of mariners he was inclined to regard smuggling leniently if not sympathetically. Moreover these did not appear to be customs officers and he resented their presence.

"It was the *Black Prince* we wanted, but we missed the customs launch that boarded it, and as we saw you leaving the ship we came after you in another of their launches," was the polite explanation of the spokesman.

"I see," grunted the captain. "And what can I do for you?"

"We're in search of a Mr. William Sanders, and thought he was likely to have come off in the tender."

"You should have stuck to the boat, then; you were nearer to him there."

A STRANGE LEGACY

"Eh? What, has he gone ashore?" Both men faced about, the larger one making a movement towards the landing stage.

"No, I don't think you'll find him there," observed the captain drily.

"Look here now," said the leader menacingly, "we're officers of the Criminal Investigation Department and I caution you not to withhold anything from us. We have to execute a warrant for this man's arrest for forgery. Once and for all, have you got him here or not?"

The captain whistled.

"Don't waste time, please. We've wasted enough already, what with missing the launch and then searching for your man just now."

"That's him! He's the one who's gone overboard."

"Who's this, then?" demanded the officer, for the first time noticing the prostrate man. Sanders was sitting up with, as yet, but a feeble recognition of his surroundings; his head throbbed unmercifully, and he was still too dazed to share in the conversation.

"This gentleman's name is Gardiner," explained the captain. "He was the other passenger who came off the *Black Prince,* and when your man was drowned he fainted. Sit down, sir," he added as Sanders tried to rise. "You'll feel better in a minute."

"Did he fall overboard, or did he jump?" asked the other detective.

The senior officer nodded. "Yes, captain, do you think he tried to jump ashore and fell short?"

"I really never noticed. I was too busy trying to get alongside the pier."

"Beg pardon, sir," interposed a sailor, "I see him standing as if he was going to jump ashore. That was after I unshipped the rail for the gangway. He was balancing on one foot, all of a shake like, as if he was very anxious to get ashore."

"And then what happened?"

"Couldn't say—I was looking at your launch."

"He must have seen us coming after him," observed the junior officer.

"Of course he did. We all saw you when you hailed us," said the captain. "Feel better, Mr. Gardiner? Just sit on this bench a bit, sir, won't you? No hurry."

Sanders, deathly pale, had now risen and confronted the group steadily.

"What is your name, sir?" the detective enquired, producing a notebook.

"John Medway Gardiner."

"Address?"

"I have none here; my last was Sekondi, West Africa."

"Where are you going to now?"

"I shall stop for a few days at the Great Eastern Hotel in London."

"How long have you known the man you came on board with?"

"I only met him on the ship."

"Was he a dark, stoutish, clean-shaven man?" The detective eyed Sanders narrowly. The description fitted him fairly well.

"No, he was rather thin with a beard." And then, remembering his own aspect at the commencement of the voyage, Sanders added, "He looked in bad health."

"Yes," the captain chimed in. "I should say he'd had a touch of fever lately—shouldn't you, sir?"

Sanders nodded, mistrustful of further speech.

The detective, as if satisfied that the missing man was his quarry, pocketed his notebook. "There was no chance of his getting on shore without our seeing him, I suppose?" he asked the captain.

"Not much," said that officer, shaking his head. "With the

tide running like that it would take the best swimmer all his time to get to land, and so slowly he'd go, in all that light you were bound to see him. But it's my opinion he must have struck his head as he went over and sank at once."

"I'll just take a look round below, captain. No one must go ashore yet," he added, with a glance at Sanders. "Jones, you remain on deck." And with that the detective went below and spent the next quarter of an hour in a fruitless search of the craft.

It was a curious sense of having undergone metamorphosis that, surrounded by Gardiner's luggage, Sanders stood a little while later upon the landing stage with his fears and anxieties, for the moment at least, behind him.

And yet he was dissatisfied. The air struck chill and a fine rain was beginning to fall. The lights shone ghastly on the water, and every now and then a passing steamer hooted mournfully. All seemed dismal and repellent. The emotional change had been too abrupt, the transition from abject terror to confidence too violent, to permit his full enjoyment of it. His name—his true identity—had disappeared along with Gardiner, and "finis" written by the waves to a disastrous chapter of his life. Before him stretched a new life, its threshold yet untrodden. Almost he feared to cross it.

CHAPTER 2

IMPERSONATION

WHEN a man has been unexpectedly rescued from a great peril, snatched from an abyss that yawns at his very feet, the first satisfaction at his escape is often followed by some return of fearfulness. So it was with Sanders as he sat in the smoking-room of the Great Eastern Hotel the next morning.

He had spent a wretched night packed with vivid dreams of pursuing boats, manacles, gaols, and the terrors inseparable from his desperate case. In all of them Gardiner's corpse figured hideous and aggressive. He saw it stranded on the beach of some faraway creek, half in and half out of a muddy tidal basin. A score of rivulets splashed from the sodden bundle with musical tinkles into the iridescent pool. The frayed, torn garments revealed the wounds and bruises sustained from passing craft in the swirling scurry downstream. The tight clenched hands stretched aloft, the legs drawn up in a last spasm as the flood roared in his ears and the sweetness of oblivion succeeded the agony of the death struggle. He saw a longshoreman wading across the mud flat, eager to gather the harvest of the flood, dragging it to his leaky skiff and rowing upstream to the whitewashed mortuary. All this he saw as

IMPERSONATION

clearly as though he stood beside the corpse on the lonely marsh.

After a perfunctory breakfast, Sanders, holding before him a newspaper of which he had not read a single line, sat racking his brains for a way out of his difficulties. True, his metamorphosis had been neatly effected. But would the police submit tamely to this loss of their prey? Impossible! A hunted felon had escaped at the very moment of his arrest. The event would surely be the sole topic in every riverside tavern and, reward apart, for some time at least each waterman and longshoreman would be an ally of the police in their search. At most he had gained but the respite of a day or two.

Rapidly he glanced down the columns of the newspaper without finding more than a mere bald reference to the drowning of a Mr. Sanders. Searching anxiously through the rest of the journals on the smoking-room table, he could see nothing to alarm him. Nevertheless, he doubted whether a prolonged stay at the hotel would be wise.

Fortunately he carried his cash on his person. It amounted to some four hundred pounds in notes and gold, all that was left of his fraudulent deal over the concession. As to the bills which represented the other half of the plunder, they were in his luggage. In any case, they would have taken too long to realise even if discounted at the most ruinous rate. But what of Gardiner's property? He went up to his room to ransack the luggage that had been landed with him. As he stared at the two substantial trunks a fresh difficulty confronted him.

It dawned on him that the keys of the trunks must be in Gardiner's possession. He tried his own keys one by one, without success. He cursed his stupidity at never having acquired the useful art of making a pick-lock. He saw that to call in a locksmith would be only a degree less suspicious than the drastic process of bursting the trunks open by main force. To wrench open the hinges would be no easier, though certainly less noticeable. As he dragged one into the light of the window the hasp rattled and he found he could lift it clean out of the lock. Neither trunk had been locked after inspection by customs. Gardiner, all eagerness to get ashore, had evidently dispensed with that operation and had merely strapped them instead.

As he strewed the contents on the floor he felt more lighthearted than at any time in the last twenty-four hours. Even if he found no money, here was an ample supply of clothing to replace his own distinctly seedy garments, for Gardiner and he differed only slightly in build. At the bottom of the second trunk was a large sealed envelope. He tore it open eagerly to find a parcel of cheques and bills of exchange, quite useless to him. He dropped the packet into the trunk again and seized some clothes with the intention of dragging them out. As he did so he caught sight of a small canvas bag wedged in a corner. Could this be cash at last? He pounced on it and felt through the cloth what seemed to be the square outline of a box. The next moment he had flung it impatiently to the far end of the room, for the squareness had resolved itself into a small parchment volume with a brazen clasp.

By the time he had repacked the trunk his irritation had given place to curiosity, and he raked the book from beneath the chest of drawers where it had come to rest. It was a fat little volume, red-edged, devoid of lettering on its covers, but opening to disclose the pages of a book of Vespers. At the beginning was the signature and date—1583—that Gardiner had mentioned. Here if not actual money was perhaps the promise of some. With a conscious quickening of the pulse he sat down and began to hunt for the mysterious cipher message.

The search was neither a long nor a difficult one, though had it not been for Gardiner's opinion he might well have regarded the writing on a fly-leaf at the end of the volume as a series of arithmetical problems. First came a number flanked

IMPERSONATION

by crosses, and this was followed by a string of figures divided by other crosses into small irregular groups. At the bottom of the page, and having no apparent relation to the figures, were the words "Cromlech" and "Beacon," each followed by capital letters which Sanders had sufficient nautical knowledge to recognize as compass bearings.

This was the cipher:

+ 3312 +
+ 32 + 2612 + 13821 + 903 + 1139 + 11310 + 11312 +1113
+ 265 + 11513 + 1134 + 1255 + 1256 + 1257 + 1112 + 7115+
Cromlech NNE.   Beacon NW+W.

Although the paper was stained and discoloured by age and damp, the script was still legible, but as Sanders stared at the long array of figures he was fain to confess that the secret they held was beyond his comprehension. He turned to the compass bearings at the bottom of the page. There was little practical information to be gathered here, either, and he felt tempted to give the puzzle up as a bad job. But something made him persist. Because Gardiner had failed was that any reason why he should fare no better? Did Gardiner possess greater intellectual powers than he, merely because he had made a bigger success of life? Confound him! Let Gardiner be the tortoise; he, Sanders, would still be the hare.

Stimulated by the thought, he mastered his irritation and resolutely thought over their final conversation. In spite of the startling events that had intervened, he still remembered fairly accurately all that had passed between them. But he could not immediately recall anything resembling a clue. Taking the book with him, Sanders went down to the smoking-room and, lighting a cigarette, began to pace mechanically up and down the room while he thought over the problem. Forced by the intrusion of three youths with a noisy gramophone to retreat to his own room, something in their overheard conversation recalled something he had recently been told. What was it? Records? Record Office! Yes. Didn't Gardiner have a friend there who might be able to decipher the message? What was his name? Of course, Blakemore.

With a critical eye Sanders examined his appearance in the mirror. For the second time in twenty-four hours he congratulated himself on his gain in weight while on board the *Black Prince.* A few days of the calm routine of shipboard had robbed him of the harrassed look he had acquired upon the Coast, although there was no smoothing where the crow had stamped in many an anxious hour. Gardiner, it was true, was slighter and his greying beard made him look older. On the other hand they were very much of a height and if, as Gardiner had said, Blakemore and he had never been really intimate, they had probably not met since boyhood.

His first intention was to take the Vespers with him to the Record Office, but as he crammed it into his pocket he hesitated. Supposing, he reflected, that Blakemore should penetrate his disguise and endeavour to retain the volume? Or that, after all, he were arrested, in which case the book might furnish evidence against him? Or even that he should lose or mislay it? He copied out the message, hid the book at the bottom of the trunk, locked the door and set out westward.

Turning down Old Broad Street, he walked on by way of Cheapside and Newgate Street to Fetter Lane, arriving at the imposing Gothic pile of the Record Office as noon was striking. His request to see Mr. Blakemore being met by a demand for his name, he wrote on a slip of paper: J. Medway Gardiner, Sekondi, Gold Coast.

He was soon being ushered into a handsome apartment on the first floor where a stoutly built man with a close-cropped

IMPERSONATION

beard rose behind his desk and returned Sanders' bow rather frigidly.

"I must apologise for intruding on you without notice," said Sanders. "I suppose you have forgotten me since we were at Gattenwood together?"

"Oh!" The other unfroze somewhat. "Are you the Gardiner I knew at school? I should never have recognised you. How are you?" He shook Sanders warmly by the hand.

"Yes. A quarter of a century has made a considerable change in us both," replied Sanders, as he took the offered chair.

"And what have you been doing all this time?" enquired Blakemore with a smile.

"Well, for the last sixteen years or so I've been trading on the Gold Coast . . ."

"Yes, I noticed the address you sent up."

". . . but I've cleared out now. I arrived home only yesterday." Remembering the scant welcome extended to would-be borrowers, Sanders made haste to add, as Blakemore's smile took on a rather fixed appearance, "I've done very well out there, you know."

"I congratulate you. A gold mine?"

"No, honest hard work. And that brings me to the object of my visit to you." Sanders, as nearly as possible in Gardiner's words, gave the history of the cipher. "Here's a copy of it." And with that he produced it and placed it on the desk.

"Hmm! Very curious," remarked Blakemore as he took it up. "But you know I don't profess to be a cryptologist."

"Quite so, but you are accustomed to read old manuscripts, and you must have come across some queer things."

"Very true, but one doesn't often meet with this sort of puzzle in state documents, with which I am principally concerned. All the same, I must confess I am interested in ciphers and codes. I never see one without a desire to discover its secret, if it has one—some haven't any! Perhaps you know that secret writing is of very great antiquity, going back at least to the Caesars. In the Middle Ages monks seem to have invented ciphers as intellectual exercises."

"To kill time!"

"Well yes, that's about it, I suppose. They used to leave out the vowels and substitute symbols, which of course had to be agreed upon beforehand. It's only when we get to the sixteenth century—and that, you say, is the date of this cipher—that any ingenuity is met with. But every one of these ciphers can be read, given time and pains. Even arbitrary signs, neither figures nor letters, can be read. The Spaniards, at the end of the sixteenth century, employed a cipher of that kind with five hundred characters."

"Like this one?" enquired Sanders, rather blankly.

"That remains to be seen. I haven't begun to consider on what principle this one is constructed—perhaps it isn't a cipher at all. What I was going to say about the figure cipher is that it's difficult to read. You put down figures, say one to ten, in proper sequence in one line, and on the next line you put the same figures in any order you please—the more erratic the better. Then you write your message out and number each letter of it in sequence. You then look at your table. Suppose number one in the first line has got, say, six below it in the second line; you select the sixth letter of your message as the first of the cipher, and so you go on. Of course your correspondent has a similar table by which he reverses the process and decodes your message."

"Do you think that is how this one is done?"

"Well, not unless it's a very complicated cipher indeed. You say you haven't any idea at all what it means?"

"No more than I got from Gar—er—Broquet." Impersonators, like other liars, need good memories.

"Did you think of comparing the numbers with the pages of the book?"

"No, in fact I noticed the pages aren't numbered."

"Hmm! You're quite sure this is an accurate copy?"

"Certainly. I checked every figure."

"And that this is the whole of it?"

"Yes."

Blakemore studied the cipher in silence for a few minutes. "Either these figures refer to something in the volume, or they were simply jotted down in the first thing handy. They must have a key, and it oughtn't to be very difficult to find. The cipher isn't very short; it's the short ones that are difficult."

"How so?"

"Well, take the case of a message constructed by substitution of one letter for another. You need only make out a table of the relative frequency of certain letters in the cipher and compare it with the frequency of those in plain language in order to arrive at a solution. But I'm inclined to think there must be some sort of secret key to this one. Is there any more writing in the rest of the book?"

"I'm almost certain there isn't."

"These figures, you see, are nearly all in groups of four or five, two have three figures, and one has two only; it's hardly possible they can stand for letters of the alphabet—the words would be too short."

"Mightn't they have been abbreviated?"

"Possibly. Shakespeare and other writers since then were fond of contractions, but it is hardly likely every word would be contracted."

"What do you think of the words at the end?"

"Well, they seem mysterious. But they confirm my belief that the figures don't stand for words, or why wasn't the whole thing written like that? Of course, the figures may contain the most important part, and that makes me believe that if there is any cipher at all it will be found in the groups of figures. Did this Frenchman—you said he was French, I think—did he attach any meaning to them?"

"No. There was simply a family tradition that they meant something of importance."

Blakemore shook his head. "I should doubt very much there is anything in it. You might let me see the volume itself the next time you come. Suppose you leave this copy with me for a week or so."

On this cue Sanders took his leave, somewhat disappointed by the outcome of his visit. He bought an early edition of the evening paper and hunted through it with renewed anxiety. But there was no word of any corpse being discovered nor of the accident itself, and, returning to his hotel, he ate a belated and solitary lunch.

Later, relaxing in an armchair in the smoking room, he turned the pages of an atlas he had found on a side table and studied intently the section devoted to Southern England. As his eye followed the winding course of the Medway it was suddenly arrested by the name of a village on the western bank—Embrook. This was the place he sought. Was there no mention of Embrook in the Vespers? He went up to his room again and searched the volume from end to end. There was no local allusion at all, unless the words "Cromlech" and "Beacon" at the end of the cipher might be so considered. Had Gardiner made no reference to them? Sanders surely would have remembered if he had. Suppose the secret lay elsewhere than in the groups of figures: in the compass bearings, for instance? He must obtain a good map and study the locality in detail. Meanwhile it was a waste of time to cudgel his brains further.

He left the hotel and walked briskly eastward. His surroundings took on more and more of a nautical air and, after

IMPERSONATION

a comparatively short walk he found what he wanted. Within forty-five minutes he was back at the hotel with several Ordnance Survey sheets of West Kent on the admirable six-inch scale, and a pocket compass.

In a quiet corner of the smoking room he spread out one of the sheets on a table and began a careful study of the Maidstone district. He soon found Embrook with a manor house a mile distant. Now for the beacon and cromlech. In an ever-widening circle he scanned the map, until away to the northeast his eye was arrested by the words "Kit's Coty House." Here was a cromlech indeed! He knew it to be, after Stonehenge, one of the most celebrated monuments of antiquity in England. All around he searched, but at no spot within a five-mile circle could he find any reference to a cromlech other than this one. The beacon of the westerly bearing was much less explicit. There were plenty of hills to the west, Wrotham, with its almost mountainous height of nearly eight hundred feet, in particular, but the most laborious search failed to detect a beacon or any hill that might reasonably be considered one. Almost despairing of success, he decided to try from the other end of the bearing. He laid one end of a strip of paper on the spot marked Embrook and placed it in a northwest direction. At a distance representing a mile and a half it struck a line of elevated ground that formed the western boundary of the Medway valley and continued to the west to form the beginning of the North Downs. His attention was attracted to a single spot of upland that reared up at the angle where the chalk hills swept round from the valley to culminate above Wrotham. This, credited by the map as being six hundred feet high, might easily be conspicuous on the skyline when viewed from the village. Although no name was ascribed to the hill, the map showed it to be wooded. Such cover would, Sanders reflected, have deprived it of the character of a beacon should it ever have possessed any.

It occurred to him to use the hill and the cromlech as starting points and measure backwards in accordance with the original bearings. He drew a couple of pencil lines, one southeast-by-east from the hill, and the other south-southwest from Kit's Coty House. The two pencil lines met at a point some three miles to the northeast of the village. Almost exactly at this spot on the Ordnance Survey sheet he read in Old English characters the legend:

ST. CRESCENTIA'S CHAPEL (RUINS)

This was encouraging. With such a foundation to build upon, the cipher lost some of its cryptic terrors. Now Sanders was half-convinced that the figures bore no occult meaning. In course of time an utterly false value might have been given to them at the expense of the actual and vital secret. A landsman beguiled by the mysterious cipher might too easily overlook the significance of compass bearings. Perhaps the rest of the message could be safely ignored.

But now his former fear again gripped him. What if the corpse should be found? He could not, after all, afford to wait for Blakemore's further study of the cipher. He had ample knowledge for his present purpose and must set to work at once. The first thing was to get out of the hotel without arousing suspicion by a hasty departure. He would leave the two heavy boxes for a few days and pack Gardiner's portmanteau with the articles he stood in most need of, including, of course, the precious Vespers and the Ordnance Survey maps.

After dark he slipped away from the hotel and was driven to the Great Northern terminus. He dismissed his cab, travelled by subway to King's Cross, and then by the Metropolitan Railway to Victoria. There he put up for the night at the Grosvenor Hotel, ready to leave by the Chatham and Dover line the next morning.

CHAPTER 3

THE RUINED CHAPEL

"CAN you tell me how long the chapel has been in ruins?" Sanders enquired.

The farmer stared. "Chapel," he repeated with a puzzled expression. "What chapel?"

"St. Crescentia's Chapel."

"Never heard of it. Is it anywhere about here?"

"Yes, not a mile away."

"There's no chapel nearer than the village, and that's no ruin! Leastways," he guffawed, "it wasn't yesterday when I passed there."

"I mean *your* chapel, the one in your field."

The farmer shook his head. "This place has been in our family nigh a hundred years, and I never heard tell of any chapel. They may have had one in the house in the old days, but there ain't none anywhere else."

"No, no." Sanders pulled a section of the map from his pocket and consulted it. "I mean in the field just by Abbot's Wood."

"Oh, them old walls? Bless you, that ain't a chapel!"

"Well, that's what they call it on the map."

"Where did you get that from? London? I thought so. What do they know about it there? Like them clever chaps that come down here lecturin', I suppose. We ain't got no call to ask none of them how to grow whops! As if we didn't know how to grow whops before their grandmothers was born."

"What do *you* call the place, then?"

"Well, I've known it, man and boy, a matter of fifty year, and never heard tell of its being called aught but 'Jacob's Wall.'"

"Well, I'm very much interested in old buildings like that, and I should like to examine it."

"Ah, do! You can't miss it. You'll see it soon as you've got clear of the orchard."

"I was going to ask if you would mind my digging a bit inside it, just to see what the foundations are like."

"Oh, dig away as much as you please. Knock it all down if you like. I can use up the stones for my yard-walls."

"I don't think I'll do as much damage as that."

"Well, I don't mind what you do. Only, if you do knock any of it down, d'ye mind chucking the stones back inside? For that's good soil all around about in the field."

Sanders had risen early, intending to explore the ruins, when he encountered the farmer in the hall. Arriving at Forbridge the previous day and walking out to explore the scene of operations, he had stumbled upon a farm whose mistress made a specialty of summer boarders, and, although the season was waning, she raised no objection to extending it in favour of Sanders. Delighted at the chance of residing barely a mile from his goal, he lost no time in shifting his quarters from the inn at Forbridge. He gave his name as Palmer and explained that he was an archaeologist engaged in a survey of the neighbourhood.

The farmhouse bore signs of having been at one time a place of some importance. It was surrounded by a deep ditch, obviously the remains of a moat, though it was now dry and grass-grown and filled with countless gnarled trunks of an apple orchard. Scattered about stood several ragged yews, which still bore traces of a topiarist's clippers. The solid red-brick house, with its massive chimney stacks elaborately carved, its square-headed windows retaining their diamond-leaded casements, and its set of three gables on each side, showed it to be an early Tudor manor house.

Within, it was full of oak, dense and fire-resistant, and of such workmanship as scarcely to reveal a single joint. The stairs, broad and shallow, showed little sign of wear from innumerable feet through the centuries, centuries that had darkened the wood throughout the mansion to the tint of rich mahogany. The balusters, each an Ionic column, supported a plain hand-rail which sprang from massive, richly carved newels. Between the latter hung the dog-gates; these, high and heavy enough to restrain the largest animals from trespassing in the upper rooms, were of a decorated portcullis pattern. Each newel also supported an escutcheon charged with the arms of the former lords: *On a field argent three lozenges gules,* surmounted by a crest of *the sun in splendour,* with the pious motto, *Spes Lucis Eternae.* Throughout the house the walls were panelled four deep and carved with a simple moulding, but the chamber doors, flanked by Ionic pilasters, were embossed by the lozenges of the escutcheon. The ceilings, on the other hand, had been less fortunate than the walls; they had not been spared the whitewash and plaster of the modern vandal. Wherever the eye glanced aloft, the linear cracks and rifts spoke of underlying woodwork, and beneath the dead white crust the delicate lines of an intricate geometrical design could still be traced. At the intersections showed the rising sun of the crest, at the centre of every ceiling the escutcheon itself.

To none of this did Sanders evince any awareness. Indeed,

the lack of interest of their new boarder was a source of wonder to the farmer's wife and daughter, for they were accustomed to the raptures of even the least antiquarian of visitors. But, with his desires fixed on a certain spot just a mile away, Sanders had no admiration to spare for anything else. After studying the map for the whole of the first evening, he went to bed only to dream of it, and rose in the early morning with his head fuller than ever of his one idea.

When Sanders left the farm it was impossible to see far through the autumn mist across the flat alluvial fields of the Medway valley; but, with a general idea of the direction he should take and with an occasional glance at his map, he was able to set a pretty direct course to the chapel. At length, he found the ruins in the corner of a slightly undulating field of stubble. The weather and human depredations had taken a heavy toll. The rubble walls, faced with flint, had sunk lower and lower until they were now scarcely breast-high. Had such fences been commoner thereabouts, it would have been easy to mistake the structure for a stone dyke or boundary.

Clambering through an irregular cleft in the wall, Sanders found himself in a rectangle about twenty feet by fifteen. A blaze of ragwort completely hid the rough ground beneath its golden mantle.

Somewhere under these three hundred square feet lay the answer to the riddle of the cipher: a small enough space, but still sufficient, he realised, to afford him indefinite employment. As he leaned against the wall and gazed around, the folly of searching without some guidance beyond his present vague ideas was manifest. If he accepted the authority of the Ordnance Survey, there were ruins of some sort of chapel, but when or how had it come to be so effectively desecrated that its very name had faded from the memory of man? Not a vestige of stonework or masonry was visible in the walls, not

THE RUINED CHAPEL

even a hollowing in the rubble where piscina or holywater stoup might have nested; only at the irregular fissure by which he had entered could the faint outlines of a doorway be imagined. As he walked dejectedly back to the manor house he resolved to acquire more data, and especially positive information about the chapel's history. The farm itself, he soon discovered, contained no county history or guidebook. Without waiting for midday dinner he hired a cycle in the village and rode into Maidstone.

At the museum in St. Faith's he spent the remainder of the day in a weary hunt through county histories and local antiquarian works for some reference to St. Crescentia's. In Richard Kilburne's *Topographie or Survey of the County of Kent* he found the following passage:

> Five miles to ye Northwarde of ye toune Embrook there is Sainte Crescente her Chapel, but being fall'n inne ruines and sore abused in ye late troubles I turne not aside thereto.

Had Kilburne "turned aside thereto," thought Sanders, he might have avoided the error of placing the chapel at nearly double its proper distance from the village. At the same time the reference was an important one, as showing approximately the date of the dismantling of the chapel, "sore abused in ye late troubles" being a very clear reference to its desecration during the Civil War, presumably by Parliamentary troops.

His curiosity whetted by this discovery, Sanders turned to the next book in his selection. This was a venerable quarto, bound in massive wooden boards covered with parchment, toned by the years to a rich old ivory. It was none other than William Lambarde's *Perambulation of Kent, containing ye Discription, Historie, and Customs of that Shyre*, in black-letter, of the year 1596. In quaint diction it asserted:

> Hard bye ye toune of Embrook toe ye Northe-Easte thereof lyeth Sanct Crescent hyr Chapelle, of ollde tyme of ease toe Sancte Vyncente. A goodlye fabrycke wherynne lye duyers of the famlye of Gardynere wythe tombes a grate nombre moste nobly chased and pleasavnte toe ye syghte wythe manye fayre brazen plattes. Wythynne ye place they calle ye qvyre was inne tyme of ye ollde faythe showne behynde an yron screne a certayne shryne, whereof ye verye menest parte was of marbel ynlayed wythe golde and jewells of pryce yncomparable contaynynge some parte of ye uerye claye thatte Adame was creyated ovt of lyk toe thatte they showed at Sanct Thomas Cantvar hys shryne, and onne yts fronte ynne precious stones moste cvnnynge wrote ye cote of Adame Escvtceoned ynne pretence wythe thatte of Eve hys wyffe as Master Gvyllyme teachyth. Butte when ye kyngis Maiestys commysyoners had dyspoyled ye same as svperstycyovse anon came others of ye common people who mad moare toe plucke uppe ye borddes and caste dovne ye leede vpon ye roofe, bvt ye knyte Sir Mydway Gardynere dydde uowe toe stryke ye hedde from offe ye sholders of ye firste thatte shovde make fvrther dyspoylmente accovntynge yt bvtte ynne defynse of ye place of beryall of hys famlye.

As Lambarde digressed into a rambling comment upon the suppression of the religious houses, in which he appeared to struggle between sympathy with "ye ollde faythe," and a natural desire to cast no slight upon the royal father of his formidable sovereign, Sanders exchanged the garrulous historian for the last of his authorities: *The History of Kent,* 1719, by

THE RUINED CHAPEL

the Reverend John Harris. This was in two volumes, the second being a folio of manuscript of *Notes and Illustrations* collected by the author but never published. In this latter volume, minutely indexed by the painful labour of some dead-and-gone antiquary, was a passage which served to fill up the gaps in the somewhat vague accounts of the two older authors.

With some difficulty, owing to fading of the ink, Sanders read:

Further account of the Parich of Embrook nr. Forbridge. The Manor-house was the hereditary Seat of the Gardyneres sometime Lords of the Manor sprung from one of the most antient Families of Kent. The last Lord, Sir Medway Gardynere fled over the Seas in the year 1583 being Attainted of treason and a price set on his Head, when his Estates were forfeit to the Crown. Tis said this Sir Medway Gardynere being a wicked Papist in league with the Jesuits was entrusted by them with vast Wealth intended to raise a rebellion here to aid the Armada which was shattered by the Divine Providence when it threatened this Protestant Realm. I visited the House last Year. Tis now a Farm, the Mote drained off and made an Orchard and the Park all turned to Tillage. A noble Mansion within, the fitting Home to a Noble Familie. But I fear me put to a seditious Purpose by this Mysguided Man, for tis said He gave secret Asylum to certain of the Society of Jesuits being Envoys of the Bishop of Rome and Instruments of the Plots to assassinate the Queen: notably one Anthonie Tyrel who when imprisoned in the Tower in 1586 did make Confession how Gregory (Thirteenth of the Bishops of Rome of that name) did assure Him that touching the taking the life of that Jezebel, as he impiously miscalled the Queen whose Life

God had preserved to their dismay so long, He not only approved the Act but held the doer if he suffered Death therefor to be worthy of being Canonized as a Saint. These same wicked Men having lately caused to be killed the Prince of Orange, were thereby encouraged in their traitorous Plots preaching that all Christendom, as they called the Peoples holding the Popish faith, would be in Peace and Quietness the once they Dyspatched that Bulwark of the Reformed Faith Queen Elizabeth. They show in ancient Manors of the Catholick Lords cells and Hiding Places in the Thicknesse of the Walls or fashioned otherwise most cunningly, where Jesuits were concealed and kept in those troublous days, but tho I make diligent Search and Question I could not learn of the like at Embrook however it be elsewhere. Doubtless it fell out after taking of the Jesuit Traitor Campion in a private Chamber that such Hiding-places were not fashioned, the Queen's Officers making so sharp a Search as rendered them of no purpose or moment, so none were made within Embrook. Howbeit I pray in all humbleness God preserve us from such Enemies to the Protestant Faith! There is no Chapel within, but a mile off was a Chapel of Ease to the Toune Church dedicated to the Popish Saint Crescentia. This was the Mortiary Chapel and Private Worshipping Place of the Family of Gardynere. In the Lamentable Civil War in the Year 1648 it was destroyed by one Baker a Captain of My Lord Fairfax, sent after his storm of Maidstone to search out and destroy the Images of Romish Worship. I cannot learn what Relics of this Idolatory were found but I opine they were Gross and Perspicuous since of all the Fabrique the Walls stand to the height but of a man's breast, and the inner part so choked with Earth and

Filth that none can tell where stood the Windows—
aye or yet the door.

Making a few notes on the salient points from the two older volumes and a careful transcript of Harris' manuscript, Sanders replaced the volumes on their shelves and hurried out of the building. He felt quite unable to reflect while at rest and, pacing rapidly down St. Faith's, he took his cycle from the shop where he had stored it and pedalled energetically out of the town, heedless of his direction so long as he had the sense of motion. At length the rhythmical action of his feet began to soothe the turmoil in his brain, and he began to appreciate the value of his new-found knowledge.

Here, he reflected, was a more distinct allusion to a treasure than he had met with since he first set out to read the cipher. If Harris' statement were to be credited, this Gardiner of Elizabeth's day had been trusted with much wealth, presumably specie. Gardiner would have been forced to place so bulky a treasure in a secure hiding place, and for the same reason could never have encumbered himself with it in his flight from England. Only two questions seemed to be worth consideration: Did Gardiner hand over the custody of the money to some fellow-conspirators? Or, if he left it hidden in the hope of future retrieval, did he carry the secret abroad with him? As to the likely hiding place, there was the fact that the chapel was regarded as an appanage of the family, so prized, indeed, that the Gardiner of Henry's reign had defended it by actual force of arms. His descendants in Elizabeth's reign still owned it with its family memorials intact. That this was the site of the treasure was made even more probable by the compass bearings.

Convinced that he was on the right track, Sanders dismounted near the top of a steep incline and, resting, admired the beauty of the landscape. The day had been fine and dry, and now, as the declining sun's rays struck brightly through the clear atmosphere, the view embraced a wide tract of level country bounded on the farthest horizon by the bold upswelling of the Downs. To the right, the hill on which Sanders stood merged with a flat-topped mass of chalk running to the west. Between them flowed the Medway, a sinuous ribbon of quicksilver, spotted by the chocolate-brown sails of a few barges. Five miles away, the flat hill was crowned by a long straight mass of timber, a few higher trees at one end giving the whole a whimsical resemblance to a church with its spire. Sanders' eye returned again and again to this conspicuous feature on the skyline. His concentration was broken by a harsh scream close at hand; a seagull, harbinger of the approaching storm, had flown inland and now circled wide above him, while its mate, sailing in a lower plane, rested for the moment upon a queerly shaped mass he had not noticed until that moment. A full quarter of a mile away, its weather-beaten surface matched the stubble field around it. Sanders could see now that it consisted of three irregular flat stones set on end, leaning towards one another to form a tripod that supported a massive horizontal slab or capstone. Long before his brain had assimilated these features, almost as soon, indeed, as his eye fell upon it, Sanders recognised it as the cromlech of Kit's Coty House. Now, where was Embrook? Eagerly he scanned the valley, oblivious of a newcomer behind him.

"Good evening, Mr. Palmer."

Starting slightly, Sanders turned to meet the blue eyes of a girl wheeling a cycle down the precipitous slope of the hill he had found so exhausting to ascend. She looked about twenty-four or twenty-five and possessed the clear complexion so often seen with blue eyes and chestnut-coloured hair. Her slight supple figure was set off by the cycling dress, and the exercise had

THE RUINED CHAPEL

given her skin a healthy glow. Recognising her to be the landlady's daughter, Sanders struggled with his tight cloth cap while the girl unobtrusively patted her hair into place.

"Good evening, Miss Siton," he said with a smile. "I was admiring the view, but I rather think I've lost my way."

"And which way is that?"

"Why, to Embrook of course. I suppose I took the wrong turning out of Maidstone."

"Yes. You ought to have crossed the river instead of coming all the way up here."

"Well, I've found something to repay me for my climb."

"Yes, it is a very nice view indeed," the other replied coolly.

Somewhat nonplussed by this, Sanders changed the subject. "I was thinking I should like to get to that hill over there, but I suppose one must cross the river? I mean that one with all those trees on top."

"Oh, that! That's Woolbeding Beacon. There's only one way of getting there from here and that's by going through Embrook."

"Oh!" Sanders started at the sound of the name. Were the day's discoveries never to end? "Do you know," he added, as, noticing the curious look she gave him, he tried to resume his former manner, "I shall be very much obliged if you will show me the way home?"

"This way," she replied simply. Sanders mounted his bicycle and followed her lead as she boldly coasted down a descent that looked all the steeper in the sudden twilight.

The storm that arrived late that night had cleared by dawn. Although the air was damp and the ground soft, there was every prospect of a fine day as Sanders set out for the chapel after an early breakfast. On his shoulder he carried a pick and shovel borrowed from the farmer, together with a six-foot length of iron rod he had found lying in an outhouse.

Consequent upon Miss Siton's information he had looked carefully over the map once more before going to bed, with the satisfaction of finding that the spot of high ground he had already fixed on as the Beacon was practically the same as that he now knew for Woolbeding Hill or Beacon. Notwithstanding, he had passed a very restless night, plan after plan suggesting itself fruitlessly, and now when he reached the chapel and surveyed the rubbish heap within, his task seemed more formidable than ever. He had settled on a method which appeared simple enough and which in his single-handed state was as likely to give as good results as any other: he would probe the whole area of the ground with his rod, and wherever it encountered an obstacle of any size he would dig down upon it. The rod, although a comparatively short one, was long enough for his present purpose since, if it failed to disclose anything of value, clearly the help of a gang of navvies was the only alternative.

As Sanders probed and probed along the walls, the rod striking upon nothing more significant than flints, doubts began to assail him. How slender was the prospect of his finding the treasure, even if it had ever existed! After three centuries what chance did he have?

As he reflected thus the rod struck some object about four feet down with a sensation quite different from any he had yet experienced. Though the object seemed hard, there was an elasticity about it that pointed to something very different from flint. Continued probing defined the object as being about a foot square and constructed of nothing harder than wood. Throwing the rod aside he seized the spade and was soon heaving up great clods of earth. Halfway down he had to use the pick as well. The actual cache was a pocket of soft clay from which he was able to lever out with the spade a heavy black lump. Carefully scraping the clay from the mass, Sanders

THE RUINED CHAPEL

reached a rounded, pot-like form which possessed a longitudinal ridge and a flexible projecting lip. He turned it over and cleaned the cavity well, upon which the object assumed the form of an iron helmet of the familiar "lobster-tailed" type. But a far more curious object was embedded in the clay and debris which had filled the interior: an irregular, jagged spicule of flint that, after wiping with a handful of weeds, was revealed as an arrowhead.

Although puzzled by this association of a prehistoric weapon and a Cromwellian helmet, Sanders hardly welcomed these first fruits of his toil. The helmet indeed seemed to prove the accuracy of Harris in crediting Fairfax with the destruction of the chapel, but the arrowhead was an ominous indication of the thoroughness with which the place was wrecked. Thus to disturb the strata so far beneath the foundations the very vaults must have been torn up, and, if so, what of any treasure concealed there?

"Oh dear, Mr. Palmer, you do look a sight!"

Startled, Sanders spun round to face the ruined entrance.

"There's no accounting for taste, but whatever you want to go making a navvy of yourself for, for the sake of a lot of old rubbish like that, I can't imagine!" Miss Siton, her skirts looped up daintily to keep them from the mud, peeped on tiptoe into the excavation.

Sanders raised his cap. "Good morning, Miss Siton, you're out early."

"Early? Why, I've been up since five helping to milk those wretched goats. I wish the doctors further with all their talk about germs and things. First they said milk ought to be boiled, and now there's nothing so good as goat's milk. Nasty dirty animals—you can smell them a mile off."

"That's because they're free from tuberculosis, isn't it?"

"That's it. You seem to know everything, Mr. Palmer."

"I've learned something since I came here, anyhow."

"Really?"

"Yes, I've learned that Kent has more to show than hops and cherries."

"What's that?"

Sanders made to take the hand that rested upon the wall, but the girl snatched it away.

"I can't bear mud!" she exclaimed.

"Forgive me," he said, in the same spirit. Then more earnestly and with the fluency of practice, "When I see you I forget everything else."

"I wonder how many times you've said that before?" she observed, and turned her gaze with a marked unconcern towards a distant point in the landscape.

"Well, if I ever said it before I never meant it."

"Amy—Amy!" called a distant voice at that moment. With a smile and a wave of the hand, the girl tripped lightly away in the direction of the summons.

Yes, she was undeniably attractive, Sanders thought as his eye followed her. The attraction lay not merely in her physical beauty, considerable as that was. She was surprisingly well-educated for a farmer's daughter. The result was a degree of refinement hopelessly at odds with her surroundings. In the contrast she presented with her uncouth father and her homely rustic mother, Amy reminded Sanders of a Kimberly diamond in its setting of dull heavy clay. Wrapped in these pleasant reflections, he placed the helmet carefully to one side and resumed his occupation.

CHAPTER 4

AN UNWELCOME MEETING

"CAN I see Mr. Blakemore?" Sanders enquired.

He set down the hamper he had brought with him and waited impatiently for Blakemore's messenger to be summoned. It was two weeks since his first visit to the Record Office, during which time he had seen nothing in the newspapers of a body being fished out of the Thames estuary. All the same, he saw no reason to return to his previous address. Had the police made any discoveries he would simply be putting his head into the lion's mouth. He had no need of Gardiner's abandoned luggage and, indeed, had every intention of returning to Embrook that night.

"Hello, Gardiner, how are you?" Blakemore rose from his chair and welcomed the impostor with a smile. He shook hands and indicated a chair.

"What's that?" he added, inclining his head in the direction of the hamper. "Another cipher?"

"Not exactly. Have you made any progress since I saw you last?"

"Well, I'll be glad to talk it over with you. Have you brought the Vespers?"

"Yes, here it is," Sanders replied, unfastening the hamper, taking out the book and placing it on the desk. A moment later he had turned the hamper upside down and with a rattle and a clank, a helmet, half a dozen flint implements, and the rusted remains of a horse-pistol rolled out on the floor.

"Here, here, hold on!" exclaimed the astonished official. "What on earth is all that? You're in the wrong place. This is the Record Office, not the British Museum."

"Well, if you don't mind I'll deposit them here all the same. The fact is, I've been prospecting for treasure."

"And is that all you've found?"

"Practically, and before we go any further I'd better tell you how it happened. After I met you and found the cipher didn't help us much, I had a good look at the writing at the bottom of the page. Here it is, you see, just as I gave it to you in the copy." He opened the book of Vespers and pointed to the compass-bearings on the fly-leaf at the end. Blakemore nodded and Sanders went on, "The more I looked the surer I grew that they were compass-bearings, but of course they were useless until I could find out what the 'Beacon' and 'Cromlech' were. It was only by the merest accident that I hit on the truth." He sat back in his chair. "Gardiner's family—my own, I mean, of course—had an estate near Maidstone."

"Had they indeed?" exclaimed Blakemore. He appeared to be quite interested and began jotting down notes.

"Yes, but it's been out of the family nearly three hundred years."

"Do you know what it was called?"

"Embrook. Well, thinking there might be some connection between that and the compass-bearings, I got an Ordnance map and found that a line drawn from Kit's Coty House, which is of course a cromlech, and another from a hill known as

AN UNWELCOME MEETING

Woolbeding Beacon, joined at a chapel—a ruin five miles from the village of Embrook."

"Really. This is most interesting. " Blakemore rubbed his hands with satisfaction. "I see great possibilities opening before us."

"Having got so far I decided to go down and investigate on the spot. The old house is a farm now. It's about a mile from the chapel, which was the burial-place of the family."

"You must have been very much moved on visiting the tombs of your ancestors," suggested Blakemore, with the sincere sympathy of an antiquarian.

"I should have been, very," returned Sanders drily, "only there are no tombs to be seen." He told of his researches at Maidstone, of Kilburne's *Topographie,* Lambarde's *Perambulations* and Harris' *History,* especially the last. Producing his extracts he read them one by one, and then went on to the story of the excavations. "I have spent over two weeks there, I think I might say without a single idle moment, at least during daylight. And here you see the result." He pointed disparagingly at the scattered contents of the hamper.

"Come, come! I don't think your time has been altogether wasted." Blakemore picked up the helmet and inspected it with a critical eye. "There's no doubt this is Cromwellian—the lobster-tailed neckpiece shows that—so the Reverend Mr. Harris may be held to have told the truth about the ruining of the chapel. This horse-pistol, too; it's a flintlock, so I should say it dates from about the same period. I don't profess to be much of a judge of these things, but I do happen to know that flintlocks were introduced shortly before the time of the Civil War, so that it corroborates the date. As to the arrowheads, they seem to strengthen the case still more, although I don't agree with you that they indicate any unusual violence on the part of the Roundheads."

"Then you think the treasure may have been undisturbed?"

"Very possibly. At least I don't think that Fairfax's men either found it or looked for it."

"But what about the disturbance of the soil?" objected Sanders. "Surely the arrowheads, if they show anything at all, show that the search was violent?"

"Quite so. That's my very point. Now, what are the facts? You've read in Harris' book that the chapel was destroyed by Baker, one of Fairfax's captains, and you found on the spot undoubted traces of Parliamentary troops, so we may consider the personality of the vandals settled. As to the chapel itself, you say the walls are only breast-high and that the interior is full of rubbish. Now allowing for all the effects of time and what we may call human agencies since then, I think you must admit that the soldiers must have been not only very powerful, but very industrious to do so much mischief in such a short time, for Fairfax would not spare them long for a mere act of Puritanical bigotry. After the storming of Maidstone there was other and more pressing work to do."

"Yes, yes, I see! You mean an explosion?"

"Gunpowder, of course. Quite a small amount exploded in the vaults would do all they wanted, and that would also account for the heaps of earth and rubbish in the interior. As for the helmet and the pistol, it's most unlikely that the troops met with any opposition, so they were probably either dropped by the soldier who fired the train as he made his escape, or were blown into the debris by the explosion."

"And the arrowheads?"

"The same thing must have happened with them. The force of the powder acting, of course, in all directions caused such a disturbance of the ground that these venerable weapons were thrown up from the subsoil to join their lineal descendants. And there they've lain, cheek by jowl, ever since."

AN UNWELCOME MEETING

"And you believe the treasure may still be there?"

"Ah, that's quite a different matter. We're talking of what happened in 1648. I think St. Crescentia has been left in peace since *then,* but the treasure dates back another sixty-five years to 1583. A great deal may happen in sixty-five years! And how do you know there ever was any treasure?"

"Well, I've been expecting to learn that from you."

Blakemore smiled and placed the book of Vespers, together with another volume that he produced from a drawer, before him on the desk. Then he took up a sheet of foolscap to which he had been referring from time to time.

"I think we have neither of us been idle during the past two weeks," he began. "When you left the cipher with me I was very much puzzled by it, and although I have made something of it now, that last line, which you say stands for two compass-bearings, was quite unintelligible. Of course, I knew nothing about your estate and your family history and all that, so I didn't have those clues to help me. Anyway, at the period this cipher was apparently written they were just beginning to be a little more complicated than the first primitive ones. All the same, if this was actually written by the owner of the book I don't think that need trouble us much."

"Why not?"

"Because it was written by Sir Medway Gardiner. If he constructed it off his own bat, so to speak, we may be pretty sure it wasn't a very learned or insoluble one. We have no reason to suppose that he was in any way different from other country gentlemen of his time. I mean, it's unlikely he was of a very inventive turn, and I should doubt he knew anything particular about mathematics. I don't think even an average present-day country gentleman would be capable of inventing an absolutely undecipherable message. Also, it's unlikely that he would have chosen his book of Vespers in which to write the cipher unless there was some connection between the two things—the book and the cipher. I wish you had brought the book with you when you came before. Then I might possibly have been able to read some sense into the message, and I can't think even now how you failed to grasp its meaning. You had the book with you all the time. Did it never occur to you to look inside? Just look here." Blakemore offered him the volume.

"But it's all in Latin," Sanders objected.

"Well, have you forgotten all you learned at Gattenwood? It struck me when you showed it to me that as the cipher occurred in a Vespers, it would be as well for me to get one for myself and see what I could mug up from that."

"Well?" Sanders prompted, as Blakemore opened the other book and appeared to read in it.

"Well," returned Blakemore good-humouredly, "I think I've now got to the bottom of it."

"You're a brick!" exclaimed Sanders.

"Don't be too sanguine," said Blakemore, smiling at his enthusiasm. "Wait until you've heard all."

"You mean, there's still some doubt about it?" enquired Sanders anxiously.

"Of course there is. You don't suppose the cipher tells you to go and dig in a certain corner of a certain field and that there you'll find fifty thousand pounds? When I had worked out the sense of it I didn't feel as if I were very much further forward, although I admit what you have discovered makes the case in favour of a treasure a little stronger—but only a little. Everything is delightfully vague even now, and you really must make up your mind for a little disappointment."

"Very well, then, I'll expect nothing, but let's hear what this wretched secret message says."

"Well now, in order that you should thoroughly understand the matter, I had better tell you how I worked it out. The

AN UNWELCOME MEETING 61

cipher is in a book of Vespers and that service is the fifth section of the Canonical 'Hours' of the Roman Church, consisting largely of Psalms. Now as soon as I got a Vespers and looked through it, I began to suspect that there was a relation between the figures and the Psalms. After all, what is more likely? The writer looks out a text in the Psalms in the body of the book, finds one he wants, and makes a note of it on one of the fly-leaves at the end."

"Just so."

"But what made me feel sure the figures referred to Psalms is the peculiar way in which the numbers run. Look here." Blakemore jotted some figures on a slip and handed it to his visitor:

113–9	125–5
113–10	125–6
113–12	125–7

"What do these look like? Don't they look like chapter and verse?" Without waiting for an answer he continued: "And if so, what alternative have you to Psalms? There is no other book in the Bible with a hundred and thirteen chapters, let alone a hundred and twenty-five. There is only one book, indeed, with as many as sixty-six chapters, and that's Isaiah. Suppose we regarded eleven as the chapter and three hundred and ten as the verse; in what place do we find three hundred and ten verses to a chapter? Where but in Psalms? It might certainly be objected that the texts I have written down in the second column there might mean the twelfth chapter and the fifty-fifth, fifty-sixth and fifty-seventh verses, but speaking from memory, I think the twelfth chapters of Luke and one of the Apocryphal books—I forget which one—are the only ones in all the Bible that have so many verses. So we may conclude, I think, that the whole passage refers to the Psalms, and indeed I have found that the only feasible place to search in."

"And did you search there?"

"I did, with a result that you will, I think, agree is very satisfactory. I must tell you though that until this morning my opinion was very different. Until I heard your story I was completely fogged! I was able to make neither head nor tail of the result and was going to tell you there was no hidden meaning in the thing—that it wasn't a cipher at all but just a collection of texts which may have hit the fancy of Sir Medway, or whoever it was who jotted them down. I was open to discuss whether the compass-bearings might have some special interpretation, but as to the rest—" He shrugged his shoulders expressively.

"And now?" Sanders asked.

"Now I'm of quite a different opinion. Those discoveries you made at Maidstone have thrown a new light on the whole thing. It seems as if you had flashed a searchlight into a dark cellar! Really, Gardiner, I must congratulate you on the result. I consider you have shown a great deal of cleverness, to say nothing of labour and industry, and you deserve all the reward the thing may bring you."

"Thank you, Blakemore. I appreciate that."

Silently, Blakemore took from a drawer a single sheet of paper which he handed to Sanders. On it was written:

Psalm XXXIII. 12—Come, children, hearken to me: I will teach you the fear of the Lord.

Psalm III. 2—Why, O Lord, are they multiplied that afflict me? Many are they who rise up against me.

Psalm XXVI. 12—Deliver me not over to the will of them that trouble me, for unjust witnesses have risen up against me: and iniquity hath lied to itself.

AN UNWELCOME MEETING

Psalm CXXXVIII. 21—Have I not hated them, O Lord, that hated thee: and pined away because of thine enemies.

Psalm XC. 3—For he hath delivered me from the snare of the hunters: and from the sharp word.

Psalm CXIII. 9—The house of Israel hath hoped in the Lord: he is their helper and their protector.

Psalm CXIII. 10—The house of Aaron hath hoped in the Lord: he is their helper and their protector.

Psalm CXIII. 12—The Lord hath been mindful of us, and hath blessed the house of Israel: he hath blessed the house of Aaron.

Psalm CXI. 3—Glory and wealth shall be in his house: and his justice remaineth for ever and ever.

Psalm XXVI. 5—For he hath hidden me in his tabernacle: in the day of evil he hath protected me in the place of his tabernacle.

Psalm CXV. 13—I will take the chalice of salvation: and I will call upon the name of the Lord.

Psalm CXIII. 4—The idols of the Gentiles are silver and gold: the work of the sons of men.

Psalm CXXV. 5—They that sow in tears shall reap in joy.

Psalm CXXV. 6—Going they went and wept casting their seed.

Psalm CXXV. 7—But coming they shall come with joyfulness, carrying their sheaves.

Psalm CXI. 2—His seed shall be mighty upon the earth: the generation of the righteous shall be blessed.

Psalm LXXI. 15—And he shall live, and to him shall be given of the gold of Arabia: for him they shall always adore, they shall bless him all day.

"Well, what do you think of that? Reads pretty consecutively, doesn't it?" enquired Blakemore with a smile as Sanders finished reading.

"It hangs together well, no doubt, but I should have liked the old boy to have been a little less ambiguous."

"Then it wouldn't have been a cipher! The very essence of a cipher is that no one shall understand it but the person it is intended for."

"And who do you think that was?"

"Why, his son—haven't you a family pedigree? No? Well, I don't think there can be any doubt about it. Just look how it begins: *Come, children, hearken to me.* It was certainly addressed to one or more sons; it would hardly have been intended for his daughters. The son must have been well aware of the causes that led to his father's exile, and with that premise would find the cipher extremely simple. Now, after what we may call the Invocation the writer goes on to lament the number of his enemies, clearly alluding to a trial with false witnesses, and implores divine aid for a devout Catholic who has adhered to the true faith. He dwells on the happiness enjoyed under special protection of the Lord, and declares he will yet be righted and his estates restored to him. Then we come, in Psalm twenty-six, verse five, to the gist of the whole thing: he speaks of being *hidden in the tabernacle,* but obviously he couldn't refer to himself since we know he fled the country. In the next verse we have an allusion to a *chalice,* and in the very next to something still more significant—*idols of silver and gold.* Finally, in the last verse someone is promised *the gold of Arabia.* We must make allowance for poetical expressions; I suppose Sir Medway couldn't find a text which described the treasure more accurately, or else he purposely wanted to make it ambiguous. It didn't matter much so long as his son had a hint beforehand."

"But that doesn't strengthen my idea of the chapel being the place where the treasure was concealed."

"Yes, it does. What else does *hidden in the tabernacle* mean? And what about your own discoveries with the compass-bearings?

AN UNWELCOME MEETING

There may have been a special tabernacle in the church before it was destroyed. The rest of the cipher is simple enough. *Sow in tears* refers to the concealment of the treasure in fear of arrest and, taken together with the remaining texts, encourages the son to search diligently so that he may attain riches and restore the fortunes of the family."

"Well, I *have* searched diligently, and you see the result." He pointed again to the melancholy assortment lying on the carpet.

"Then you must persevere. I'm sure you are on the right track. But I must warn you of one important matter you have overlooked."

"What?"

"Just this. Like many other people you seem not to be very clear about 'findings being keepings,' as they say. Suppose that everything turns out as I suggest: suppose there really is a treasure in that ruined chapel; and suppose you are lucky enough to find it—what then?"

"You mean I can't claim it?"

"I do," said Blakemore quietly. "I'm no lawyer, but I know enough to tell you that if you find property of any kind in a public place you are entitled to keep it only so long as the real owner can't be discovered, and if you find property on private ground the title to it rests with the owner of the property."

"Oh." Sanders' shoulder sagged perceptibly. "I didn't know that."

"Few people do," said Blakemore with a smile. "Of course, if you bought the land, that would go a long way towards simplifying matters, and were I in your place I should seriously consider doing that. It might not be the best possible investment, but even without the treasure it *is* your ancestral estate, after all."

"You advise me to purchase, then?"

"I think so. But excuse me, I hear my messenger's bell.

Someone is waiting to see me. Are you still at the Great Eastern?"

Thus reminded of the waste of public time to which he had been accessory, Sanders rose to go. "No," said he, "I've moved my headquarters to Embrook."

As he walked down the gloomy corridors of the Record Office, Sanders began to see that the reading of the cipher had not cleared every difficulty from his path. To buy the land was a counsel of perfection; he had neither the money nor the time for such a transaction. Plunging into the twilight of the stairway, Sanders sought the handrail, but he relinquished its aid halfway down when he moved aside to allow a messenger following by the dim form of a visitor to pass him. In the darkness the newcomer lurched heavily against the almost invisible Sanders, and, muttering an apology, continued his upward climb.

Against the further wall, Sanders had staggered back in a state of utter shock. He had recognised in the visitor the figure and voice of Medway Gardiner.

For several minutes he leaned against the wall, paralysed by a sickening dread. Then he tried to pull himself together. For an instant he was seized with the idea of rushing to justify himself before the two men who were even now discussing his theft, his treachery and his fraud. But the gulf between them seemed suddenly too wide to bridge. Instead he turned and ran down towards the entrance hall. Near the foot of the stairs he hesitated once more. Might his fears be groundless? Were it not better to return and face the consequences? His offence, he tried to tell himself, was a venial one. He had stolen nothing— nothing but a man's name, and that was none of his seeking. But he was not convinced. His mind turned to the possibility of a police trap. How had Gardiner's survival been hushed up? Might a cordon have been placed round the building?

Slowly he descended the stairs and reached the inner lobby

AN UNWELCOME MEETING

whence, at the end of a short vista, he could see the doorkeeper nodding in his chair. The hall was otherwise quite deserted. He gazed through a glass door towards the silent vestibule. That way might be immediate disaster, but to retrace his footsteps would be to risk running into Gardiner. While he stood irresolute, a door slammed far above. Footsteps could be heard on the stairs. On an impulse he darted through the glass door and turned off short into the adjoining museum. In an instant he had bought a catalogue and begun a conscientious study of the exhibits with an eye cocked towards the doorway across the hall.

At last, after spending the greater part of an hour in this peripatetic fashion without being rewarded by any sign of Gardiner, the suspense became intolerable. He flung down the catalogue and walked boldly out of the museum. He encountered not a soul but the porter, who held the door open for him. On the steps he paused to give his adversaries their opportunity. Far down the approach stood a policeman on point-duty; nearer, a postman was emptying a pillar-box; no one else was in sight.

Mechanically he turned into Chancery Lane and at the bottom bore round into Fleet Street. On and on he strode in expectation every moment of an arresting hand upon his shoulder, till at length he found himself at the top of Broad Street within sight of the hotel. Dare he call there? Did an ambush await him? Turning, he retraced his steps, uncertain of his destination.

A cab stopped nearby and, with a sudden resolution, he hailed it.

"Victoria—Chatham and Dover line," he cried and leapt into the vehicle.

CHAPTER 5

QUESTIONS OF IDENTITY

WHEN Gardiner was thrown from the tender he struck his head against a sponson and, after only a moment's submersion, floated face upward, unconscious and unresisting. The fast-moving tide swept him along until, about half a mile higher up, he collided with a boat that was being rowed across to an outward-bound steamer. As he fouled the starboard line, the sailor pulling it seized him by the hair and supported his chin upon the gunwale.

"Is he dead?" asked the steersman.

"No sir, I think he's just got into the water." He pushed a leathery finger inside Gardiner's collar. "He's still warm."

"Hold him up then, we're just on her. Oars!" They rubbed along the side of a large steamer whose Plimsoll mark was barely above the water-line.

"*Amazon*," hailed the steersman. "Send a light down."

"Aye, aye, sir." A man holding a lantern descended the rope ladder above them.

"What've you got there, captain?" asked a voice from the deck.

"Dead man, I think," replied the captain. He tore open

Gardiner's vest and felt his chest. "No, he isn't."

"Nasty cut, sir," observed the man with the lamp.

"Someone's cracked his head and tried to drown him. Got his watch on, so it wasn't robbery. Looks a respectable man, too."

"Hurry up there, please, captain; the tide's just turning for us," warned the man on deck.

"All right, pilot. Sling a chair down. Lively now."

The still unconscious Gardiner was soon lashed in a chair slung from a davit and hoisted on deck. After the boat had been hauled up in its turn, the fifteen-hundred-ton ship, cleared for Rio with machinery, began to hoot her way down the crowded river.

The *Amazon* carried no regular passengers, so there was plenty of room for the unconscious man. He was undressed, had his wound bandaged, and kept warm in a cabin adjoining the captain's. During the night, a natural sleep replaced the unconscious state. Early the next morning, as the ship rounded the North Foreland to enter the Channel, Gardiner woke up and was able to learn from the steward what had happened. The appetising smell from the galley made his mouth water and, feeling little the worse except for a headache, he joined the captain at table.

Off Deal they slowed up to land the pilot, and Gardiner, having no wish to go on to Rio, was eager to accompany him. His head began to ache severely as he tottered up on deck, and the captain forbade him to attempt the rope ladder. Instead, after goodbyes had been exchanged, money offered and declined, and Gardiner's heartfelt thanks patiently heard out, the involuntary passenger was lashed into the chair once more and slung over the side. It was almost with regret that, as the little boat danced across the Downs, Gardiner watched the *Amazon*, her exhaust pipe spuming vigorously, double the South Foreland.

Had the ship been a passenger steamer with a surgeon on board, or had the captain possessed even a smattering of medical knowledge, Gardiner would have been spared the error of leaving his bed, or of eating so heartily so soon after a head injury and partial drowning. Nature soon exacted the full penalty. As Gardiner, leaning on the pilot's arm, crawled out of the boat and tried to mount from the beach to the Esplanade, he staggered and fell senseless on the steps of the sea-wall.

Twelve hours' delirium were succeeded by as many days of slow recovery before Gardiner was able to sit at the window of his room at the Beach Hotel. The bright noonday sun seemed to heighten his pallor and deepen the hollows of his cheeks as the surgeon applied a final dressing to the nearly healed wound on his brow.

"But surely I shall be fit to travel tomorrow, doctor? I have most important business in London."

"Well, maybe London, but mind—no further!"

"Very well. But I must at least claim my luggage. You can see what a condition my wardrobe is in." He held his arms out to display his stained and tattered clothing.

"Yes, but an overcoat will hide all that. There's a shop in the High Street where you can get a ready-made one good enough to travel in. I suppose your things are at the docks?"

"I haven't the least idea. I last saw them on the tender going ashore."

"Hmm!" The doctor eyed his patient uncertainly for a few moments. "I never asked you before, but can you explain why they called you 'Sanders' in the newspapers?" Gardiner looked blank at this. "The account in the *Telegraph*—it was only a few lines—said that a 'Mr. Sanders' had fallen overboard from the tender. It has puzzled me rather, but I didn't care to go into the matter before."

"I really can't account for it at all."

"Most likely they mistook his name for yours, eh?"

"Yes, that must have been it. Of course, they didn't know either of our names on the tender."

"Perhaps an error of the reporter's."

"Perhaps. All the same, I can't think how Sanders let them take the wrong name, unless he fell into the river at the same time!"

"Well, you'll be able to investigate all that tomorrow. Don't go out today and take things very quietly tomorrow. Above all, live plainly and abstemiously."

About noon the next day, Gardiner called at the shipping office in Leadenhall Street where his seedy clothing won him scant attention or respect. After explaining his business half a dozen times over to as many different officials, he was at length curtly referred to the authorities at Tilbury Docks. Annoyed and perplexed, he took a cab to Fenchurch Street and ate a quick lunch at the refreshment bar while awaiting his train. All the way along the weary and depressing route he puzzled over the curious ignorance of his catastrophe that prevailed at the shipping office. Even supposing the captain of the tender had failed to report the accident, it was strange that no word should have reached headquarters from other sources. Altogether, matters seemed very unsatisfactory. He felt doubly anxious now about his luggage, especially his papers and a certain small parchment volume.

It was nearly two o'clock when he arrived at Tilbury and was directed to the tender. He found it lying at the landing stage in obvious disappointment of work and with no sign of life beyond a single deck-hand dozing on a bench.

"Is the captain on board?" Gardiner hailed.

The man sat up and, removing an extinguished pipe from his mouth, gazed blearily about him. "Yes," he yawned, when at length he had located the questioner. "He's down below."

Gardiner climbed on board and descended the stairway. When his eyes had grown accustomed to the cloud of tobacco smoke, he made out a man seated before the fire with his back turned towards his visitor.

"Excuse me," said Gardiner rather loudly. "I want to see the captain."

"That's me," growled the man, without deigning to turn round.

"Do you remember a passenger falling overboard a fortnight ago?"

"What!" Springing to his feet so abruptly that he upset a kettle which simmered on a small stove, the captain advanced threateningly. "Look here. I told the last of you 'tecs what came smelling round here like a crab goin' to a lobster's funeral that I wasn't goin' to have my time took up with answering any more questions unless I was paid for it. My time's as valuable to me as your'n is to you, and don't you forget it, neither."

"I'm not a detective," Gardiner protested. "Don't you remember me?"

"No, I don't, and I don't care what you are. I've heard nothing for the last five minutes about the blasted case and I thought it was blowing over, but if people keep on coming here forever, and worrying me about any more of it, I shall turn vicious, I shall." He picked up the kettle and replaced it on the stove with a savage clang. Then he went down on his knees and fished up from among the ashes the fragments of his pipe.

"I'm really sorry to bother you," said Gardiner placatingly. "Here, try one of these cigars."

"Thanks," said the captain, somewhat mollified. "What do you want, anyhow?"

"My name's Gardiner. I'm the man who fell overboard."

The captain started and edged away uncomfortably.

"No, I'm not a ghost!" laughed Gardiner. "I'm just as much

alive as you are." And in a few words he described what had happened to him since the accident.

"Well, I'm . . . . But look here, what did you say your name is?"

"John Medway Gardiner."

"Well, that can't be right. It was Mr. Sanders who fell overboard."

Gardiner's headache returned. He felt his way to a chair. "Excuse me," he said, lying back. "I . . . I haven't quite recovered. I'm still rather weak at times."

What could be the meaning of it all, he asked himself. The newspapers had reported that Sanders had fallen overboard, and now the captain declared the same thing. Was everybody mad, or had his own brain been affected by the accident? "Did we both fall overboard, then?" he asked at length.

"No, only Mr. Sanders."

"And who was he?"

"Why, the gentleman with Mr. Gardiner," was the dogged reply.

"But I'm the one who fell overboard, and *my* name is Gardiner!"

"He said you were Sanders and he was Gardiner."

"You must have mistaken him. His name is Sanders."

"No fear! The police took care of that."

"Police?"

"Yes, they boarded us just after Mr. San—er, you fell over. They came to arrest Sanders."

"Arrest him? What for?"

"Forgery," said the captain grimly.

"Oh! And did they?"

"No, he was in the water—at least so the other one said."

Gardiner rose and walked shakily to the doorway. The fresh air from the river blew gratefully upon his aching brow. Slowly he mounted the stairs and, stepping out on deck, stared absently at the foam-topped wavelets. What villainy was this? Had Sanders stolen his name? A mere acquaintance, yet a man he had befriended. Robbed of his name, was he now to bear the burden of another's crime?

"What became of the gentleman who called himself Gardiner?" he asked the captain, who stood enjoying his cigar at the top of the companion.

"Oh, the police took his address and then he went off. Said he was going to the Great Eastern Hotel."

"And his luggage?"

"Took it with him, of course! What do *you* think?"

"And what became of the other—Mr. Sanders' things?"

"Police took charge of them. But not till I'd made 'em give me a receipt." The captain puffed his cigar and chuckled at his own smartness.

"And that's all you know about it?"

"Yes, that's all I know. Police'll be able to tell you more, I reckon." He watched Gardiner with a sidelong look.

"Well, captain, I'm much obliged to you," said Gardiner with as much cheerfulness as he felt able to assume. "By the way, do you know where Captain Norris of the *Black Prince* lives when he's ashore?"

"No, I don't, but you'll likely find him on board the *Black Prince* now. I heard she was going a little way up the river to adjust her compasses. She'll most likely go down with the tide this afternoon."

Gardiner thanked the captain, offered him another cigar, and took his leave. As he walked on to the landing stage, the captain beckoned to the sleepy deck-hand. "See where he goes and mind you don't lose him! He's wanted by the police. It'll be worth a good drink to you."

Gardiner took the steam ferry across the river to Gravesend and made his way to the police station.

"Can I see the officer in charge?" he asked the sergeant.

"What name, please?"

"Gardiner. I want to see him about the accident on the *Black Prince's* tender a fortnight ago."

This statement appeared to excite some interest, for he was immediately shown into an inner room where an inspector received him.

"But you're not Mr. Gardiner!" exclaimed the officer as Gardiner sat down and faced him.

"I assure you that is my name."

"You wanted to see me in reference to the accident on the *Black Prince's* tender?"

"Yes. I am the passenger who fell overboard."

The inspector gave a slight start before asking rather unnecessarily, "Then you weren't drowned?"

"No," replied Gardiner with a smile. Briefly he sketched the story of his adventures. "And now," he concluded, "I have come to ask your assistance in recovering my luggage."

The inspector pressed an electric-bell push. "It is all here," he said rather drily, "but—"

"Pardon me, I believe that what you have here belongs to Mr. Sanders. I understand he has assumed my name and taken possession of my luggage."

The sergeant entered the room and the inspector rose. "Is there anyone outside?" he asked.

"Yes, sir, P. C. Davis."

"Wait here, then," ordered his superior and, turning to Gardiner, "I am sorry to inform you there is a warrant issued for your arrest on forgery and other charges, and I must detain you until the arrival of an officer from London."

"But this is a very extraordinary proceeding. You have no warrant for my arrest. My name is Gardiner!"

The inspector produced an official looking buckram-covered

volume which he consulted before replying. "My instructions are that your name is William Sanders."

"Nothing of the sort," protested Gardiner. "Sanders was a passenger I met on the *Black Prince*. I had never heard of him seven weeks ago."

"Well, sir, I don't disbelieve you, but I can't go beyond my instructions. You admit you are the man who fell overboard? Very well, I am instructed his name is Sanders, for whom a warrant is out."

"See here! Will this convince you?" cried Gardiner despairingly, as he tore apart his clothes and, baring his breast, showed the name upon his undervest.

"Yes, I see 'Gardiner' written there plainly enough," agreed the inspector as he examined the marking, "but that isn't proof of your identity."

"And so you arrest me on another man's warrant?"

"No, no." The inspector laughed and raised his hands. "Bless you, sir, I don't arrest you at all, but it is my duty to detain you until an officer arrives from London with the warrant. It is he who will decide whether you are to be arrested or not." He turned to the sergeant. "Telephone at once," he ordered.

"I warn you this is a complete mistake," Gardiner protested.

"I hope it is, sir, and when the officer comes I hope you will be able to convince him of it."

Gardiner's head throbbed unmercifully. "But how am I to do that?"

The officer found something convincing in Gardiner's show of sincerity. "Is there no one who can identify you?" he suggested. "If there is, we'll be happy to help you communicate with him. Someone of position is best."

Gardiner considered a moment, and then suddenly sprang to his feet. "Why, of course—Captain Norris. I'd forgotten all about him. Would the captain of the *Black Prince* do?"

"Perhaps so," was the cautious admission.

"But how can I communicate with him?"

"We will send a telegram if you pay for it."

"I don't know his address. Oh, yes I do, though. He's on board his ship just off here. Can someone take a message to him?"

"I can't spare one of my men at present, I'm afraid." He raised his voice. "Davis!" The constable from the outer office entered and saluted. "Is there anyone who can take a message to the *Black Prince,* out on the river?"

The constable considered a moment. "I think, sir," he said, "there's a man outside who might do. Shall I call him in?"

When the man shuffled in, Gardiner found his face vaguely familiar, but he did not recognise the deck-hand from Tilbury.

"Are you willing to take a message for this gentleman to the captain of the *Black Prince*?" enquired the inspector.

The man looked at Gardiner in obvious doubt. Consent would mean losing sight of him. He was conscious of a thirst and had tantalising visions of the reward promised by the tender's captain. He was hesitating when Gardiner interposed.

"Here is a sovereign," he said. "I now hand it to the inspector to give you as soon as you bring me back a written answer."

The man's face brightened. "All right, sir. Where's the message?"

The inspector supplied an official sheet of paper on which Gardiner wrote as follows:

Gravesend Police Station

Dear Captain Norris,

I am detained here in error on a warrant concerning another person. As there is no one else I can apply to, may I ask you to come here as soon as possible to identify me?

Yours truly,
J. Medway Gardiner.

Placing the note in an official envelope, Gardiner handed it to the sailor, who departed with an alacrity to which he had been a stranger since boyhood.

"Now, Mr. Gardiner," said the inspector, "I am sorry, but I must ask you to step this way. I have a lot of things to see to and it may be some time before the officer comes from London."

"Are you putting me in a cell?" asked Gardiner.

"No, sir, I won't take that responsibility. We'll put you in the officers' mess-room. You'll find it comfortable enough, though I am afraid I must lock you in." He followed Gardiner along a whitewashed corridor to a room furnished with a long table and several chairs. A fire blazed cheerfully in the grate, and the walls were hung with several gaily coloured prints from illustrated papers, but the barred windows overlooking a narrow whitewashed court subtracted from the room's brightness. After the inspector had gone, Gardiner paced dejectedly up and down the room. His position, he realised, was a serious one. Clearly he saw the whole chain of circumstance, beginning with the story of the Futenta concession. Despite Sanders' denial, he now knew him for the swindler he was. And now Sanders had managed to shift his name and responsibilities on to his, Gardiner's, shoulders. What devilish ingenuity and what a preposterous situation! Surely it could not last. Norris would arrive soon and in an hour or two they would be laughing together at his predicament.

But as he continued to pace, doubts assailed him. Suppose Norris was not to be found? Was there any other method of proving his identity? Was the official mind so crassly impermeable to the truth that he would have to go to prison? Unthinkable! Even if Norris were to fail him altogether, even if he had actually sailed, Gardiner would sooner or later prove his identity and expose the error. He must communicate with his London agents and get a good lawyer. Thank God, he could

QUESTIONS OF IDENTITY

afford the expense. But the humiliation, the unspeakable degradation, in the interval!

Nearly two hours passed before the inspector unlocked the door and told him a Scotland Yard officer was expected at any moment.

"No word of Captain Norris yet?"

"Not yet, sir. I'll send you his reply the moment it comes."

"Suppose the Scotland Yard man arrives first? I hope you won't let him take me away until the captain comes."

"If the officer decides to arrest you on the warrant, you will pass the night here."

Gardiner was somewhat cheered by this prospect and by the kindly offer of some tea. At a quarter to six he was taken to the inspector's office where he found the inspector in company with a smart-looking man in mufti. Had he encountered him in Pall Mall, Gardiner would have put him down as a member of one of the service clubs.

"This is Inspector Saxby of the Criminal Investigation Department," said the inspector.

Gardiner bowed and the new arrival, after a keen look at him, moved to the window. "Will you kindly step over here?" he said. After carefully scrutinising Gardiner's features, he said, "I understand you claim to be Mr. Gardiner?"

"That is my name."

"You know I hold a warrant for the arrest of Mr. Sanders. Can you describe his appearance?"

"We were about the same height, but he was darker than me and a little stouter, especially by the time we got to London. He was growing a beard at first, but shaved it off when we got into the Channel."

"I see. Now, did you ever notice the colour of his eyes?"

"Oh, brown—very deep brown!"

The detective seemed impressed by this remark. He excused

himself and held a whispered consultation with the other officer.

"I think," he said to Gardiner, "that there has been a mistake. There is no doubt about your description not tallying with that of Mr. Sanders. Among other differences, your eyes are blue, and his are recorded as dark brown. That was a matter easily overlooked at night, and as the captain of the tender assured us that it was Sanders who had fallen overboard, we didn't examine very closely the one who claimed to be Gardiner."

He paused before continuing, but Gardiner did not speak.

"I must apologise for your having been detained, but you see how it is; the inspector here would have been seriously to blame if he had let you go. All the same, it will be more satisfactory if you can be positively identified as Mr. Gardiner. I understand you have sent—"

There was a quick rap at the door, and the constable entered. "Captain Norris, sir; will you see him?"

"Why, inspector," enquired the captain breezily as he bustled into the office without waiting for the officer's reply, "what are you going to do with my friend Gardiner? How are you, Gardiner? What's all this about? As you seemed to be in a bit of a scrape, I thought it best to come in person."

A little later, as Gardiner and his identifier were crossing Woodville Road on their way to the railway station, a sailor lurched beside them and, pulling his forelock, hiccupped, "Where yer goin' to, guv'nor? I wasn't to lose sight of yer."

"Well, well," said the captain of the *Black Prince* good-humouredly, "Mr. Gardiner is going to dine with me in London, but here's something to get *really* drunk with."

CHAPTER 6

A NEW ALLY

AS soon as they arrived in London, Gardiner lost no time in buying new attire and a portmanteau to put it in. Then he drove with the captain to Norfolk Street, where, in a quiet hotel at the Embankment end, he secured lodging for the night. Abandoning his problem for the rest of the evening, he followed his companion's prescription of "a nice little dinner with the Alhambra to follow."

The following morning, after a late breakfast and a leisurely study of the newspaper, he determined to put off his visit to the Record Office no longer. His disagreeable experience of the previous day had shown the urgent need of his securing evidence of identity. Although he had satisfied the police of their mistake, it was still possible for some zealous subordinate officer to fall into a similar error and, since Norris was on the point of sailing, a substitute witness must be found at once. It was barely eleven when he left the hotel, too early to intrude upon a highly placed government official whose morning would scarcely have commenced. He therefore turned towards the Embankment and walked westward, inhaling the cool breeze from the river, and enjoying the half-forgotten spectacle of the apparently clumsy barges deftly shooting the bridges. For a while he enjoyed his ramble. The continuous drone of traffic, the clangour of hoofs, the distant shouts: these sounds were less melancholy to him than the incessant roar of surf. He would settle in London, he decided. He had long promised himself a hansom-cab ride. But first he must straighten out the muddle in his affairs, including the question of his luggage. He hailed a cab and was driven along the cheery, bustling streets to the Strand. When the cab turned into Chancery Lane the clock at the Law Courts was chiming a quarter to one. Because lunch-time was near, or because his interest in the cipher was waning, Blakemore gave the messenger an impatient reception.

"Who did you say? Mr. Gardiner? No, no, it can't be. I'm really very much occupied. . . ."

But the messenger was already retiring, leaving the embarrassed visitor in Blakemore's doorway.

"Yes, my name is Gardiner, but if I am intruding I will call another time," he said rather stiffly. And with that he turned on his heel.

"Oh, pray don't go, sir. I mistook you for someone else. Please sit down and tell me your business."

"No doubt you've forgotten me," said Gardiner, taking the indicated chair. "We were at Gattenwood together, but that's many years ago. I've been abroad a long time and have only just come back from the Gold Coast."

Blakemore gave this latest visitor a hard stare. "No, I don't remember you," he replied. "Whom did you live with?"

"I boarded with old Hayes, you know. I remember you were one of Green's lot—'Tunk' as we used to call him."

"Yes, that is so," agreed Blakemore, thawing a little. "I remember Gardiner quite well, but I never should have thought you were he."

"Well, it's been a long time, of course. And I've been rather ill lately."

A NEW ALLY

"Hmm, I thought you were looking seedy. The Gold Coast climate, I suppose?"

"No, it's nothing to do with the Coast; I was always pretty well there. I've been laid up since I came home, and it's partly in connection with that that I came to see you."

For the third time in twenty-four hours Gardiner told his story. This time its effect was profound. Blakemore sat in open-mouthed astonishment, his lunch-hour forgotten.

"You amaze me, sir," Blakemore responded, when the recital came to an end. "And this man Sanders is going about impersonating you?"

"That I can't say, but I fear he may be, and it's because of that, and my being detained by the police yesterday, that I came here today. I wanted to make myself known to you so as to have a witness of position to my being the man I claim to be. It would be almost farcical if it were not such a tragedy for me. I'm glad you understand my position. The curious thing is that I intended to come and see you over a very different matter."

Blakemore had some difficulty in preserving an impassive countenance as Gardiner retold the story of the cipher. Though the account was similar to the one he had already heard, this one was altogether richer in circumstantial detail.

"And when did you last see the volume of Vespers?"

"Well, it's seven weeks since I left Sekondi, and I didn't look at it for some time before that. I presume it's in my trunk now. That is, unless Sanders has made away with it."

"Is this anything like it?" enquired Blakemore, placing the book on the desk in front of Gardiner.

"I— how on earth—? Where—? Whatever is the meaning of it?" stammered Gardiner as, trembling with excitement, he seized the book. Turning over the leaves he assured himself that it was indeed his own copy, with the cipher still intact.

Blakemore laughed heartily, enjoying his bewilderment. "I haven't had it in my keeping more than half an hour," said he.

"But who gave it to you?"

"Who else but this fellow Sanders? You must have passed him on the stairs."

"Oh! I did pass someone, but it was too dark for me to recognise him. What did he come for?"

"To discuss the cipher."

"But what excuse did he make for having it in his possession?"

"None at all. Why should he? He represented himself as the owner."

"And you treated him as such?"

"Certainly," assented Blakemore, a trifle stiffly. "How was I to know otherwise? He gave your name and trotted out all the details of Gattenwood and so on, in all respects exactly as you have been doing."

Gardiner rose and walked to the window. Only now did he appreciate the depths to which Sanders had fallen. Hitherto he had almost condoned the pilfering of his name as a desperate subterfuge to avoid immediate arrest. But this plot to profit from the cipher was an affair of far greater moment. For a few minutes he was angry. And then, gradually, more charitable thoughts prevailed. Was there so much dishonour in his treatment of one he honestly believed to be dead? Of a man, as Gardiner had given him to know, without heirs or relatives? He turned from the window and resumed his seat.

"I ask if you have any doubts about my *bona fides*?"

"No, no," protested the official. "I am perfectly satisfied you are the Gardiner I knew at Gattenwood. As the police admitted, the colour of the eyes decides between you. Why, I remember now we used to call you 'Blue-eyes.' But what I want to know is how this fellow Sanders got to know all about the school? Did he pump you for those details as well?"

A NEW ALLY

"Oh, no; he was a Gattenwood boy, too."

"Never! I don't remember any boy of that name."

"Well, he was rather junior to both of us. You know how a year or two's difference makes schoolboys perfect strangers. I never knew much of him myself."

"Well, he played his part very cleverly, and he was actually here until the moment before you arrived. However, what are your plans now?"

Gardiner sighed. "I really don't know what to do," he confessed. "Ever since I came home there seems to have been nothing but one worry after another. When I came to you today I thought my difficulties were over, but now I see they're only just beginning."

"Come, now, you mustn't be downhearted."

"I can't help it. My head aches and I can't think, especially when something like this is sprung on me."

"Let me think for you, then," said Blakemore kindly. "We'll put our heads together and if we can't go one better than Mr. Sanders it'll be a wonder. Now, this is how we stand." He described Sanders' discoveries at Embrook. "But after all," he commented, "they amount to very little. There's his treasure-trove, look at it!" Blakemore pointed to the helmet and the other objects. "He seems to be on the right track, but there may be a weak link in the chain somewhere, and you must remember that we have the cipher."

"Yes, I should like you to keep it for the time being. But it seems to me Sanders has worked it all out very cleverly, and those extracts you read me all dovetail into one another."

"No doubt, but I'm not satisfied. Since you've been here, it's occurred to me that those compass-bearings may be wrong. You see, their instruments in those days were clumsy and inaccurate, and a few yards would make all the difference."

"So?"

"So I'll ask my friend Rees about it. He's assistant astronomer at Greenwich Observatory, and he'll be able to tell us if any man can. I'll telephone to him presently, and you should lose no time in letting the police know about Sanders."

"But won't that be telling them of the treasure?"

"I don't see that. Just tell them you've heard Sanders is down at Embrook."

"Not at the Great Eastern Hotel?"

"He told me he was making Embrook his headquarters."

"But suppose he's found the treasure when they get there?"

"All the more reason you should hurry up. But he's found nothing yet."

"I'll go to Scotland Yard, then."

"Wait a bit! Didn't you say the police took Sanders' address when he left the tender?"

"So the captain told me. He said Sanders went straight to the hotel."

"With your luggage?"

"Yes—the scoundrel!"

"Well, he had to keep up the character. So he constituted himself your residuary legatee!" chuckled Blakemore. "Depend upon it, as soon as the police found out their mistake from you yesterday they would make a bee-line for the hotel. The place is likely being watched now. It strikes me from what Sanders said that he must have cleared out lock, stock and barrel."

"Yes, there's a good deal in that," agreed Gardiner. "If I don't find the police at the hotel I may be able to get my luggage at last."

"Take care you don't land in difficulties again. I shall be expecting a wire to come and identify you later on." Blakemore stood up with a smile. "Now come and have some lunch. Don't stand on your dignity just because I thought you were an impostor at first."

A NEW ALLY

"Dignity forsooth!" exclaimed Gardiner, grasping his hand. "I can never thank you enough for all your advice and help. But I want to get this affair over and done with. If I have any appetite for lunch, I'll get some at the hotel."

In less than an hour Gardiner had made himself known to Blakemore, secured him as a witness to his identity, and discussed the cipher with him. In short, he had accomplished more than he had come for. Yet he left the Record Office more depressed than ever.

A lonely, self-contained man, absorbed for many years in the winning of a moderate fortune, Gardiner made friends only with difficulty. It had needed the constant association of shipboard for a stranger to penetrate his outer shell of reserve. By the end of the voyage Gardiner had felt a sincere friendship for Sanders. He had been profoundly sorry for him on hearing the tale of his being duped over the concession. The contrast of the other's plight with his own rosy prospects had troubled him, and a nebulous plan of setting him on his feet again had been in his mind as they boarded the tender. These memories returned to Gardiner as he bitterly reviewed the other man's villainy. Gardiner arrived at the Great Eastern Hotel in a sombre mood.

"Is Mr. Gardiner still staying here?" he enquired of the clerk.

"Mr. Gardiner?" He thought a moment and he referred to one of his books. Then with a sharp glance at his questioner he closed the volume. "He left here a fortnight ago."

"Did he take his luggage?" Without replying the clerk looked stonily past Gardiner's right ear. A second later he felt a grip upon his shoulder. Half paralysed by fear, he turned to meet the gaze of Inspector Saxby.

"Do you mind coming over here for a minute?" said that officer. He led the way into a small room adjoining the entrance hall. Only when they were both comfortably seated did he unbend.

"Well, Mr. Gardiner," he grinned, "you seem to be on the same errand as myself."

"Not quite, I think," said Gardiner with a deep sigh of relief. "I'm anxious to get hold of my luggage with all my clothes and paraphernalia, while I take it you are waiting for the gentleman who brought it here?"

"Well, yes, I suppose I may as well admit it. I'm glad you came here, because I think we may be of some use to one another."

"Just so. Well, I want to know if my things are still here."

"Oh, yes, they're still here." He paused. "But I am afraid you can't take them away."

"Oh?" Gardiner's tone was sharp and questioning. "You have no doubt of my being the rightful owner?"

"Certainly not. But I think they're likely to be more valuable to me than to you."

"I don't see that. All my clothes are in the trunks. I certainly don't propose to go to the expense of buying new things just to suit the convenience of the police. Besides, all my private papers and securities are with them." He rose to his feet. "I simply must have them. I can't consent to this for a moment. I've been put to quite enough worry and trouble over the affair already."

"Now, now, sir, that's all right. There's no objection to your taking all your property away as soon as you like, but I must ask you to leave the trunks and boxes here." And lowering his voice, he explained his need of them as a decoy.

"But surely Sanders won't know if they are removed."

"I don't know that. He's pretty acute and may be watching the place, or perhaps even bribed an employee."

"In that case it would be just as easy for him to find out that I had emptied the trunks."

"Quite so, sir, and that's why I want you to do it at night."

A NEW ALLY

Gardiner was silent for a few moments. "May I ask how long you've been here?"

"Only since I saw you yesterday. As soon as I found out the confusion we had been making between the two of you, I saw what a mistake it was not to have kept a close eye on Sanders. He's slipped through my fingers, I'm sorry to say."

"You know," said Gardiner, "I'm sure he did it on the spur of the moment."

"The neatest thing I ever heard of," remarked the detective admiringly. "Where he's been spending his time the last fortnight I would give a great deal to know!"

"Perhaps I can help you to find out," said Gardiner, gravely.

"I should be grateful if you would, sir. I was going to say, it seems to me your interests are as much concerned as anyone's, seeing that he's going about using your name."

"You are quite right, inspector. Now this is what I heard about him this morning." And he recounted the story of Sanders' visit to Embrook, suppressing, however, all reference to the cipher or the treasure.

"Hmm." Saxby stopped writing notes and tapped his teeth with a pencil. "Have you any idea what made him think of that place?"

"Only that I once told him it used to be the property of my family. Do you think what I have told you will be of any use?"

"Certainly, sir. I'm only wasting time here if Sanders has gone back to the country. Would you be good enough to wait here a minute or two?"

In the inspector's absence Gardiner asked himself whether he had more to gain or to lose by Sanders' arrest. The impersonation was annoying, but now that the police knew of it Gardiner almost regretted that he had mentioned Embrook. From the standpoint of Gardiner's interests, Sanders' proceedings had had a certain value. They had helped to clear up much that was obscure, and his very failures were useful in restricting the area of future searches. His reverie was disturbed by the inspector's return.

"I've been talking the matter over with my colleague," he said, "and we both think you'd better send a trunk here addressed to yourself. We will send it back to you with all your property if you'll leave your address."

"Very well, but you'll need my keys as well."

The detective smiled. "Our friend has been beforehand with us. The boxes are open."

"Did he burst them open?"

"No, they are simply unlocked."

"Oh, I remember now," said Gardiner. "I never locked them after they were examined by the customs."

The inspector nodded. "I see. I've arranged that my man here will send off your things this evening."

"Are you leaving for Embrook?"

Saxby merely smiled.

"I only ask," said Gardiner, "because I'm thinking of going there myself. I have some important business to see to."

"Well, I would much rather you didn't do it without first communicating with us. If Sanders saw you he might take alarm and get clear away. I don't mind telling you that I'm going down there tonight, and if I do manage to run him to earth, I might want you to identify him before I arrest him."

With agreement reached on this point, Gardiner left. As he turned into the approach from Chancery Lane, he espied Blakemore descending the steps of the Record Office, his official labours ended for the day.

"So you've not been arrested again," was his jocular greeting. "I've been anxiously awaiting a telegram to come and bail you out."

"No, but you were right about the police," returned Gardiner.

"They're in possession of the hotel, but I've got everything cleared up."

"Well, come and dine with me at the club and we'll talk over everything." And this time Gardiner did not demur.

CHAPTER 7

A TUDOR INTRIGUE

BLAKEMORE was bubbling with good spirits when Gardiner entered his office the next morning. Always placid, today he beamed. So contagious was his elation that Gardiner's lingering depression was soon dispelled.

"Things are moving," said Blakemore. "I have a lot of papers I want to show you and I've arranged to devote the entire morning to your affairs." As he spoke he laid his hand on a portfolio from which sundry ends of discoloured parchment peeped out.

"Have you heard from your astronomer friend?" enquired Gardiner.

"Oh, yes. I spoke to Rees on the telephone this morning."

"Was he helpful?"

"Yes. I asked him if the old compasses of three centuries ago were reliable. His answer surprised me; he said, 'Certainly,' but that one must allow for 'secular variations,' as he called them. He tried to explain what he meant, but I couldn't quite catch what he said, and the young lady at the exchange broke in just then, so I told him I'd send him a copy of the bearings. That's all we can do for the present, and we couldn't have got hold of a better man, for what he doesn't know about that sort of thing isn't worth knowing. Meanwhile, if I were you I should go down to Embrook and find out what our friend is doing there."

"Not just yet, I'm afraid. I promised the police I wouldn't go till they gave me permission."

"So you did; I remember now. Well, I've got quite enough here to keep us employed." And Blakemore undid the fastening of the mysterious portfolio and picked out a few sheets from the contents. "Now here," he said, "are papers which have a most important bearing on the case. Hitherto I've been a little sceptical about this treasure. Sanders is a shrewd fellow and he certainly worked up what we may call the local colour of the cipher very cleverly, but when all is said and done he has no direct evidence of the treasure's existence. It's all surmise and rests only on the unsafe foundation of old Harris."

"Is he unreliable?"

"I should be sorry to rely on any uncorroborated statement of his. Sanders said he found the reference in a manuscript book of *Notes and Illustrations* to Harris' *History of Kent*. If they had not been written by Harris but by someone else, that, in my opinion, would favour their reliability."

"Was he such a liar?" persisted Gardiner.

"I won't say that. He was an industrious compiler of books and wrote a *Lexicon Technicum* which was the first encyclopaedia of all. He was also a great mathematician, which should have inclined him to favour the truth. But there's no getting over the fact that he flourished just after the Revolution when party spirit was very bitter, and as he was a violent Whig and Low-Churchman, one feels unable to put faith in much that he says about the Jesuits. Furthermore, even if all he wrote was true and, as the cipher seems to say, the treasure was hidden in the chapel, how do we know it's there now?" He laughed.

"But don't look so miserable, old chap. I hope to send you away far happier than when you arrived."

"I'm glad to hear it. I thought you were going to say the whole thing was moonshine."

"Far from it. I've had a careful search made through the state papers of 1580 and thereabouts, especially the documents in cipher—they're in the section we call Domestic Manuscripts—and I've made some important discoveries."

"About the treasure?" asked Gardiner eagerly.

"About what *was* a treasure. Of where it is now I can say nothing. I don't know if you learnt anything about it at school; if so, you've probably forgotten by this time that Queen Elizabeth, beginning to fear a Spanish invasion, had Leicester fit out an expedition under Drake to make a raid on the Spanish possessions in America—to create a diversion and also to capture some of the gold and silver which were to be had for the mining. So in 1577 Drake set out for South America, where he seized Spain's trading ships, fought their galleons, held up towns for ransom, intercepted cargoes that were being brought down to the coast, and altogether played the very deuce along the Pacific shores."

"Rather cool, what?"

"Oh, quite routine for the 'Spacious Days of Elizabeth!' No doubt Drake considered himself the avenger of the English captives who had been imprisoned, tortured and burnt by the Spanish Inquisition. As to the Queen, she, like most other sovereigns, had always refused to acknowledge that America was a Spanish colony, and it's pretty certain that all three of them, the Queen, Leicester and Drake, went into the affair as a speculation. Although Drake started with only five small ships, which in the course of events got reduced to a single one—his own flagship, *The Golden Hind*—he managed to defeat or escape from all the Spanish warships sent to capture him, and arrived home safely in 1580 after a voyage right round the world."

"Did Spain do nothing about it?"

"Oh, yes. There was a tremendous to-do. The Spanish ambassador threatened to leave England unless the plunder was restored. Elizabeth refused to admit any knowledge of the treasure, although it was landed from the *Golden Hind* in accordance with her own instructions. The ambassador claimed it to amount to three million ducats, or about a million and a half pounds sterling."

"Phew!"

"And worth about eight or ten times that in modern terms. The Spanish claimed to have been robbed of wedges of gold by the hundredweight, silver ingots by the ton, bushel measures of pearls and diamonds and emeralds, to say nothing of jewelled crucifixes and church plate, bales of silks and velvets, and any amount of private property. Drake was said to have been worshipped as a god by the Californians, who made over their country to him, besides giving him substantial presents. Altogether, it was what Drake would have called a very successful voyage."

"Sounds more like piracy."

"Yes. That's just what it was—piracy, pure and simple. But you must remember that the *Golden Hind* with her four consorts were the nucleus of our modern navy. Anyway, the ambassador insisted on restitution of the treasure, but as the Queen was expecting a thumping commission on the affair, that didn't suit her; Drake, too, had made handsome presents to several courtiers who didn't want to give them up. On the other hand, the Queen was afraid to refuse point-blank, and Burghley and some of the more honest members of the council supported the ambassador, Mendoza. So Elizabeth agreed to have the plunder registered as it was landed at Plymouth, where the

Golden Hind lay. Then, to make the whole affair look open and above-board, a local magistrate, one Tremayne, was appointed to superintend the registration, but Elizabeth determined to have someone she could trust who should take toll of everything in the interests of herself, and Drake and Leicester as well. And the personality of that man is of the utmost interest to us."

"Who was he?"

"Sir Medway Gardiner! I find he was one of the Queen's equerries, so he was evidently a person she felt able to trust. Tremayne, the Plymouth magistrate, was, I should think, an ordinary respectable country gentleman whom Gardiner could easily humbug. And that brings me to the first of the documents. It's a letter from Sir Francis Walsingham, the Secretary of State, to Lord Burghley, who luckily was ill at the time."

"Luckily?"

"Because otherwise Walsingham would have communicated with him orally and we shouldn't have had the documents. Burghley wanted to know what had been done about Drake's piracy, a matter he felt strongly about—at least he refused a handsome present from Drake. Here's the letter." Blakemore held up a stained sheet of paper with faint yellow characters upon it and a splash of sealing-wax in one corner. "It's in cipher, the normal official one of the time, but I've had it written out in literal translation. Here, read it for yourself." He handed Gardiner a sheet of foolscap which read as follows:

For the Right Honorable the Lord Burghley at his House near Savoye

28 day of July 1581

My very dear Lord

I am now to acquaint you as you desire regarding the enumeration of Sir Francis Drake his treasure. It is valued by the King of Spain at iii million ducats, a return

A TUDOR INTRIGUE

will be made to Don Bernard de Mendoza of xx tons of silver bullion, and many diamonds and pearls and precious stones, but there remaineth over and above the same iii wedges of pure gold, many bales of silk and velvet, some scores of crucifixes and swords set with emeralds and diamonds, and precious stones in several sack measures. Would that Her Highness would look to her own estate considering the many evil subjects she hath. The peril cannot be redeemed at too dear a price though I fear the treasure will be preferred before surety. When Her Highness sought some trusty person on whom she could rely to look to it and take toll upon the treasure landed in Saltash Castle, she chose the one your Lordship suspecteth always, that sad Papist Sir Medway Gardiner being still of her household since that Her Highness will always be seeking to cure disloyalty by trust. (Thou and I dear Lord could haply find a trustier steward from they we wot of) nathless was he sent though had I in the choice no word of council. Of a truth he hath shown himself busy and prone to go beyond his commission having sent as well an inventory of the treasure for furnishing to the King of Spain's Ambassador as of the secret portions of the same which was not in cipher, a double folly. Her Highness now would continue him in charge of this privy portion to bring it nearer to London as though poor he is held an honest, but it is a perilous custody and I would it were returned to Don Bernard. Yet is it a hard and grievous trial for Her Highness to part therewith since fair words come ever cheaper to her. And now to conclude making haste, I pray this findeth you easier of your grievous affliction. God bless you as I wish myself, my good Lord your faithful servant

                         Fr. Walsynghame.

"So, we've got some positive evidence at last," Blakemore observed as Gardiner finished reading.

"Yes, this certainly tallies with all you were telling me about Drake's expedition."

"Ah, but more than that, we have now for the first time a connection between Gardiner and the treasure."

"But we knew that before. There was that extract from Harris' *History*."

"Yes, but the old fanatic had got hold of the wrong story. He said it was money sent here by the Jesuits, and now we find it came from a very different source, and you must remember that this letter of Walsingham's is an official secret, so we can believe it absolutely."

"And do you think this is the treasure to which the cipher refers?"

"I'm inclined to think so, and when you've seen the rest of these papers I think you'll agree. Whether the Queen was justified in thinking Gardiner loyal it is difficult to say, but you can see that Walsingham didn't trust him and Burghley evidently had a poor opinion of him, perhaps because he was a Catholic. Anyhow, when Walsingham says they could 'find a trustier steward from they we wot of,' he evidently alludes to the secret police they both had in their pay—Walsingham to spy on the Jesuits and other possible conspirators, Burghley to guard the Queen against assassination."

"But how came Gardiner to retain possession of the treasure? This letter is dated 1581 and the cipher is 1583, so that between the two he must have got hold of it somehow."

"Quite right. We shall be able to trace it step by step, I think. Just look at this. It may take you a little time to read, but I wanted you to see the original document, not a copy." He produced a dirty-looking paper covered with sprawling laborious writing which a careful scrutiny resolved into the following:

A TUDOR INTRIGUE

Toe Hys Excelencie Syr Fr. Walsynghame—
Moste secrete.

Fayre Syr Gode my Lorde I moste humlye besche y'r Excelencie toe knowe her Highnesse plasur concernynge the coste I was putte atte Plmouth and Saltase as moche by resonne of the harde & heauie task of enumer'n. I wolde humlye besche her Majestye toe pardonne her olde seruante been thus bolde my stewardshyppe remaynge wythout fee or recompens. I wille not denye thatte itt greveth mee toe see my desyre to do the Quene seruyce so grately cross'd. Methink her Highnesse predecess'rs dyd neure loke toe chargis when affayres of moment dyd soe compasse them & I humlye praie y'r Excelencie toe presse on her Highnesse mi sore strait. For mi owne parte tho mi estat be poore & mi dettes grat yette wolde I myselfe selle eurythynge I possess'd than perswade the openyng of her Highness purse butte rather choos a meer heui burdenne upon my weke backe toe answere all thynges in mi care & charges. Moreouer touchynge the dystynie of the thynges twoud comforte mee toe knowe her Majestie her gracyous wille as toe the place I purpos'd toe convoie them. I haue especialle cawse toe knowe them a faire marke & not impossyble toe hitte atte presente soe praie moue her Highnesse toe deale therewythe. If her Majestie hathe not truste in mi dyscretyon & secrecie I wolde faine bee relyued of the burdonne butte if peraduenture she ranketh mee not the leste faythfulle of her slaues the Lorde wyllynge yow shalle not nede toe fere butte wyth alle mi hartie thankfullnesse I wyll holde mi tyme to serue yow and the Quene her Highnesse beyng the chyfest thynge inne thys worlde I doe praie for. I besche y'r Excelencie toe dyspatche mi busynysse & toe bee plaine wyth mee soe I maye lerne whatte her Highnesse wolde hauc mee doe & I dar assur yow of mi secrecie in alle thyngs. My tyme biddes mee hast toe ende & soe I comytte thys toe y'r care & hope of y'r helpe. Y'r faythefulle seruante inne alle humylytye

MYD. GARDIN'R

"Well?" said Blakemore, as Gardiner laid down the document.

"I should call the spelling queer and the composition very poor," said Gardiner.

"Nonsense," said Blakemore, impatiently. "You must remember it was only very highly educated people who wrote or spelt well in those days. For a country gentleman of the sixteenth century I call it a very creditable performance. I could show you a letter of Mary Queen of Scots which is hardly an improvement on it. You must admit Gardiner goes straight to the point, and I've no doubt he made his position perfectly clear to Walsingham."

"And that was his want of money."

"Clearly. He says plainly he's hard up and in debt; he complains that he can't get his expenses paid, and hints that he might do a great deal more for the Queen if she would only pay up. Everyone seems to have discovered, as Walsingham told Burghley in the letter, that it was a hard matter to get Elizabeth to part."

"I wonder how he got so hard up? Surely he had a good enough estate."

"Probably it would have been enough if he had lived quietly in the country; but, you see, he was one of the Queen's equerries and must have lived expensively. It was a very brilliant Court around 1580, and dress, to mention only one point, was luxurious and costly. I've been wondering whether the Queen in any of her Progresses ever visited Embrook, but I can't find any record of her coming any closer than Rochester. Besides, it would have taken an enormous manor house to accommodate all her retinue. That letter of Gardiner's is undated, as you see, but it was possibly written after Walsingham's letter, and at any rate before the beginning of 1583, when Gardiner's fortunes changed drastically. Here, read this."

"This" was a large sheet of yellowish parchment, still full of crackling life, with a formidable seal attached to it by a broad riband, and covered with beautiful black-letter script which Gardiner could read easily.

ELIZABETH BYE THE GRACE OF GOD OF ENGLANDE SCOTLANDE FRAUNCE & IRELANDE QUENE toe all Justices Maiores Sheryffes Constables Hedd-Boroughes & others Oure offycers & toe the Lieut't of Oure Priuie Councylle thatte Syr Mydwye Gardinere of Embrooke in Oure Countie of Kente Kn't hathe ayded and concealed certayne beynge preestes pretendynge powere of absoluynge Oure faythfulle subjects from theyre due allygance to Ourseselues, ALSOE thatte the sayde Syr Mydwye Gardinere hathe atte diuerse seasonnes permyttedde the ydoltrous righte of ye masse wythyn hys priuye Chapelle, ALSOE thatte the sayde Syr Mydwye Gardinere hathe ajoyonede toe hym certayne rebellyous & traytors as hauing justlye bene condemmede bye lawe & fledde oute of thys Our Royaulme haue priuelie ryturnedd toe compasse hurtte to Oure Personne the styrrynge uppe of rebellyonne & the ouerthrowe of the state of true Christianne Relygyonne, & WHEREAS the sayde Syr Mydwye Gardinere for all & singulare the sayde mysdymenoures is suspect of Sydytyone Tresonne or Mysprysyonne of Tresonne NOWE Wee commande you the sayde Justices Maiores Sheryffes Constables Hedd-Boroughes & othere

Oure offyceres you & euery of you toe straitwaye arrestte the sayde Syr Mydwye Garinere & Wee commande you the Lieut't of the sayde Oure Honoure of the Toure toe receve the sayde Syr Mydwye Gardinere & hym safelye toe kepe untylle suche tyme as shalle bee ordered bye Oure Councylle. FOR Alle the wyche thys shalle bee youre suffycyente warrantie & dyscharge. Gyuen undere Oure Sygnytte atte Oure Manoure of Grenwyche thys fourtynth daye of Janurie inne the twentiefyfthe yere of Oure Raigne.

      BYE THE QUENE
      FR. WALSYNGHAME
        Her Majestie Pryncypalle
        Secretarie of State.

Gardiner laid down the parchment and gave a long whistle.

"Rather a change, isn't it?" said Blakemore. "As Shakespeare says, 'All gone and not one friend to take his fortune by the arm.' I wonder if he was thinking of Gardiner when he wrote that, for although of course they never met, he may have heard of Gardiner at the Court."

"What on earth is the meaning of it?"

"Well, we must try and fill up the gaps between the two letters and the warrant. These three documents are all we have to work upon, for I've been unable to find any other papers bearing in the slightest degree upon the case. First we have Walsingham's letter to Burghley dated 1581, then Gardiner's letter to Walsingham. That must have been written either at the end of 1581 or the beginning of 1582, and for this reason: When Gardiner wrote it he was still in charge of the secret part of Drake's plunder, and he evidently was in some doubt about what he should do for its safety. It's clear that it hadn't been going on for long, as he doesn't seem to have very often before asked to be repaid his expenses. His letter reads to me, indeed, like a second application. On the whole, I think we are justified in regarding it as written no later than the beginning of 1582. We have to imagine what happened in the next twelve months to change the Queen's feelings towards him. Here she is issuing a warrant for his arrest as a traitor, when we had last heard of him as a secret agent entrusted with the most delicate and responsible piece of business imaginable. And you must remember, too, that neither Walsingham nor Burghley, for all their power, were able to prevent his receiving the commission."

"But how did he manage to get over to France? Did he escape from the Tower?"

"He never was in the Tower," said Blakemore quietly. "Just look at the back of the warrant. Do you see the note endorsed there?"

"I can't quite make it out. It's not in such clear writing as the front of the warrant."

"No. The warrant was made out, I suppose, by a man whose business it was to engross documents of state such as this, a kind of law-stationer, but the endorsement is in the same hand as the signature. It was added by Walsingham. See, here are his initials. It reads, 'Not putte in exycutionne. Fr. W.' "

"Then he was never arrested after all?"

"No. He either got away just in time, or else was warned by some friend at Court. As to the charges in the warrant, I'm convinced there isn't a genuine one among them. They have a spurious air."

"What we might now call a put-up job?" suggested Gardiner.

"That's it. The Act under which Gardiner was supposed to be arrested was passed early in 1581, but it was not carried out rigorously until after Campion, the Jesuit missionary, was executed the following December. After that, Catholics had to attend services of the Established Church. But something much more serious than religion must have destroyed the Queen's trust in him. Elizabeth cared about as much for Protestantism as I do for Buddhism. She used religion as her father did, to further her own ends. She had all the pagan ideas of the Renaissance, and her Court was as lax on matters of faith as any other before or since. The act of 1581 was aimed at the foreign priests who plotted to assassinate her with the blessing of Gregory XIII, and so long as Gardiner enjoyed her favour, he might have heard Mass every hour of the day for all she cared. When he was sent on his confidential mission, everyone from the Queen downward knew he was a Catholic. So we have to ask ourselves what caused them to trump up these charges against him within a twelvemonth afterwards. We know that Gardiner was hard up, and the Queen was notoriously grasping and avaricious, so perhaps she may have taken offence at his demands for money. Another possibility is that Elizabeth, with her usual double-dealing, may have tried to deceive her councillors about the part of the treasure she was appropriating. If she could induce Gardiner to hide it in a place known only to the two of them and then frighten him out of the country, she would not only secure the treasure without anyone else being the wiser but would get rid of an inconvenient witness."

"Why not have him assassinated?"

"Well, to do her justice, Elizabeth, for all her crooked ways, would never consent to murder. Again, if Gardiner was shown to have escaped, she could claim he had made off with the entire treasure. In that way she might avoid a showdown with Spain."

"Perhaps he did make off with it."

"Possibly. Honesty then was not quite what we understand by the word now. Gardiner had told Walsingham that 'his estate is poor and his debts great,' and he may have been tempted. He may even have tried to blackmail the Queen, though that *would* be dangerous!"

"And unlikely, I think."

"Yes. Well, now, we've exhausted every theory for Gardiner's quarrel with the Queen except the most probable one. Suppose he really was an honest man, after all; he couldn't well refuse the office that was thrust on him, however much he objected to such dirty work. It was intended as a compliment, he must have realised. He may have seen a chance of restoring the treasure to the rightful owners. He could have accepted the commission with the full intention of doing so, and have seized the first opportunity of hiding it in a secure place. Again we must never lose sight of the fact that he was a Catholic—possibly a devout one. Just think what his feelings must have been on seeing the crucifixes, the jewels and the other loot torn by Drake's band of pirates from the churches of the Pacific Coast!"

"Yes. Of course. And that's the theory you favour yourself?"

Blakemore put on an inscrutable expression. "I don't say so, but the bare facts are that there was a treasure in 1581 of which Gardiner was given charge, that he hid it in a place of safety, and that he fled soon afterwards. The cipher shows that he left the treasure behind him; it also shows that none shared the secret of its hiding place with him, for if they had, the secret message would have been unnecessary. To this day the whole of Drake's treasure has never been satisfactorily accounted for, and it looks as if you and I are the only people who hold the key to the mystery. Whatever his motives may have been, Gardiner concealed the whole or part of the Queen's share without letting her know of its whereabouts. She would resent such an apparent breach of trust and, when you remember her avaricious disposition, and especially her inability to disclose the nature of Gardiner's offence, you can imagine how she must have raged like a lioness deprived of her cubs."

"Then," said Gardiner, "you have no doubt of the treasure's existence?"

"None—in 1583. As for the present—" Blakemore shrugged. "All I can say is, if the treasure is still there it is likely to be more valuable than any Jesuit's war-chest could possibly have been. I think you really ought to go down and find out what Sanders has been up to. I advised him to purchase the ruins, for the reason that when property is found on private grounds the finder as such has no claim. But since I explained that to him I have looked the point up, and I find that I told him only half of the truth. The case seems to be this: unless the owner of the treasure is known, it becomes 'treasure-trove' and the landlord must surrender it to the Crown. Of course, the owner of *this* treasure is not known, so if Sanders has bought the land, we may score off him yet!"

CHAPTER 8

A WOMAN'S HEART

"AND you went away without saying one word to me," said Amy reproachfully.

"Good heavens! I was only going for a single day," Sanders protested.

"You never said so—you might have been going for a whole week for all I knew," she pouted.

"Well, Amy, I had a lot on my mind when I left."

"But even when you came back I never saw you. I haven't set eyes on you for two whole days!" She stared intently into his face before turning on her heel.

"But I can see you don't care," she said over her shoulder, upon which she burst into tears and buried her head in her hands.

It was the day after his encounter with Gardiner on the staircase. He had risen late after a disturbed night and wandered across the fields towards the ruined chapel, uncertain of his plans. There he had come upon the girl, sitting despondently on a heap of rubble within the shattered walls. Now faced by this outbreak, he put his arm around her and tried to console her. But it was in vain that he explained that it was too late to meet her when he returned from London the previous evening, that her parents would surely have objected. He discovered at last, as others have done, that silence is sometimes more effective than conversation. Little by little the girl's sobbing ceased, and they sat quietly together, each busy with his own thoughts. Sanders found it agreeable to be loved by this comely girl, so much younger than his own forty years. She in turn had quite lost her heart to her dark-featured, handsome admirer. His thoughts soon took a more melancholy turn. Though he dreaded the prospect he must confess to her the guilty secrets of his past. By doing so he would, he felt quite certain, lose her, yet it was inevitable. The sacrifice must be made; the hand of the iconoclast must not tremble. With his fortunes at their nadir, he would act honourably. Holding her more tightly he murmured, "Dearest, listen to me!"

He felt her body stiffen, but she made no reply.

"Tell me, could you love a criminal?"

"A what?"

"A felon—a jailbird."

"Oh, Willie." She turned her face towards him with wide anxious eyes. "I don't believe it."

He smiled sadly and kissed her cheek. "It's only too true. Listen carefully, and I'll explain. I was managing a business on the Gold Coast. I wanted to grow rich. I speculated and lost, and paid my losses with my employers' money. They were dissatisfied with my accounts and gave me notice to leave, so I was forced to replace the money or they would have prosecuted me."

"So you repaid the money?"

Sanders shook his head. "Where could I get it? I needed a large sum. I hadn't sixpence of my own."

"You stole it?"

"Practically." He released her and turned his face away.

"A man I knew died. He was said to be the owner of a mining concession. I forged his signature, transferring the property to myself, and then resold it."

"But I don't understand. Is it known you did this?" asked the girl.

"Yes. The real owner has the same name as the dead man. The fraud was discovered soon after I left."

He stopped. In a soft husky voice Amy prompted him to continue.

"When I landed at Tilbury nearly three weeks ago, two detectives were waiting to arrest me. But as they came on board the tender, a fellow-passenger—a man named Gardiner—fell overboard into the river and was swept away, and the captain in the confusion gave my name as his, and they didn't interfere with me."

For a moment they sat in silence. Sanders, with a certain dull satisfaction that the worst was over, continued to stare at the wall immediately in front of him. Amy, her face pale and drawn, looked aside upon the ground, absently plucking at a weed. She was the first to speak.

"I can't understand why you came to this place," she said quietly.

"To seek a treasure."

She turned suddenly and stared at him. He hastened to explain.

"No one knows of this treasure but you?" she asked, as he concluded.

"Until yesterday I thought so, but as I left the Record Office I ran against a man in the passage. I know it sounds unbelievable, but it was Gardiner. He must somehow have been saved from drowning."

"Did he see you?"

"Not to recognise me, but he must have learnt everything

from the man we both saw at the Record Office. The police must have heard it too. I came down here with no plans made, except to tell you everything before I went away."

He rose and turned towards her, but she neither stirred nor looked up.

He paused a moment, then: "Goodbye," he said softly, and turned to walk across the enclosure. He had almost reached the ruined doorway when he heard her call.

"Willie! Willie!"

Quickly he turned and looked back. The girl was on her knees with her arms outstretched towards him. He sprang back and helped her regain her seat on the pile of rubble. She was shuddering from cold and shock. He whipped off his jacket and wrapped it around her, then rubbed her hands briskly to restore some warmth to them.

"Don't ever leave me," she murmured, as she leaned heavily against his supporting arm. He whispered tender assurances and endearments into her ear.

"Can you still believe in me?" he asked at length.

"Why not?" she returned softly.

"Even the name you know me by is not my own."

"Isn't it Willie?" she exclaimed anxiously, sitting upright.

"Oh, yes, that's right enough." He smiled at her alarm. "The surname is what I meant."

"Oh, that's not important," she sighed, and relaxed in his arms again.

"Darling," he said presently, "I must leave here as soon as possible."

"For where?" she faltered.

"I must get out of England. Do you love me enough to come with me? To leave your home—your parents? Will you come with me and share my life?"

She did not answer, but drew him closer. Their lips met

A WOMAN'S HEART

silently and for several minutes they did not speak.

"But what about the treasure?" asked Amy at last.

"Well, yes, that's disappointing. I was hoping to find something of value that would help me to settle the affair on the Coast. Lewis—the man I sold the concession to—only wants his money back. But the main thing now is to get away from here."

"But the other man whose name you took? Won't he come and search for the treasure too?"

"Gardiner? I don't think so. He must have heard all about my failure from Blakemore—his friend at the Record Office—so he's unlikely to do anything himself. Besides, there's little more to be done. You know how thoroughly I've dug every square yard of the place. There remains only that piece over there." He pointed to a part halfway along the wall, where a hillock rose several feet above the general level. "I'm beginning to think, though, that if there's any treasure at all it's too deep down for anyone to reach single-handed—and I don't want to employ any labourers."

"But Gardiner might do that, mightn't he?"

"Perhaps, and that's one reason I don't want to leave the neighbourhood altogether. I should like to stay and have a last try for it."

"Then where can you go? The village is too small." Suddenly she disengaged herself from his embrace and stood up. "Any stranger coming there would be noticed at once and talked of everywhere. Darling, it's dangerous for you to hang about. Let's go right away—at once, and then we needn't part at all."

He smiled at her impetuosity and shook his head. "No, I'm determined to finish the search. I'll stay in Maidstone for the present. I'll walk there by way of the riverbank and when I get there I'll find lodgings. As a last resort I'll stay at a hotel."

It was agreed that he should leave at once. Amy would steal out of the house with his portmanteau containing some essentials and bring it to him on the village cart.

"Meet me at the three-mile stone from Maidstone," he said, as he scribbled in his pocket-book. "Here's a note for your parents explaining I've been suddenly called away to London. Be sure to retrieve it later and destroy it. None of my writing must be found."

He clasped her fervently once more and bade her farewell. Watching her from the ruined walls as she walked back across the fields, Sanders felt a tug at his heart. Stunned and shocked though she undoubtedly was by his confession, not a hint did she convey of anything but love and infinite pity. And this was the little country girl whose aid he once would have disdained to seek. Now she was his colleague, the partner in his enterprise, the cherisher of his hopes, and the comforter of his fears.

If his luck turned, he would repay Lewis and, with the few hundreds he already owned, he would settle in Paraguay with Amy. If he still drew blank in his search he would be no worse off. Lewis, paid or unpaid, could not withdraw from the prosecution and thereby compound a felony. He, Sanders, would remain an outlaw. But he would put up a good fight with Amy to back him. Such were his thoughts as he walked at a good pace towards Maidstone.

Towards seven that evening a sharp "trit-trot" echoed along the high road some two miles west of Maidstone. Faint moonbeams, reflected from the chalky way, revealed the figure of a girl driving a village cart drawn by a little mule, as neat and well-groomed as a thoroughbred. As she approached a railway arch her pace slowed, and a man emerged cautiously from the shadows.

"Amy, is that you?"

The girl started and reined up the mule. "Yes, Willie. Has anything happened? Why were you not at the milestone?"

"I thought it better to hide under the arch, where I could

see anyone who came along from either direction. I just can't afford to take risks. Any news?"

"Yes. Someone came to the farm this afternoon and—"

"Asked for Sanders?"

"No, just asked if any rooms were vacant. He had heard of the place in the village and wanted to see them. He saw the room and admired the place and said he would think it over. I'm sure he didn't ask about you."

"Hmm!" He looked worried.

"By the way, I got your note back like you said. I burned it."

"Good girl!"

"And I went over the rooms and hunted up every scrap of paper I could find—"

"And burnt them, too?"

"No, I thought some of them might be important, so I packed them all up."

"And you've got everything in the portmanteau there?" He pointed to the cart.

"Yes; I took out some of the heavier things. I'll bring them later. But you must let me drive you at least to the beginning of the town; you can't carry it all the way."

"No, dear, I think you'd better come no further. You haven't got any lights."

"Oh, I'll light up going back; I didn't want to be seen as I came along. I had to sneak out of the house."

It was agreed he would walk part of the way and get a fly across town. She would come to the same meeting place the following night and make final plans to leave the country with him soon.

"But if you must go on with your digging," she told him earnestly, "do start tomorrow and clear it up quickly. I shan't have a moment's rest while you're in danger."

He did not demur, but reminded her of an important matter she had overlooked.

"Oh, dear! Something serious?"

"Very," he said, with a smile. "Can't you guess?"

"No, Willie. Please don't tease me. What is it?"

"Well, I don't mean to travel with Miss Siton."

"Oh! Willie! Do you mean— Oh!" Dim as the light was he saw the crimson flood into her face.

"When is it to be?" he asked, bending down beneath the hat brim.

"When you please." The answer came softly, but without a trace of shyness. So quickly had the girl become a woman.

"That's another reason against my leaving the neighbourhood. The Registrar requires a few days' residence, even with a special licence."

"Oh, must it be done like that?" She sounded distressed.

"Darling, we can hardly go to church and have the banns read, and all the rest of it, can we?"

"There's nothing nice about the other," was the feminine lament.

"I understand, old girl, I do, really. But I'm sure you're too sensible to insist on flowers and bridesmaids the way things are. And you couldn't have a more legal or binding ceremony than before the Registrar."

"I know, my sweet. I see it can't be helped." She sighed and gave him a rueful smile. As he bent again beneath the hat the pink and white had reappeared upon her cheeks, and her lips felt cool to his in the chill of the night air.

CHAPTER 9

THE OLD MANOR HOUSE

JUST two days after Gardiner's encounter in the Record Office he received a laconic note from Saxby, withdrawing the official objection to his visiting Embrook. The following morning, as he stepped onto the platform at Forbridge, he directed a keen glance at a middle-aged gentleman ostensibly browsing at the bookstall. There was something familiar in the man's appearance, but Gardiner could not immediately identify him. He had left his luggage at the cloakroom and was hesitating outside the station over the best route to Embrook when the stranger strode by him, muttered "Follow me," glanced up and down the street as though looking for one who had failed to keep an appointment, turned briefly on his heel and retraced his steps.

"Why, inspector, is it really you?" asked Gardiner, as the other closed the waiting room door carefully behind him. "Your get-up is perfect, but now I look at you close up your eyes and the upper part of your face give you away."

"Yes, that generally is the difficulty," remarked Saxby with a gratified smile. "You've lost no time in coming down, I see."

"No, I'm anxious to see the place." Gardiner went on to

offer an explanation that was at least half the truth. "My family used to own the manor house and, as I've heard a great deal about it from my father, it occurred to me that this would be a good opportunity to come down and see it for myself." Saxby nodded solemnly. "I assume from your note that Sanders is gone?"

"Look here, Mr. Gardiner, you've taken me into your confidence, and I'll do the same. It's unusual, of course, but the whole case is a queer one, and the fact is I want your help. I came down here the same night I met you at the hotel and went out to the farm the next morning. I wasn't able to find the place at first; the local superintendent was away and I didn't want to go out there with a constable, so I managed to lose myself. When I finally got there in the afternoon, the bird had flown!"

"When?"

"Just a few hours earlier. I've been wondering what scared him. Can you suggest how he might have learnt you'd come back?"

"Not unless he saw me at the Record Office. My friend told me that he left just a moment before I arrived, but I didn't notice him."

"That's it, then. He must have seen you, come straight down here and then cleared out the first thing in the morning. Was he acquainted with your friend at the Record Office?"

This was an awkward question. Gardiner hesitated. "He was impersonating me, you see, and—"

"Just so," interrupted Saxby, intent on the one idea. "Trying to keep up the character, of course. Well, it'll take us all our time to put salt on his tail. If only I could find out what direction he's gone. That's where you can help, Mr. Gardiner. When you go to the farm, please try and find out where he said he was going and let me know, care of the superintendent at Forbridge."

THE OLD MANOR HOUSE

With the help of Saxby's directions, Gardiner, more fortunate than that officer himself, found his way to the farm without difficulty. He approached it with a thrill of conscious pride. Spacious, its position enhanced by the slight rise of the ground on which it stood within the deep wide moat, it was indeed a handsome house. The exterior, which had acquired that claret tint possibly only to the very oldest of red brick, glowed warm and cheerily in the autumn sun, which was reflected brilliantly from the numberless panes of the diamond-leaded casements.

But there was an air of vanished splendour about it. The broad stone steps leading to the porch were cracked and sunken, the lichenous balustrades broken and tottering. The square dripstones above the windows had crumbled away, some of the window mullions had even been repaired with wood, and many a chimney had been replaced by common clay cylinders which contrasted absurdly with the handsome carved brickwork of the original shafts. It was borne in upon Gardiner that the days of his family's property had long since departed.

With slow step he mounted to the porch and enquired of Mrs. Siton if there were any rooms to let. That good lady, secretly puzzled at the procession of out-of-season visitors, was content to accept her good fortune without question. It had been, she confided to Gardiner, a bad season, cold and wet. The twenty chicks had all succumbed to chills, the ducklings and fowls and goslings largely to the depredations of rats. So absorbed was she in the catalogue of her woes as she conducted her visitor to his room that she quite failed to notice the backward glances he cast along the hall. Amy, eager to note the appearance of this new arrival, had shot past Gardiner just as he began to ascend the stairs. So unexpected was the vision, so lasting and vivid the charming impression, that Gardiner paid little attention to his guide's woes.

The striking exterior had prepared him but little for the

beauties within: the array of massive oak, the panelling, the imposing stairway with its dog-gates. But it was the twin escutcheons in the hall, and especially the Gardiner badges, reiterated at every turn, which aroused all his latent pride of race. What though the mansion belonged to another? His by inalienable right were these emblems, and even were the place levelled to the ground, its very name forgotten as the corn waved upon its site, there remained to him that which no wealth could purchase—his ancestry, his descent from those who had flourished great and powerful when the fathers of many a present-day noble were still but serfs and villeins.

The panelling, well preserved in the lower rooms, was missing from the upper ones. Those into which Gardiner was shown had little but the low ceilings, with their massive cross-beams and diamond-leaded casements, to distinguish them from the most suburban of lodgings, so thoroughly had the old-world atmosphere been dissipated by the cast-iron fire-stoves and crude wallpapers of early Victorian taste. For the rest, the sitting room furniture was mercifully draped in a hard, staring chintz, while the profusion of white dimity in the bedroom was at least clean and spotless. Gardiner, half-expecting to see some traces of his predecessor, was almost disappointed with the neatness and tidiness of the place.

Hoping to learn something of Sanders' movements, he asked carelessly, "Are these the only rooms you let?"

"The only ones."

"I suppose they haven't been occupied lately?"

"Indeed they have," exclaimed Mrs. Siton, all smiles. "It's only two days since Mr. Palmer left—as nice a gentleman as I ever knew."

"Oh. You must have been sorry to lose him."

"I was indeed. A real nice gentleman was Mr. Palmer, but he was called back to London in a hurry. He used to make the place a bit of a mess with the mud he brought in, but he was that civil about it one didn't mind what one did for him. He was taken up with digging after 'fossils,' as they call them, and he used to spend all his time at Jacob's Wall out there in the meadow. Not that I think he ever found very much. But he was a nice gentleman."

By interjecting an occasional remark, Gardiner kept the stream of chatter going, hoping to extract further information, but it soon became clear that once "Mr. Palmer" had left the house, Mrs. Siton was careless of his further movements.

Thanks to Blakemore's notes and Sanders' narrative acquired at second-hand, he had a fair idea of the chapel's locality, and within a day or two of his arrival he had found it and learnt as much about it as mere inspection could impart. Hurried as his visit was, it was long enough for him to appreciate the difficulties of searching for treasure in such an unpromising spot where Sanders with all his energy had evidently failed. Gardiner's only doubt related to the purchase of the land. That Sanders had paid anything for it was most unlikely, but he might have opened negotiations with the farmer, perhaps might even contemplate some new swindle. Then there was the riddle of his whereabouts. Saxby would be expecting to hear from him. Having drawn blank in his cross-examination of the wife, he must make haste to gain the confidence of the husband. Gardiner saw that he had quite enough to occupy him for the moment without troubling his head about the treasure.

Siton was a farmer of the old school, which is as much as to say that he sniffed at the scientific approach to farming and tolerated machinery just enough to make such sparing use of it as the paucity of labour and his inability to pay for what there was necessitated. His fixed and undeviating principle was that what was good enough for his father was good enough for him. Siton was nearing the end of his tether, his land mortgaged to the last halfpenny, his feet fast in a quagmire of debt. To economise he had dismissed his labourers one after another and himself attempted to do the work of three men. The result was that the place grew more and more neglected. The stable and yards were choked with filth and rubbish, the fields were stony and undrained, the hedges ragged and broken, the boundaries marked by cheap and unsubstantial 'faggot-fences.'

Gardiner, who at first dreaded that his ignorance of things agricultural might be a bar to familiar converse, soon found that the old man was far from unapproachable. Indeed he hungered for an audience. In vague reminiscence of his father's tales of good old days, he inveighed against 'the foreigner,' but with his hazy grasp of economics he included in the term his own countrymen as well, resenting the competition of Sussex 'whops' as fiercely as that from overseas.

There was the Ground Game Act—much good that was! His best land was only one field wide and, as his neighbours on either side of him preserved everything, the rabbits ate every root he grew! That meant he was paying for other people's sport. And when they did have a shoot, did they give him any birds? Not they! They sent them all into the town and sold 'em to the dealers. Yet they called themselves gentlemen! Hunting? Well, no, there wasn't much hunting just thereabouts, to break down fences, leave the gates open and frighten the ewes.

That animal over there? Oh, that was his daughter's mule, drove it in her cart—or used to. Things was so bad he was afraid they'd have to sell 'em both, with the crops failing from the blight and the mildew and the red spider. As much as one could do to keep paying the interest on the mortgage—as bad as paying rent for his own land that had been in his family a matter of nigh on a hundred year. And as to paying 'em off—not a chance! In fact if he was going to do any good next year he'd have to raise another to replace stock! But that Lawyer Hay

THE OLD MANOR HOUSE　　　　121

was a hard man—hard as nails! Said last time he couldn't advance more money on the estate. And now the bank was just as bad. Even the wife's rooms hadn't let this year like they used to. That young chap that's just left didn't stay long. Artist? No, one of them scientific fellows. He was always pottering about down at the old walls—he called them a chapel!

Buy the place? No, Mr. Palmer hadn't said a word about that—not he! Why did he leave? Couldn't say. Went off one day all of a sudden. Didn't know where—London, most likely; all them scientific chaps came from London.

The neglect of the farm was quite apparent. The silence that brooded over the land and buildings was broken only by the discordant screaming of half a dozen geese, the remnant of a large flock. The eye sought in vain for any sign of honest toil, and but for the polo ponies and a few other horses at grass, the goats represented the only livestock about the place. The antics and skirmishes of the kids, now approaching maturity, gave a cheerful movement to a scene otherwise solemn, even funereal.

In his daily rambles, Gardiner's thoughts were largely occupied by the affairs of the Siton family, but he was not altogether forgetful of the main object of his visit. The old manor house and its lands were in possession of one who plainly was unable to stagger much further beneath their burden. As to the treasure, the old man, even if he were to find it, certainly would not know what to do with it, and might be trusted to blunder into legal complications that would rob him of any gain.

Now, Gardiner's capital, though by no means large, was sufficient to permit him to consider the purchase of the estate as an investment. True, any cash return would be meagre, but other advantages would accrue. In the first place there would be the material profit of the treasure, with none to dispute his right to it. Secondly there was the sentimental pleasure of gaining possession of the family seat. Finally was the consideration, which weighed with him as heavily as either of the others, that his interceding and buying up the mortgage might rescue the old couple—and the daughter too—from beggary or the workhouse.

Since his first glimpse of the girl as she flitted through the hall, Gardiner had been disappointed in his hope of seeing much more of her. Although it was impossible for her to avoid meeting him occasionally, she restricted their intercourse to the barest and briefest civilities. She seemed always to be in a condition of breathless haste, never scrupling to retreat if she could do so before he had spied her. The natural result of all this was that Gardiner was seized with a piquant curiosity which burgeoned into an attraction and finally into an affection for the tantalising, elusive phantom. He found nothing incongruous in his falling in love with such a young girl, grey and worn though he was by the passing years and his recent illness. He basked in daydreams in which he saw himself the master of a golden treasure. He saw the old manor house reverently restored to its Tudor splendour, over which Mrs. Siton would preside as matron. Her husband would run a restocked farm. Best of all, Amy would be mistress of the mansion—*his* mansion. Vividly he imagined it all, until at last the fairy castle collapsed, and he remembered that not only had Amy not said yes, but he had scarcely yet gained a speaking acquaintance with her.

Although his stay at Embrook was short, so great had been the expansion of his mental horizon, so wide the prospect which began to open before him, that in a few days he felt a different man from the newly arrived convalescent. He remained unconscious of the animating effects of his new aims and projects and credited his improved tone to the change of air.

Filled with boyish enthusiasm, all thoughts of Sanders and Saxby were forgotten; the treasure dwindled to minor importance as his thoughts ran on Amy. So insistent became his one idea that the twelfth day of his visit found him cycling through Forbridge in search of Hay, the lawyer. The interest had not been paid with such regularity, nor was the security so absolute, that the mortgagees would resent the return of their capital. Indeed, had Gardiner been less eager to complete the transfer, he might have made a much better bargain.

A little later he found Siton in a distant field gazing ruefully at the depredations of the moles. Undisturbed amid the general neglect, Moldiewerp, as he was known thereabouts, had bored his tunnels in all directions, the out-throw heaps dotting the green of every field. Now, as the season advanced and the worms became fewer, he worked nearer the surface, and the close network of runs was witness to the insatiable hunger of the little engineer. As if this misfortune were not enough, a valuable polo pony sent to Siton only yesterday had gone lame.

The old farmer's latest troubles provided Gardiner's opportunity. Much explanation was needed to make Siton realise the full extent of Gardiner's benevolence. The old man had met with so little consideration in his troubles that he could hardly believe he was not exchanging one creditor for another. When he did grasp the fact that he would be after all be able to end his days where his youth and manhood had been spent, he was forced to turn away to conceal his tears of gratitude. Affecting not to notice these symptoms, Gardiner told of his ancestral interest in the place and his plans to win back prosperity to the farm. Then he came to the subject nearest to his heart.

"Now, Mr. Siton, there is another and most important matter I want to speak to you about."

For a frightening moment the farmer's heart was jolted.

His face fell. So there was a catch in it after all. Eviction, want, a pauper's fate—ideas he had lived with for so long would not be so easily dismissed. But Gardiner's next words reassured him.

"It concerns your daughter."

"Oh!" He brightened visibly. To the mind of her father evidently nothing unpleasant could attach to Amy, and he nodded with a half-smile.

Gardiner hesitated, for as the other's confidence returned, his own began to leave him. Then haltingly, diffidently, as though his station, his fortune, the obligation he had just rendered, all had no existence: "Mr. Siton—I haven't spoken to her yet, but—I should like to know—if Miss Amy consented, whether you and her mother would welcome me as a son?"

"God bless you, sir. I wish with all my heart it might be. I should die happy if only I could live to see her married to such a man as you." He extended a gnarled paw. "There's my hand on it," he exclaimed heartily, "and God bless you again!"

CHAPTER 10

SOME MIDNIGHT ADVENTURES

IT is given to few men to know the secrets of the feminine heart. Some pass through life unaware that there are any such secrets to be discovered, while others acquire the knowledge too late. Gardiner belonged to neither category. He had no sister or other female relative; his mother had died when he was very young. So he grew up without losing the curiosity and something of the awe of a schoolboy for womankind. His years had been too much occupied with the building of a fortune to permit him much feminine society. His attitude to women was the sum of the generosity he displayed to all his fellows added to a simple old-fashioned chivalry.

A more experienced man would have known how slight were the prospects of a middle-aged suitor such as himself. Crabbed age and piquant youth seldom have been united save by youth's self-interest. His romantic illusions blinded Gardiner to the fatally clumsy manner in which he paid his addresses: so formal and frigid an approach would have damaged his chances with any maiden of spirit, even one already inclined in his favour. Neither the old man nor his wife was an ideal ambassador. By the time the proposal had filtered through to its goal it had lost not a whit of its diplomatic formality, while it bore the clumsy marks of a proposed deal in livestock. When Gardiner was represented as the family saviour, Amy not unnaturally resented deeply this gross appeal to her gratitude. Its only effect was to enshrine the image of Sanders the more inexorably in her heart.

Loath to undeceive Gardiner and fearful that he repent of his generosity, the old man was careful to avoid the subject of Amy when they met. For his part, Gardiner, diffident as ever, made no reference to it, lest he embarrass the delicate negotiations he imagined to be in train. In his heart, Gardiner felt some misgivings at Amy's reluctance to speak with him or even to see him. She was now more than ever eager to avoid him. A distant footfall upon the stairs, or at most the flutter of a skirt round a bend in the corridor, were his only assurance that the same roof continued to shelter them both. He could only ascribe these alarms and excursions to an excess of maidenly modesty under pressure of his addresses by proxy, and he endeavoured to await patiently the progress of events.

In the meantime he drew comfort from Mrs. Siton's attitude. Her attentiveness to his wants, her anxiety to anticipate his wishes, her placid amiability, all bore witness to the favour with which she regarded him.

The simple life suited Gardiner. His recent accident had impressed its necessity, and now the lack of society assured it. But, although he was always asleep before the old clock in the hall chimed eleven, he regularly heard it announce midnight. On the first occasion he blamed his strange surroundings for his wakefulness, but when the phenomenon was repeated he began to wonder. On the third night, as he opened his eyes once more, he felt rather than heard the stealthy passage of someone along the corridor. His curiosity aroused, he sprang out of bed and gently opened the door. In the faint moonlight which shone through a corridor window, he could just perceive the denser black of a figure, muffled and shrouded in a mass of drapery, that glided silently along.

Shivering, and with a premonition of evil, Gardiner locked his door and returned to bed. Was the house haunted? Did the ghost walk every night? Uneasy thoughts such as these kept him awake for many long hours, but towards dawn he fell asleep.

The next evening he spent a little time working the locks and hinges of the door until they acted silently. Lying down without undressing, he waited until his watch showed the quarter before midnight; he then stole to the door, and, opening it a crack, commenced his vigil. He had not long to wait. His heart beat loudly in his ears as the shadowy form again glided silently past, disappearing in the direction of the stairs. The next night he repeated his watch with the same result, and he resolved to speak to his host on the subject at the first opportunity.

"Ha'nted!" The old man was taken aback by Gardiner's question. "No, no! That's rubbish." But after the first startled glance at his questioner he failed to meet his eyes.

"Well, then, can you explain what I saw last night and nearly every night I've been here?" And Gardiner described his nocturnal discoveries.

"Well," said Siton, "you're the first who's ever seen it. Leastways, I never heard tell of it before."

"Strange that I should be the only one," observed Gardiner.

"Ah, you're right! Perhaps it's a family ghost, an' no one can't see it 'cept one of the old stock." He grinned at this, but still looked uneasy. This was a theory that had not occurred to Gardiner, and he found it strangely appealing.

"They do say," continued Siton, "there's been a sight of doings about the place in old times what ought to've made it ha'nted if 'tisn't!"

"You don't use all the house, I suppose?"

"All t'other side of the house 'sbeen cut off this many a year. Amy's room, beyond yours, is the only one that's been used near that side for longer than I know of."

"Has she ever seen the ghost?"

The farmer shook his head, pursing his lips as if to strengthen the denial, and then, with a noticeable access of formality at the approach to the dangerous topic, he added: "She must have seen it if 'twas walking, for she's been sitting a great deal with one of the goats. It had three kids last week an' one of 'em's that weak I'm afeared we shan't rear it."

"And you say no one before me has seen it?" Gardiner persisted.

"Never heard anything on't if they did. Mr. Palmer said nothing on't."

The mention of Sanders turned Gardiner's enquiries in a new direction. "Do you happen to remember where Mr. Palmer went to when he left here?"

Siton was doubtful at first, then thought maybe Mr. Palmer had said he was going back to London. With this Gardiner had to content himself. Taking his leave of Siton, he walked across the fields wondering how Saxby—supposing the detective had been in his place—would have acted. Detective procedure was not his long suit, or it would have occurred to him it might be worth questioning Amy.

"Hulloa, there!"

Gardiner turned round sharply at the sound of a low-pitched voice, but could see no one.

"Here, Mr. Gardiner!" That gentleman answered the summons by striding to the hedge and peering over it into the road. His eye met that of Saxby, who was crouching in the lee of a bush.

"Anyone with you?" was Saxby's eager question.

"No."

"Any news? About Sanders, I mean?"

SOME MIDNIGHT ADVENTURES

"Not a word! He talked of going to London; that's all I've found out."

"I don't think he's as far away as that," observed the detective dryly.

"What! You think he's somewhere near?"

The detective drew as close as the hedge permitted. "I'm sure of it," he said impressively.

"What makes you think so?"

Saxby smiled. "Perhaps *you* can tell me what the attraction is." Gardiner stared blankly. "I mean, what keeps him hanging about here?"

The ruined chapel was all Gardiner could think of. He could just see it if he turned his head. There, if the detective but knew it, lay the magnet that attracted Sanders. Should he tell what he knew? No, better keep the secret to himself.

"No," said Gardiner at length. "I'm not good at riddles. What do you think yourself?"

"It beats me! Do you happen to know if he had much money while he was on the boat?"

"He seemed to live as well as anyone else, so far as I could see. Wait a bit, though. Yes—I do remember when we went ashore at Madeira he spent a good deal, and I had trouble making him let me pay my share. Why do you ask?"

"Because if it's want of money that keeps him here it will also prevent him getting out of the country. I have information about some bank-notes he has, but he may have gold as well."

"Do you know where he is? Can you arrest him any time you like?"

"Ah, you want to know too much," laughed the detective. He straightened up, waved his farewell and turned up the road.

Gardiner resumed his walk with a more definite goal. The associations of the old mansion and the intrusion of Amy had distracted him recently from the original object of his visit.

He was not a covetous man. His means were sufficient to meet his simple wants. That the chapel harboured no riches, or, alternatively, that Sanders had succeeded in making off with the treasure would not have devastated him. On the other hand he owed it to Blakemore's efforts to make some attempt.

Since his first survey of the scene he had visited the chapel but seldom, and never doing more than cast his eye over the site. Now he stood well within the enclosure and gazed around the surrounding hills. Away to the right the autumn sun shone full upon the weather-beaten mass of the cromlech high up on the hillside, looking just as it must have done when it caught the eye of Sir Medway as he sought a bearing for his cipher message.

On the heap of rubble near the centre of the area Gardiner took his seat, with gaze intent upon the ground. All at once he noticed something. In a trice he was on his hands and knees beside the wall. Everywhere else the earth was dry, brown and caked, but here it was loose, moist and almost black. And more, behind a heap of new-turned soil was an excavation, but a foot or two deep, clearly formed by a human agency, and recently.

So he was not mistaken. Here was the attraction which so puzzled Saxby to explain. Sanders was still faithful to his early love and still she baffled him. The treasure was as yet unfound. But Saxby's claim that the missing man was still in the district was proved accurate. Here was the proof. The earth had been dug no more than a day ago. It was clear that Sanders must come by night, and that it was time for Gardiner to act. He had a good deal to ponder as he retraced his steps to the farm.

That night, Gardiner retired at his usual hour and sat reading in his bedroom until nearly the time for the spectre's appearance. Muffled in a greatcoat and wearing rubber overshoes, he stole down the stairs just as midnight was about to strike. The ghost was nowhere in evidence; its tour must have ended by now.

The moon shone brilliantly into the hall, bathing the garden front of the house. Shunning its light, Gardiner turned to the door opposite the porch that gave on to the open court around which the house was built. The court was in deepest shadow and, crossing it, he traversed the passage opposite which led to the old carriage entrance. As he picked his steps through the litter and confusion of the yard a sudden clatter, as of falling staves, brought him to a halt. The sound appeared to come from an outhouse; tiptoeing towards it, he put his eye to a crack in the boards. Within, he could see by the light of a lantern a woman piling fallen rakes and tools, the evident cause of the noise. She worked quickly and quietly. Then, bundling a spade and pick under her arm, she lowered the light to a mere spark. At first Gardiner was unable to identify the woman, but as she held the lantern to turn it down, he recognised Amy. As she passed out he shrank behind a corner of the shed and then, in a tumult of excitement, followed at a safe distance.

What could she be about? Surely not to seek the treasure? Was she aware of Sanders' proceedings? Onward he hastened through the mist wreaths hanging white and ghostly over the fields, keeping in sight the speck of light which flitted ahead of him like a will-o'-the-wisp.

It seemed to Gardiner that the girl was leading him anywhere but to the chapel, so erratic was her course. With his gaze fixed on the spark ahead he tripped over an errant branch of a fallen tree and found himself wallowing in a muddy ditch. By the time he could scramble to his feet again, the light had disappeared. For a moment, like a hound at fault, he paced to and fro; then he mounted the trunk, hoping from there to see the light in the hollow. Not a glimmer could he see. Doggedly he set off again, as nearly as he could judge in the direction Amy had taken. A few minutes later his heart gave a bound. For a moment the mist lifted, and the moon shone full upon a landmark he remembered well: an oak tree, seared and riven by lightning years before, that stood gaunt and misshapen at the hither end of the field containing the chapel. Familiar with every step of the way, Amy had headed straight for St. Crescentia's and must even now be within its walls.

Gardiner felt that a crisis was at hand. Stepping cautiously, he skirted the field until, some twenty yards from the ruin, he was forced to leave the shelter of the hedge. The moonlight, subdued and mellowed by the mists and the constantly drifting clouds, was insufficient to betray him as he darted across the open space. Reaching the wall, he looked in vain for the glimmer of the lantern until, shifting his position beyond a jutting buttress, he caught its flash as Amy increased its light to its fullest.

The girl was alone. Plainly he could see her grasp the spade and, with a power highly creditable to her slight figure, throw aside a considerable amount of earth. She was working close to the spot he had noted in the morning, shovelling the loose earth away from her. Presently he saw her lay aside the spade and, stepping lightly over the heap, half-disappear as she seemed to tread down the soil she had already thrown. She was filling up the excavation. Suddenly she reached for the lantern and, bending down, inspected something just turned up. The silent watcher leaned forward but, strain his eyes as he might, the object, whatever it was, lay too far off to be identified. It seemed she held a mass or rounded whiteness in her hands. Could it be a skull? Or was it something costlier and rarer?

The situation was tantalising. He dared not approach nearer; yet here, almost beneath his eyes, was a discovery he would have given worlds to assist at. Had she found any part of the treasure? At all hazards he must know. As he leaned further over the wall he dislodged a loose stone. Striving to replace it, he sent it crashing down. Paralysed, he saw the lamp abruptly extinguished. A heavy cloud just then obscured the moon. He dropped into the shadow outside the wall and ran stooping towards the hedge. A backward glance revealed the ruins to be now all dark and silent. He shivered in the night air. Why did he run from this girl whom he had lately striven so eagerly to meet? Was she so formidable?

He felt humiliated. He could not show himself to the woman he loved and forfeit her esteem, if indeed she entertained even that cold sentiment for him. He could not justify his presence there. He stood self-confessed as a spy. There was nothing for it but to return as silently as he came, praying that he could do so without discovery.

CHAPTER 11

A FOOTPRINT

GARDINER awoke at his usual hour. Notwithstanding the excitement of the night before he had enjoyed a dreamless sleep. Yet he felt dull and jaded and, prescribing for himself a further rest, it was far into the morning before he finally rose. It was for this reason that he encountered Amy in the corridor. Aware of his regular habits, the girl was taken unawares. With a slight inclination of the head she sought to pass on but, disconcerted as he was, Gardiner mustered his courage to take advantage of the occasion.

"Miss Siton—I—er—I hope you will pardon me. I have been trying to speak to you for some time, but—" He paused awkwardly. "But you have never given me an opportunity." It was not an auspicious opening.

"I was unaware there was any occasion for us to speak," was her frigid reply.

"I thought—I was under the impression your father—that Mr. Siton might have said—explained—"

Amy frowned. "Do you refer to my father's difficulties?"

"Well, that, and also—"

"I think I understand," she broke in, preventing him from

A FOOTPRINT

approaching the forbidden subject. "I suppose it is in the nature of an ordinary business transaction?"

"I hope you will give me credit—"

"I know your interest in the place," she interrupted once more. "I believe it once belonged to your family, and that you are anxious not to lose any opportunity of getting possession of it."

Gardiner winced. A wiser man would have ended the conversation at that point, but Gardiner's passion was too deep; he had waited long for this opportunity. He tried a different tack.

"Have you ever heard of the house being haunted, Miss Seton?"

"Certainly not." The reply was sharp as the crack of a whip.

"You have never seen a ghost here?"

"Never."

"This is a very old house. Surely it is at least possible it could be haunted?"

"I know nothing about it. Why do you ask?" Her evident curiosity caused her manner to appear a trifle less ungracious.

"Well, for several nights, just before twelve, I've seen a figure pass along the corridor outside my room and disappear towards the stairs."

"What sort of a figure?"

"Like a woman muffled up in a shawl."

"No, I know nothing of it." Amy's tone was dry, but Gardiner noticed her voice trembled and for a moment she failed to meet his eye.

Still eager to prolong their conversation, he blurted out: "You know St. Crescentia's Chapel?"

"You mean the place they call Jacob's Wall?" She met his gaze unflinchingly now, and there was an edge to her voice.

"Do you ever go there?" His nervous smile added insolence to the question.

For many long seconds Amy was silent, the blanching of her cheeks the only sign of her emotion.

"You have referred to your family once or twice, Mr. Gardiner, as if you were proud of it. I wonder if this is the first time it has produced a spy?" She spoke quietly but with a bitter intensity. "I know perfectly well what happened last night. What right have you to spy on me? Thank God, I'm not answerable to you for my actions! It was a mean and despicable thing to do. Would you have insulted like that any woman you thought your equal? You may buy the house and the land too; you may take advantage of my father's poverty and debts, and buy him as well! You may take advantage of my mother's good heart and buy her as part of the furniture, but you haven't bought me yet. You are a coward! You have been afraid to speak to me face to face. Instead, you go crawling to my parents to sell me to you. You are a coward and a cad! Don't ever speak to me again while I'm here. I shan't trouble you long with my presence. The day this place becomes yours, I leave it!"

Another word and she would have choked on her tears. She swept past him, leaving him stunned and shaken.

"Amy, where are you?"

He was brought back to his senses by Mrs. Siton's voice echoing up the stairs. Slowly he descended and at the foot turned away to avoid meeting her.

He walked distractedly across the fields, uncertain of his next move. The place was distasteful to him now, and he was sorely tempted to leave it and return to London. If it were not for his promise to Siton he would cancel his arrangements to purchase the manor house, but that would be too cruel.

How stupidly he had acted. If only he had made sure of Amy's feelings first, everything would still have been well. As it was, he had made her his implacable enemy.

It was the treasure that had been the source of all his troubles from first to last ever since he came home from Africa. Accursed thing! He wished he had never heard of it, or the ruins. As he looked towards the chapel he saw a man coming across the field towards him, the rural letter-carrier taking the shortest path towards the farm. As the man came up he sorted the bundle of letters he held and, without a word of greeting, handed two of them to Gardiner. As the man went on his way, Gardiner looked after him thoughtfully. Barely a fortnight had passed since he arrived in the district, yet his name and figure were familiar. For aught he knew his business was discussed as freely as his appearance. The average human being, having no rational source of entertainment within himself, must have it supplied. In the town this is not a problem, but in the country he needs must turn to peeping and prying upon his neighbours.

It occurred to Gardiner that the doings of Sanders might possibly have aroused an even greater curiosity among the country folk, so difficult is it for the movements of a stranger to escape notice.

He walked slowly to the ruins and sat down in the enclosure to read his letters. One was a blue envelope with "Record Office" stamped in the corner. If it was from Blakemore regarding the treasure, it could wait. The other, endorsed "Local" with a Forbridge postmark, was from his solicitor. He opened it and learned that matters were taking the usual course. The affair was practically settled, but one of the mortgagees was abroad and his address was doubtful. The solicitor feared this would cause a postponement of several weeks, or even months. The message ended with apologies and regrets.

Here shone a slender ray of sunshine to lighten the general gloom. With the purchase of the house delayed indefinitely, there was no need for him to cajole Amy to remain with her parents. The letter was as satisfactory as anything could be at present. The rest of the business could be conducted quite easily from London and, if necessary, he could run down to Forbridge at any time. In a word, the letter had removed the only inducement for him to stay.

He got up, shivering slightly. The air was damp and so was the place—damp, rank and depressing. As he walked briskly up and down he tried to make plans. The country, he now saw plainly, was for the light-hearted and the happy. He would return to London and maybe put his affairs in order and travel; it mattered little where he went, for he had no ties. The solicitor at Forbridge seemed a sharp and businesslike man. He would employ him to look after all his affairs, and Blakemore might help, too. But before he went up to London he would thank Siton and his wife and assure them their worries were indeed over.

A last look round. There, right opposite him, was the spot where Amy had dug, the soil still moist and heaped in irregular masses. To one side lay something round, glistening and white. He walked across and picked it up. It seemed but a shapeless piece of marble, stained and discoloured by a long stay underground. He was about to let it fall when his eye caught the faint outlines of a pattern that covered one side. Turning it so that the sunlight fell on it, he could make out the device: "On a field argent, three lozenges gules." Puzzled, he turned the marble this way and that, until he realised that the block represented the torso of an effigy clothed in a surtout on which the Gardiner arms had been emblazoned. Doubtless the effigy had served to decorate the monument of some old-time Gardiner buried beside his fathers in the chapel, his family's likeness sculptured on the plinth in the attitudes of prayer. Here was further evidence of the devastation wrought by Fairfax's troops in what must have been a noble cemetery.

But was this mere block of marble the reward of Amy's

A FOOTPRINT

search—the find he had seen her scrutinising with such rapt attention the night before? Could curiosity, not a treasure hunt, be her motive? A curiosity aroused by Sanders' mysterious acts?

He cleaned the fragment as best he could and placed it in his pocket. Midday was not past; he must get back to the farm, for there was much to do before his departure. As he turned to go he noted all about the spot the footprints of the graceful digger. Then, looking more intently, he saw that which sent his blood racing through his temples. Intermingling with Amy's footprints, here overlapping them, there almost obliterated in their turn by the slender prints of the girl, were the bootmarks of a man! And had they been stamped with the owner's name, they could not have been more clearly identifiable.

Gardiner remembered himself back in Madeira, landing from the steamer with his new-found companion. They had traversed the narrow streets with their prison-barred houses and poorly kept shops, their slow bullock sledges and quaint hammock bearers, his companion in quest of something less clumsy for the promenade deck than the stout shoes in which he had come aboard. He remembered so clearly the buying of the Belgian tennis shoes, the rubber soles stamped with a spiral trademark like a Lituus or query-point. The marks of interrogation later left by the shoes upon the moistened decks had been the occasion for waggish comment. How trivial had it all seemed then—of what tremendous moment now! There before him lay the question mark, Sanders' calling card. This had been no solitary midnight excursion of the girl's. It was a tryst. No curiosity inspired her movements. She knew as much about the treasure hunt as Sanders himself. The allies had been present together as they pursued their work. With a spasm of jealousy Gardiner recalled the bitter words of Amy, the taunts and insults she had heaped upon him. It had been solicitude for her lover that prompted the outburst. She had dreaded that, with her own secret known, Gardiner should discover that of Sanders as well.

Now that the first shock of the discovery had passed he was able to think clearly. He would not give in yet. Tamely to submit would be to abandon Amy to this forger, this thief. Amy—poor Amy, how devotedly she must love Sanders! No matter, she must be saved at all costs. He would help Saxby to arrest Sanders. Already Amy hated him; he had nothing to lose whatever happened, nothing to hope for at her hands. Someday perhaps she might be grateful for what he was about to do. It was not four weeks since the two men had arrived in England. Was he always fated to be forestalled by Sanders? He smiled bitterly, remembering with what ease Sanders had wormed into his confidence by the facile charm of his manner, the smoothness of his speech. And now he had charmed the girl, so that they seemed almost constant companions. How often, he wondered, did Amy come here? Every night? He started at the thought. Back went his thoughts to the ghostly figure in the corridor. How obtuse he had been! Of course, the apparition came always from the direction of Amy's room. Every night she crept out to help her lover, losing precious hours of sleep. How deep her affection must be for the scoundrel!

Unnoticed, the sky had clouded over, and now rain had begun to fall. He would be drenched before he could reach the farm, and there was no shelter in the ruins. He looked about for some nearer refuge. Barely a hundred yards to the right stood a small haystack, honeycombed and derelict like everything else upon the farm. Scudding across the field, he shot round the lee side, nearly colliding with a cyclist who was already sheltering there with his machine.

"Good morning," said a well-known voice as Gardiner pressed himself against the side of the stack. He turned and

A FOOTPRINT

looked at the youth, but failed to recognise him; only the voice was familiar. In another moment he remembered where he had heard it before. At Gardiner's sudden look of intelligence the other spoke rapidly. "No names, please, and speak low. One never knows who's listening."

"Admirable, inspector!" murmured Gardiner, won to a more cheerful frame of mind by the piquancy of the situation. "You look about eighteen. I was coming to see you."

Saxby nodded. "Just missed him again. Ran him to earth beautifully. Never saw such luck as he has. I believe he came in this direction, for one of those wooden-headed local fellows thought he saw him and says he didn't recognise him until he'd gone by. Have you any news of him yourself?"

"Yes. I believe he comes here to the ruin every night about twelve." And when the inspector shot him an impatient look, he added, "I only discovered it this morning."

"But why? A woman?"

Gardiner hesitated. "I think it must be," he admitted.

"Good! I'll try my luck again. Wait here a little until I've got clear away. I don't want anyone to see us together." He wheeled his cycle over the sodden grass and dragged it through a gap in the hedge. Having thus regained the high road, he pedalled off towards Maidstone.

As Gardiner sheltered beside the stack he remembered Blakemore's letter and felt in his pockets without finding it. He had had it at the ruins. Could he have dropped it on the way from there?

As the rain began to slacken he left his shelter and retraced his steps through the drizzle. Beside the mound on which he had sat lay the blue envelope, sodden but still legible.

CHAPTER 12

THE AMBUSCADE

WHEN Gardiner took his leave of the Sitons, there was more than a hint of restraint on both sides. The farmer was apprehensive that Gardiner might make the gaining of Amy's hand a condition of his aid. His wife sensed rather than knew that Gardiner's suit with her daughter was beyond hope.

The departing visitor himself had already reached a level of dejection which nothing could well deepen. As he sat in his room sorting out a few necessaries from the bulk of his luggage, he looked aged and careworn. The rest of his belongings were to follow him to London, in which city, he had assured his hosts, urgent business awaited his attention. Actually, he had no intention of leaving the neighbourhood before the next day. His plan was to put up at a Forbridge hotel and start out for the ruins about ten o'clock. The two miles back to Embrook and the three from there to the chapel could be walked easily by half-past eleven, which was early enough for him to join Saxby's party. For he had resolved to take a hand in the evening's programme, whether or not his company was welcome.

Ever since his meeting with Saxby, Gardiner's thoughts had dwelt only upon the forthcoming arrest and the despair it would cause Amy. He only hoped Saxby, that humane and courteous officer, could be trusted to act tactfully. His subordinates were local men who would know Amy well; details of the incident would be sure to leak out, and Amy's reputation would suffer severely. Clearly, Gardiner's place, he felt, was by her side.

As he stooped to lock the last portmanteau, a paper fell from his breast pocket. It was the blue official letter, crisp and dry again, but still unread. He sat down and perused its contents.

In a covering letter, Blakemore did little more than explain that he had passed the cipher bearings on to his friend at the Greenwich Observatory—without giving him details—and that he now enclosed Rees' reply. "You will see," wrote Blakemore, "that the chapel is hopelessly off the correct bearing." With his appetite thus whetted, Gardiner turned to the enclosure:

Royal Observatory.
Greenwich.
Tuesday.

Dear Mr. Blakemore,

I must apologise for not answering your letter before, but press of work in connection with the recent eclipse must be my excuse.

The enquiry you asked me to undertake was very interesting, but before I tell you the result perhaps I had better explain certain astronomical facts. Just as the sun does not rise invariably in the geographical east nor always set in the west, the compass needle does not invariably point due north and south. The magnetic north or meridian does not coincide with the geographical north or meridian except on rare occasions, and over long periods the magnetic needle oscillates slowly about $24° 38'$ either side of the true geographical north, the rate of movement being about $14'$ a year.

In the year 1580 the needle pointed 11° 15′ east of north; in 1657 it pointed true north. It then moved in a westerly direction until 1818, when it pointed 24° 38′ west of north. Since then it has been returning, and now points at Greenwich about 18° west of north; the place you refer to is so near London that its variation may be considered identical with the latter.

In making observations with a compass for the purpose of map construction, it is usual to reduce magnetic bearings to true, *i.e.,* geographical ones, by applying the known variations at the time. The bearings you have sent me as having been taken in 1583 and which I will now call (A) are:

(A) CROMLECH NNE–BEACON NW by W. In that year the error or deviation of the compass was 10° 51′ east, and allowing for that, the actual bearings on a map would have been these, which I will call (B):

(B) CROMLECH NE by N–BEACON NW. Inasmuch as the deviation at the present time amounts to 18°W, the bearings, taken with a compass, would be these:

(C) CROMLECH NE ¾E–BEACON NNW ¼W. Now if you wished to take the bearings with a compass on the land, they would give the result as (C), but if you wished, as I take it you do, to find the exact spot on the map which is referred to in (A), you must disregard the compass and consider the true bearing to be (B). (B) is therefore what we must work from, and on the Ordnance Map I find that it lands you at a place marked Embrook Manor Farm, just one mile SW ¼W from the ruined chapel.

Any further help you want I shall be very glad to give you.

With kind regards, yours very truly,
Lionel Rees.

THE AMBUSCADE 145

Gardiner read the two letters with a strange jumble of emotions, and when he had finished he read them over again. At first, disappointment at this new complication predominated, but as he regarded the situation calmly from every side, this feeling gave place to a sense of satisfaction. It was now clear that Sanders, for all his shrewdness, had been completely misled; he and Amy had been digging a mile away from the correct site! And yet how simple did it all seem in retrospect. Where could a more secure hiding place be found than within the walls of the manor house? And what more natural than that his ancestor fix upon it? Gardiner threw a mental glance around the rooms of the house, trying to imagine a likely place of concealment. Secret rooms and passages probably abounded in the ancient structure, in which case the treasure doubtless lay mouldering and forgotten in one of them.

The old clock struck four. With a sigh he took up his bag and went down. The place seemed deserted. Somewhere at the back of the house the farmer whistled a fragment of an old ballad. He, at any rate, was happier than he had once been. Gardiner hesitated at the door, hoping in spite of himself to catch a glimpse of Amy. A second later, angry at himself, he undid the latch and passed out.

He crossed the orchard moat by the mound that marked the site of the drawbridge. Upon the further side he stopped to look back at the mansion. Although the sun was gone, a rosy light yet lingered. The old brickwork glowed like rubies. Sturdy and square, its lines broken only by window bays and chimney flues, three centuries had left so little mark of their passing that the house stood solid enough to endure another three.

In and out between the grotesque yews something flickered whitely. It was Amy, crossing from the house towards the stables. Upon his departure she had lost no time in resuming her household duties. Lest she suspect him of spying on her again he turned and sped away.

During his stay at the farm the oncoming winter had grown more assertive. From every hedge the spiders sent tentative cables in search of anchorage to stream upon the wind and flash like spun glass in the sun. Between the newly naked tree-tops the wood pigeons lumbered in their noisy flight towards the turnip fields; the rooks paid fitful visits to their nesting trees in the line of elms bordering the high road; and the partridge, solitary and wildly apprehensive, flapped nervously from copse to copse in search of the security and peace gone with the days of his recent domesticity. The last swallow had disappeared in graceful flight towards the south, its place taken by the robber gang of hooded crows.

Night was closing in before Gardiner reached Forbridge. He left his bag at the station and dined at the hotel. He had little appetite, but the time must somehow be spent. Afterwards he managed to dawdle away the evening in the smoking room. Close on ten he set off for the chapel. Because he had plenty of time he elected to follow the high road part of the way and then to strike northward along the road where he had met Saxby in the morning. As he came in sight of the sheltering haystack, half-past eleven chimed from a distant clock tower. Scrambling through the gap in the hedge, he tramped across the grass and sat down in the stack's shadow.

Now that he had arrived at the theatre at last, it occurred to him that he had not made up his mind from where he should view the drama, or how to make his entrance upon the stage. It was useless for him to remain where he was, for it was impossible to see or hear what might pass in the ruins. As he sat there hesitating, the knowledge came to him that he was not alone. Pressing his cheek against the stack, he was able to perceive a darker projecting mass distinguishable as the figure of a man seated like himself upon the ground. It was impossible to suppose that this other was unaware of Gardiner's presence; the stranger in the shadows must have seen him as he crossed the field. Was he asleep? Not the faintest sound of breathing could be heard. Did he think himself unseen? Gardiner's heart thumped at the idea. Could it be Sanders, and if so, how could he take him single-handed?

At that moment a man came into sight round the corner of the stack. It was a uniformed policeman. As Gardiner rose to his feet he was amazed to see the newcomer salute the silent stranger.

"Beg pardon, sir, but Mr. Jones thought I'd better come and tell you he thought I'd made a bit of a mistake over this 'ere."

"Mistake! Why, you—you idiot! What on earth do you mean by coming here and telling me such a thing as that?" It was Saxby's voice.

"Why, sir, I was coming along the road according to orders about an hour ago, and as I got near the railway bridge I heard voices. I crept up and listened, but I couldn't get near enough 'cause they was talking so low." The constable paused.

"Yes, yes. Go on!"

"Well, sir, I made out as it were a man and a female, and after a bit I recognised Mr. Sanders."

"You dunderhead. And you let him go?"

"I heard as how he was to be arrested here."

The inspector groaned. "Go on."

"That's all I see, sir."

"Did they see you?"

"No, sir; I followed them in the rear."

"Then why don't you say all you saw?"

"I've told you all I see," said the man, with an air of injury.

"No, you haven't! How long did he wait under the arch? Where did he go when you followed him?"

"He didn't wait more'n a minute or two after I came up, and then they walked away together, he and the female, and I followed 'em up as fur as this."

"And no further?"

"My orders was to report myself here at eleven-thirty, an' I done it."

"Did you ever hear of such a fool in your life, Mr. Gardiner?" exclaimed Saxby. To this hint that he had been seen and recognised Gardiner could find no appropriate reply, and the inspector resumed his cross-examination: "Where were they when you left them?"

"Going along the road towards Embrook."

"Was the woman anyone you knew?"

"I couldn't get near enough to make sure, sir, but she looked to me like Miss Siton from Manor Farm."

"And you heard nothing they said?"

"Only some place name or other I caught once or twice— Southampton, I think it was. If I'd got close enough to hear better they'd have seen me."

"A nice kettle of fish you've managed to cook for us all! You'd better go back to your post. Tell Mr. Jones I'll come and speak to him presently."

By this time Gardiner had recovered from the series of surprises this interchange had given him. As Saxby still fumed silently at the crassness of his subordinate, Gardiner spoke. "I'm afraid you're going to lose him again."

The detective ignored the remark. "Look here, Mr. Gardiner," he said, "what on earth are you doing here?"

"I have my reasons," Gardiner replied stiffly. "I presume there is no objection to my taking a walk this way?"

"If I hadn't let you know my plans I take it you wouldn't be here?"

"Perhaps not. But have you forgotten you said you would

THE AMBUSCADE

be glad of my assistance?"

"That was before I knew the man so well. There's such a thing as too many cooks spoiling the broth."

Gardiner frowned. "Look here, inspector, I object to your tone."

"No, no. I beg your pardon. I'm upset over that fellow's stupidity. I must say, though, when I saw you coming across the field, I did wish you further."

"Had you been here long?"

"Yes, I'm making this haystack my headquarters. Jones, my sergeant—it was he who boarded the tender with me, you know—he's got the Malling men posted all about, and it really looked as if we'd got a nice little surprise ready for Mr. Sanders. But when you turned up, I thought the whole affair was going to be upset. I was afraid to speak to you in case it gave the whole show away still more. But it looks now as though we shan't be seeing him. Is that the girl he generally meets—Miss Siton?"

"Yes, I think so."

"I wonder why they altered their plans."

"I think I know. She saw me follow her down to the ruins last night."

"There you are, then. Great heavens! Why couldn't you let me see to it?"

Gardiner felt resentful, but he was also embarrassed. He could not justify his actions without telling Saxby too much. So he said nothing.

The pause was broken by Saxby. "Sanders is probably on his way to Southampton by this time, and it looks as though he has the funds to get clear away."

"Oh?"

"I suppose I may as well tell you, but let's not talk so loud. Sanders received much of the money from the Gold Coast swindle in English bank-notes, and we have the numbers.

Some were changed in Maidstone, and that told us where Sanders was lying low. We had the place surrounded by six o'clock this morning, but I suppose his usual luck came in again, for when Jones and I searched the house, the bird had flown. He really is as slippery as an eel!"

Saxby shuddered with the cold, and both men crouched deeper in the stack. The minutes lengthened into hours. Twice the detective made a cautious circuit of the field to confer with his lieutenant, but when three o'clock came and brought nothing to disturb the monotony of the watch, he abandoned it in despair. Leaving orders with Jones to withdraw the bulk of his forces in daylight, Saxby invited Gardiner to return with him to Forbridge. There, at the police station, they spent the remainder of the night more pleasantly before a good fire. Then, tired and drowsy, Gardiner took an early train up to town.

CHAPTER 13

A PLAN OF CAMPAIGN

"IF she'd only been more your own age—" Blakemore shook his head disapprovingly.

He was imparting his advice to Gardiner at the club over a bottle of Chateau Rauzan '75. "The fact is, my dear fellow, at our time of life a man is anything but wise who allows himself to think of such things. Our salad days are over, and the time has come for us to resign sweets to the boys and girls who can digest them. Not that we've either of us got one foot in the grave yet. But here we are, a couple of middle-aged bachelors, and the wisest thing we can do is to remain just as we are." He took a pensive sip.

Gardiner sat in gloomy silence, lacking both the energy and the inclination to reply. His companion leaned forward and grasped his arm. "For heaven's sake, old man, snap out of it. Go for a brisk walk. Anything rather than sit and brood. A man I used to know recommended taking a bath when you were in the dumps. He said you always came out thinking of something quite different from when you went in."

Gardiner smiled at last. "I'll make a note of the remedy."

"Now, fill up. Here's to the right Mrs. Gardiner when she

comes along. Let's be practical and talk of money—the root of all happiness."

"It used to be the root of all evil."

"No, the want of it is that. Money gilds every pill. Tell me what it can't do? I can conceive of no misfortune it isn't able to mitigate."

"Death?"

"I said mitigate, not prevent! Anyway, pass the bottle this way and let's be thankful we're able to do ourselves so well. Nice little dinner, wasn't it? You really must join this club— I can get plenty of men to second you. Here, waiter! Where's the Candidate's Book? In the smoking room? Then we'll go in there."

Under the influence of Blakemore's impulsive good humour and a final glass of the excellent wine (the club was noted for its cellar), the last shreds of Gardiner's depression vanished.

London that day had had its due share of wet and cheerless weather. The newspapers and some perfunctory shopping in the foggy streets had helped him to pass the morning. Then, after an early lunch, he had set out to find his friend.

Of Gardiner's treasure hunting at Embrook there was little that Blakemore had to learn and that little was soon told, but about his relationship with Amy, Gardiner was inclined to greater reticence. Despite Blakemore's amiability—even jollity, his genial shrewdness and his common sense, Gardiner had a lively dread of his ridicule. Still, Gardiner was not adept at concealment. The tale of his adventures at the ruins, including his discovery of Sanders' traces, made little sense without mention of Amy, and an innocent question or two from Blakemore soon brought forth the embarrassing remainder.

But romance, as Gardiner should have learned, is not the monopoly of any period of life. His narrative was listened to with a concern as unexpected as it was cheering, and it was in

A PLAN OF CAMPAIGN 153

a sincere spirit that Blakemore offered his sympathy. For he, Blakemore, the browser in musty parchments, had also suffered, and, confidence begetting confidence, he told of his own tragic romance of a quarter-century ago. Later that evening, in the seclusion of the club library, the two confidants discussed the treasure again. Blakemore recommended that Gardiner, with the field deserted by Sanders, should forthwith make an effort to discover it.

"Where's the hurry? Surely it would be better to wait until I've bought the place."

"But if you can locate the treasure immediately, so much the better. We've never yet had positive proof that it's there at all, and supposing it is, you've still got to find it, which may take time."

"And if it's been removed it will take longer still!"

"As to that, I hope you'll be able to settle the question quite shortly. If it hasn't been removed in these three hundred years, you'll find it in one particular part of the house."

"You mean in the 'tabernacle,' as the cipher calls it?"

"Yes; that is to say, some sort of private chapel."

"Well, how would you advise me to begin?"

"I've found a document in the office which I thought might give you a few hints." Blakemore drew a paper from his pocket. "Here's a copy of it. It lists the instructions from the Privy Council to Sir Henry Bromley, the magistrate who was told off to search Hindlip Hall at the time of the Powder Plot. After telling him to surround the place, to guard every door, to allow no one to pass, to watch the movements of the servants, and so forth, it goes on like this:

> First observe the parlour where they dine and sup; in the east part of that parlour it is conceived there is some vault which to discover you must take care to draw down the

wainscot whereby the entry into the vault may be discovered. The lower parts of the house must be tried with a broach by putting the same into the ground some foot or two to try whether there may be perceived some timber, which if there be there must be some vault underneath it. For the upper rooms you must observe whether they be more in breadth than the lower rooms and look in which places the rooms be enlarged, by pulling up some boards you may discover some vaults. Also if it appear that there be some corners to the chimneys and the same boarded, if the boards be taken there will somewhat appear. If the walls be thick and covered with wainscot, being tried with a gimlet if it strike not the wall but go through, some suspicion is to be had thereof. If there be any double loft some two or three feet above one another, in such places any may be harboured privately. Also if there be a loft towards the roof of the house in which there appears no entrance out of any other place or lodging, it must of necessity be opened and looked into for these be ordinary places of hovering.

"Is that all?" enquired Gardiner sarcastically as Blakemore stopped reading.

"Yes, all that concerns the hiding place, at least."

"But if I did all that there wouldn't be much of the house left standing! Pulling down the wainscot, tearing up the floor, then broaching—I suppose that means probing—the ground in the cellars, then trying the walls with a gimlet, and then the measuring of the rooms. Why, it will take a lifetime!"

"Not a bit! There's a very simple operation you can begin with."

"The measuring?"

"Not exactly. I should start by making a rough sketch-plan of the house and comparing the windows that show outside with those in the rooms. If there's any discrepancy you have proof at once of a forgotten room. And there, ten to one, is where you'll find the hiding place."

"And if the windows correspond?"

"That doesn't disprove a secret chamber. It's unlikely to have much light, perhaps no window at all, wedged up in a corner between several other rooms. But if the windows fail, then you'll have to fall back on full internal measures, and that of course will take a little time."

"But Siton said there were several disused rooms cut off from the rest of the house."

"Did he know where they were?"

"Yes, I think he said all one side of the house was cut off."

"Then it's easy enough for you to do as I say. There's no earthly occasion to talk of pulling the house down until the windows and then the measurements fail you."

Gardiner looked distinctly unhappy. "Somehow I don't relish the idea of searching the place just yet."

"Why not?"

Gardiner was silent.

"My dear fellow, you've told me all about the lady, so you won't mind my saying that the situation has radically altered. You haven't got her feelings to consider now. She can be left out of the calculation altogether. You say the old gentleman is hardly ever in the house, and surely the mother is not so very formidable?"

"Oh, quite the contrary. It's the secrecy and mystery that worry me. How would *you* feel?"

"But the house is going to be yours. They know you're going to have it, and you'll want to furnish it. Consider the carpets and blinds and things. Won't they be excuse enough for any amount of planning and measuring?"

Gardiner laughed at his friend's solution. "I wish you were coming down with me," he pleaded.

"I wish I were; perhaps in a few days I could manage it."

The club's staff, waiting to close up for the night, were now eying them with the acidulous glances reserved for those who have overstayed their welcome. The friends bade one another goodnight at the club entrance and made for their respective beds.

Next morning Gardiner received a telegram from the Forbridge solicitor:

MR. WEST RETURNED PLEASE COME AT ONCE IF BUSINESS IS TO PROCEED AS ARRANGED–HAY

West, he remembered, was the name of the mortgagee whose absence abroad had delayed transfer of the mortgage.

After last night's talk with Blakemore, much of Gardiner's interest in the treasure had revived, and with it his desire to purchase the old house in which it was possibly still hidden. The telegram thus arrived at an opportune moment, and, whether Blakemore was able to come with him or not, he decided to return to Embrook at once. As he walked along the Strand he thought of Amy—not entirely dispassionately—but less sentimentally than in the past. He hoped she would not regret her choice, that Sanders would treat her honourably, that her old parents were not taking her sudden departure too hard. Deep in thought he was startled by a sudden grip on his arm. It was Blakemore, on his way to lunch.

"What's the matter, old man?" he grinned. "By Jove, you look serious enough for anything; *l'amour* again?"

Gardiner grunted noncommittally and handed him the telegram.

A PLAN OF CAMPAIGN 157

"Of course you'll go down at once?" said Blakemore as he returned it.

"Yes, now that Am—er, Miss Siton isn't there, I shall go straight on from the station."

"I wish I was coming too."

"Can't you possibly get away?"

"Well, let's have a spot of lunch together, and then I'll see."

Later, as they walked back to the office, Blakemore raised a related matter.

"Have you considered whether the secret of the treasure is still a secret?"

"Oh, I'm sure it is." Gardiner was shocked by the question.

"I admire your confidence. In a little country place like that, Sanders' movements can't have gone unnoticed. The farmer and everyone about the place knew he was digging for something, and a search for treasure is just what the bucolic mind is able to appreciate. Everyone has heard of pots of coins being discovered now and then in a field."

"But Sanders was digging fully a mile away from the house."

"Quite near enough to set all the yokels agog."

"With the secret known to only four people in the world?"

"I hope it is, certainly, but there's a saying that a secret known to more than two people is none at all. Besides, there have been far too many police about the place to suit me, and I know what officials are when there's any question of the Crown's prerogatives."

"Well, if the worst comes to the worst I shall have to give it up, that's all."

"If you're satisfied to surrender the treasure when it's found I shan't have a word to say, but I can tell you one thing: I mean to get a sight of that treasure somehow. After that, you can please yourself what you do. Now if you'll excuse me?"

They had reached the Record Office. Gardiner waited in

his friend's room while the sudden absence from duty was arranged, filling in the time by sending a telegram to Hay and a letter to his London bankers.

On the journey down, some of Blakemore's jubilance was transferred to his companion, and it was in a frame of mind very different from the melancholy of his recent departure that Gardiner approached the manor house again.

The untended approaches, the neglected fabric, the crude and clumsy attempts at reparation, all so palpable at midday, were now discreetly veiled by the shadows of the waning afternoon. Blakemore was lost in admiration of the massive red walls, the mullioned windows with their leaded casements, the rows of jutting gables, and the red-tiled roof topped by the clustered chimney shafts of chiselled brick. Within, he found other and more delicate attractions, and it was lucky for the success of their plans that the hall and staircase claimed so much of his attention, or not even the presence of Mrs. Siton would have restrained him from commencing a treasure hunt forthwith.

As usual, the farmer was out of sight, but his wife received them with a placid welcome in which Gardiner was puzzled—but greatly relieved—to note no hint of grief at the shipwreck of her daughter's life. For all the philosophy Blakemore had managed recently to instil, Gardiner was unable to repress a surge of poignant memories as he entered the scene of his shattered hopes. Back in his old rooms again, Gardiner might well have relapsed into his former melancholy had not Blakemore's presence provided an antidote. That gentleman eagerly awaited the next day's dawning and declined to be lured by any other topic from the discussion of his plans. In his baggage he had packed a bicycle lamp "to light any secret passages we may find," a huge case-opener—practically a burglar's jemmy, a large leather-cased Chesterman tape measure

A PLAN OF CAMPAIGN

and a folding surveyor's rod. These, among other appliances, were the fruits of a hurried call at an establishment in Victoria Street on his way to meet Gardiner at the station.

"I don't know what difficulties we may have to meet," Blakemore explained, "maybe none at all. But supposing we find it necessary to go through the Privy Council's formula I read to you—well, we shall be prepared, that's all!"

"Look here," said Gardiner at the display of tools, "it's all very well for me to tell the old people I'm measuring the house with an eye to furnishing, but how can I explain your presence? Are you to figure as an upholsterer?"

"Simple, dear boy! Tell them I'm an architect. They'll think I've come down to advise you on the alterations you're going to make in the house. They won't see anything odd in that, for it's just the sort of vandalism they would go in for themselves if they stood in your shoes."

Blakemore discussed the morrow's doings well into the night. Gardiner had fallen asleep in his chair and wakened again at least three times before Blakemore, garrulous to the end, could be persuaded to turn in.

CHAPTER 14

A PIECE OF PARCHMENT

BLAKEMORE was up at the crack of dawn and, despite the persistent rain, poked into all corners of the big house and its outbuildings, notebook in hand. Industriously he jotted down sketches and ideas. Siton, who had not found such a listener since the early days of Gardiner's visit, poured out his woes in a prolix stream. Much of what he said was useless for Blakemore's purposes, but by a shrewd comment or question when the opportunity offered he was able to keep the monologue on a fairly relevant tack. The morning was well advanced when he received an inner reminder that he had not yet breakfasted. Hurrying indoors, he found his friend finishing eggs and bacon and asked the good Mrs. Siton for some of the same.

"Hello, old man, what's the latest?" was Blakemore's salutation.

"Nothing much. I went for an early walk while you were sleeping."

"Sleeping? Nonsense, I've been up for hours. In fact, I've put in a whole day's work already."

As they ate, Blakemore told Gardiner of his latest ideas.

"Do you know," he remarked thoughtfully, "I've been wondering whether Nicholas Owen can have had anything to do with this place?"

"Nicholas Owen?"

"You know! The Jesuit—a colleague of Father Garnet—the Gunpowder Plot Garnet. To all intents and purposes he was an architect, and the cleverest inventor of priests' holes and secret rooms that has ever been. He was arrested after the Powder Plot and ended his days in the Tower."

"Was he executed?"

"No, he killed himself. He had been tortured and evidently feared his resolution might fail under further pressure, so he opened an artery in his leg and bled to death. Other reports say he actually died under torture."

"And you think he had a hand in building this place?"

"Not in the actual building. That was all over and done with, I should say, before his time. But he might have been called in as consulting architect to devise a secret chapel or priest's hole." Blakemore chewed a piece of bacon thoughtfully. "It's a curious thing that he fell victim to his own contrivance."

He explained that Owen was arrested at Hindlip Hall, near Worcester, with Garnet and Oldcorne where they had taken refuge after the arrest of Guy Fawkes. That house had been built entirely from Owen's plans, and there was hardly a room that did not possess a concealed door leading to a secret room or passage. Even the chimney flues were reputed to have been double.

"And yet they were still discovered?"

"After a fashion. The priests were betrayed by a servant, but Owen and another man were starved out. They had had to bolt suddenly to the hiding place, which had never been victualled for a seige. It's hard to see how the matter was overlooked. Garnet and Oldcorne seem to have lived on some marmalade they found, but of course that wasn't very sustaining. They were in a dreadful condition when discovered."

"Heavens! If Embrook is anything like Hindlip, it will take months to unearth all the hiding places."

"I don't think so. Hindlip was Owen's masterpiece and an exception. There's not likely to be more than one hiding place here; it was only intended as a temporary refuge in an emergency. The priest would live and move and have his being with the family most of the time."

After breakfast the two friends rose from the table. "Now," said Blakemore, "I've got something of great importance to tell you. What I discovered this morning will greatly simplify our work. It's this: almost every window in the house looks out from one of four sides; in fact, only three rooms in the place look into the courtyard. Here they are." He walked to the door and set it open.

The corridors which threaded the mansion ran squarely round the open court in its centre. Because the sitting room lay in the northeast angle, the junction of two of these corridors confronted them as they stood at the door. The one in front ran shortly between three rooms and a row of windows in the northern facade to end at a wall. On the left a longer one, without windows except at the end, lay at right angles to the first. It was the one they came and went by to the stairs, and that their own rooms opened into. Next to the sitting room came Gardiner's bedroom; after that Blakemore's, and at the end nearest the stairs was a vacant bedroom Mrs. Siton would gladly let had another tenant been available. On the ground floor were the various rooms occupied by the family.

"And what are these three rooms?"

"Miss Siton's in the middle and a lumber room on each side, I understand."

Gardiner pondered this information. Though he had lived so

close to them for several days, a natural delicacy had restrained him from even trespassing in the shorter corridor. A moment's reflection would have told him that because the ghost, identified as Amy, had passed the door, her own must be somewhere near, but he had given it no reflection until now.

But Blakemore was still speaking. "—the partition, there—the partition at the end. It cuts off this little corridor from the one at the other side of the house. It looks like a wall, but it's only wood and plaster." He rapped sharply with his knuckles. "This one is pretty solid, but Siton says that the one at the other end near the hall is rickety, so we ought to get through it easily. And we shan't be disturbing anyone by working there, because it's a fair distance from the living rooms."

"Then we shall find the same number of rooms on the other side as on this?"

"Well, I counted four windows, and the rooms all open into the corridor that's cut off."

"And what about the large one underneath? The banqueting hall, as Mrs. Siton calls it, and the little drawing room beyond?"

"I don't think we need trouble about them yet. They haven't been cut off from the rest of the house and so are unlikely to conceal any secrets. Now let's have a look at the other partition."

He strode back into the sitting room and handed Gardiner the Chesterman tape measure and the bicycle lamp. Taking the surveyor's rod and the formidable case-opener himself, they started off down the long corridor.

A stretch of eight feet brought them to the head of the stairs. From this point the corridor was continued along the garden front of the house by a gallery above the hall. Light and graceful, with a balustrade similar to that of the stairway, the gallery was dusty and untrodden. It formed practically a *cul-de-sac,* then ended at an apparent wall, which was betrayed by extensive shedding of plaster to be a mere partition.

"This is our mark," said Blakemore. With a tap he sent the greater part of the remaining plaster tumbling to the floor. The laths behind were thick and closely set, and when he twisted a handful the last scraps of plaster fell, leaving a satisfactory gap between the partition and the wall.

"Catch hold!" Blakemore cried. "And shove when I give the word! One, two, three, go!"

The two men flung themselves upon it and the partition shivered. A rush of plaster was heard behind. Dust poured out and almost choked them. Covering their faces, the two men rushed to fling open the casements.

The corridor they stood in a few minutes later had a musty tang, as of an overcrowded room. The walls and ceilings were hung in rich profusion with cobwebs that waved like banners at their approach. The floor was thickly carpeted with dust that rose about their advancing footsteps. But, as the air cleared, the sunbeams sent a cheery glow along the mouldering panels of the walls.

"Four rooms, just as on the other side," remarked Gardiner, pointing to the four doors that could now be seen. He tried the nearest door, but it was fast. "Shall we have to do any more housebreaking?"

"I hope not," said Blakemore. "Try the next one."

That, too, was locked, as was the third. But the handle of the fourth yielded, and with a sharp crack the door opened.

There was little enough to see inside. The room was empty but for odds and ends of timber, laths, a great heap of plaster, a bent old trowel and a scattered nail or two. It had evidently been used as a workshop for constructing the partitions when the corridor was closed.

"Now measure from the door to the dividing wall," said Blakemore.

"Five feet," Gardiner announced. "It was twenty feet outside, so that leaves fifteen."

"Is that so?" said Blakemore eagerly. "And we're above the division between the two lower rooms. So unless the next-door room is larger than your bedroom on the other side of the house, there's a good deal of wall to be accounted for."

"Shall we try and get into the next room and measure it?"

"Wait a minute," said Blakemore. He struck the panelling in the corner with his fist, and as it emitted a drum-like note the two exchanged a glance of triumph.

"See here." Gardiner showed him two cracks barely visible in the panelling, one running horizontally six feet above the floor to join the other at a right angle.

"A door, sure enough," cried Blakemore. "And here's the lock."

Gardiner thrust the case-opener above the bolt and began to lever, at first tentatively and then with all his force. The wooden mortice snapped, the bolt tore through and the door opened. An exclamation of disappointment escaped them as a shallow cupboard was revealed, the shelves occupied by several curiously shaped implements covered by dust and cobwebs.

"Well, well! What have we here?" Careless of the grime, Blakemore lifted down one of the grimy objects. "Musical instruments, and very old ones, too!" As he examined one after the other he mused delightedly: "Elizabethan, every one of them. This is a shawm, the ancestor of the oboe; and here is a pommer, an early bassoon. This fish-hook affair is a cromhorn, and this huge thing is a bass recorder. And here are the tenor and treble. Ah, this is really interesting; look: a pipe and tabor!" Blakemore, his eyes bright, waxed enthusiastic on these discoveries. "I must really buy these from the old gentleman; I don't suppose he will object to parting with them."

He was replacing the instruments in the cupboard when the bass recorder slipped from his grasp. Steadying himself with a hand upon the shelf, Blakemore stooped to recover it. Behind him Gardiner uttered a cry of astonishment. The cupboard with its shelves swung inwards upon hidden hinges to disclose a narrow passageway beyond.

"The cupboard is even more interesting than its contents," exclaimed Blakemore excitedly. He pushed the shelves further back. The hidden space was quite narrow, a bare three feet in width, but when they had passed in and forced the shelves back into position, they found it to extend backwards for twenty feet or more; that is, for the whole length of the partition-wall between the rooms.

Some attempt had been made to render it comfortable. The floor was covered with a strip of tapestry evidently clipped from a larger hanging that represented a hunting scene. Along one side was ranged a carved oak table upon which rested a heavy lamp, an embroidered leather glove, rigid as a steel gauntlet, and a horse-pistol with a tarnished silver-inlaid stock and rusty graven barrels. Beside the table stood an oaken chair of the old double egg-cup shape, the arms and seat covered with stamped leather, soft and well-padded. Above it hung a most delicately modelled silver crucifix.

The further end of the chamber was filled by a dark oak chest: a massive cube, three feet in each dimension, which came flush down to the floor without any intervening rest. Its front was deeply carved in a geometrical pattern of the late fifteenth century, but the lid, a solid piece of planking, was planed smooth and secured by two long hasps engaging in a pair of hooks. The hasps were honeycombed and deeply rusted, and great rifts stretched across the carving of the front.

"Here," said Gardiner, "what do you make of this? I found it underneath the glove."

He held out a narrow strip of dirty paper. Taking it, Blakemore recognised it to be the outside of a folded parchment, soiled and brown with age and fused together by the

A PIECE OF PARCHMENT

damp. Drawing the chair up to the table, he sat down and smoothed the parchment, gently separating the folds. The folio sheet was faintly covered with a large untidy script which had none of the precise alignment of a legal document. So long was he in conning it that Gardiner took a seat upon the chest and awaited the result with an outward show of patience he was far from feeling.

At length Blakemore turned to Gardiner with a seriousness he had not displayed before. "Here," said he, laying his hand upon the parchment, "here is the Queen's Treasure."

"That piece of parchment?"

"This is the inventory."

"But where's the treasure?"

"It doesn't say. But here is proof at last that what we've been searching for did exist, and for anything we can tell, exists still. There's a date at the end—1583—with something that may stand for 'M. G.' It reminds me of Sir Medway's writing, and the spelling is odd enough to be his. Listen, and I'll condense it for you in modern English:

" 'Three gold wedges; ten silver bars; sixteen bags gold pistoles; twelve bags gold escudos; one parcel topaz and amethyst; one parcel pearls; twenty-two sword hilts; one salt, a ship; another, enamelled; two candlesticks; one cup, St. James; another, rubies; a ewer, chased; a beaker, enamelled; a diamond belt; a pouncet-box; a crucifix seal; a pearl brooch; another, diamonds; four pearl earrings; a pendant, emerald; another, rubies; fifty-two rings; six pairs diamond buckles; eighteen spoons; a gold reliquary; five cruets; two thuribles; eight handbells; a crucifix, emeralds; another, pearls and rubies; a paten; three chalices; a monstrance.'

"Then there is a note, 'The vessels are all of gold.' "

Before Blakemore had half read through the list Gardiner was on his feet striding up and down the narrow space, and, as the other stopped, he cried, "But this is terrible! Is that all it says? Not a word of where to find it?"

"Not a word. It's an inventory pure and simple. But does it really matter?" And then, as Gardiner stared at him blankly, "Look around you. What is this but 'the tabernacle' of Sir Medway's cipher? A priest's hiding place if ever there was one. And there will be the treasure, if there is one." He pointed to the chest at the end.

Silently Gardiner took the case-opener and forced it under the rusty hasps of the chest. The first snapped readily, and the second spun in fragments across the chamber. Thereupon, with Blakemore's help, he levered up the heavy lid.

"So this is all!" was Gardiner's bitter comment.

The chest was empty but for a mass of black drapery at the bottom. Blakemore dragged it out. "A cassock!" he proclaimed. But even as he held it, it fell asunder.

Leaning over, Blakemore swept the rotten fragments to one side. "Nothing more of the priest's property. Hullo! What's this?" He rapped with his knuckles and the bottom of the chest rattled loosely. "Lend a hand with that jemmy."

The bottom boards had shrunk away and left a gap towards the front, just wide enough to receive the claw of the case-opener. A wrench, a loud crack, and then the bottom heaved upwards like another lid. It was a trap door, until now secured upon its underside by a bolt that now hung by a single screw. Underneath was darkness, dense and unrelieved. The two men peered eagerly down. The top of a ladder could just be discerned. Though sturdy and substantial, it was roughly constructed from a pair of ponderous beams now wrinkled and warped with age and full of wormholes. But the steps, solid and three-sided, afforded a better foothold than most latter-day rungs.

"This is where the lamp comes in," said Blakemore, and

A PIECE OF PARCHMENT   169

taking it from Gardiner he lighted it and held it down at arm's length. "Strange that I can't seem to see to the bottom. Why don't you try?" He straightened up and handed the lamp to his friend.

"I think I can see the bottom," Gardiner reported, after several athletic contortions. "At least I can make out the end of the ladder, and that must be resting on something solid." He grasped one of the cross-pieces and shook it.

"Yes. Most likely there's another chamber under this. If so, it's between the banqueting hall and the parlour, and we may expect some interesting developments. Now, Gardiner, will you go down first with the light? You're lighter and more active than I am and won't strain the ladder so much if it's rotten."

The ladder was short, of only some eleven rungs, but as they were each quite a foot apart the descent was not an easy one. It ended in a room, if such it could be called, of a size equal to that above, but unlike it in being absolutely clear and empty. The walls were bare brick without a trace of door or opening, and it was not until they had searched the floor many times over that they found a section of the boards looser underfoot than those around. It was a square of flooring near the middle—another trap, but without the looseness; a dozen lamps would have failed to show it, so neatly was it joined in.

"You'll have to use the jemmy again," said Blakemore. "I hope the bolt isn't too strong for us this time."

But the trap came up with very little levering and showed another ladder, just like the first.

"That's queer," Gardiner remarked. "Hasn't it a bolt?"

"Yes, there it is," said Blakemore. "But it wasn't shot. Whoever used it last must have been in a hurry. Of course the glove and pistol he left upstairs show that."

"And the inventory, too," suggested Gardiner.

"Yes, he certainly was pressed for time, this priest or whoever he was. But if he thought he was being chased he was mistaken, for it's quite certain the hiding place upstairs was never found."

"Could it have been Sir Medway himself?"

"As likely as not," Blakemore agreed. "Who can say now? But the air in here is anything but sweet. Will you go on?"

The second ladder was half as long again as the first, and being so much less firm it swayed uncomfortably as Blakemore followed after Gardiner.

"I want no more of this!" he panted on the last rung. "Is there another ladder? If so, you'll have to go on alone."

But fate, or rather, the architect, had not been so unkind. The second ladder had brought them down a well-like shaft, and now, as they stood at the bottom with scarcely room to turn, a narrow arch in front opened on to a stone flight of steps, very steep, that wound quickly out of sight around a newel.

"Ah, this is more to my taste," Blakemore chuckled. "Lead the way, old man, but not too fast. I suppose these damnable steps go down to the bowels of the earth."

Round and round and down and down they went, and Blakemore almost began to regret the straight simplicity of the ladders, when Gardiner called back to him, "Here's a door! Take the light while I have a look at it."

Blakemore came down to him but, as he took the lamp, it was evident that no violence would be necessary. At a little distance the door looked solid enough and, indeed, it was well studded with nails, but at closer range it showed rotten in every part, and hung by one hinge only. Gardiner easily pushed it aside, and the two men entered a stone-flagged passage that stretched away in front beyond the utmost beams of the lamp. It was over six feet wide and built of good red brick, the roof a four-centred vaulting rather higher than the hand could touch.

The air, which hitherto had shared the musty, mildewed

odour of the closed up rooms above, now struck their nostrils with a freshness that increased with every yard. The amount of daylight also increased, until after sixty yards of slow ascent the lamp became unnecessary. At the same time a current of air was distinctly felt.

"This must be the end," exclaimed Gardiner, stooping as his head struck the roof. "But what on earth is this?"

"Better put the lamp out," said Blakemore. "Is it a window?"

Gardiner stooped and felt about him. "It's only a hole with a shrub growing in front."

Crawling on his hands and knees, Gardiner forced his way up and through the lower branches of a yew tree to the open air. With his friend's arm to help him, Blakemore, after several vain attempts, made shift to scramble after. They were standing upon the sloping wall of a deep trench that was thickly planted with fruit trees.

It was the moat.

CHAPTER 15

A MYSTERIOUS LETTER

"THESE are all I could find, sir," said Mrs. Siton. "They've been hanging in the harness room as long as I can remember." She held out to Blakemore a set of keys, old, rusty and many-sized, that jingled on a leather strap.

"I suppose you don't know what any of them belong to?"

"Indeed I don't, sir! But they fit none of the rooms we use. Siton might know, perhaps, but he's gone to bed again. I don't like to disturb him, him having such a bad night with the sciatica."

"I think we shall be able to make something of them," Blakemore observed to Gardiner when the two investigators were alone again. "Some look old enough to be contemporary with the house, but even if they can't help us, these old doors shouldn't hinder us much."

"Except that we don't want to cause unnecessary damage."

"Careful man! But the house isn't yours yet, you know! Anyway, let's waste no more time."

Although the search had been so far abortive, neither felt discouraged. Blakemore's good humour was of a kind that no reverse seemed likely to dissipate, certainly not since he had read the inventory, while Gardiner, with its every word clear in his memory, was even keener to resume the search.

As they passed into the disused corridor, Blakemore pointed to the end room, which stood open as they had left it. "I never thought of closing the door."

"Neither did I, but no one is likely to have been here."

"All the same, let's lock it if we can. I'm not satisfied we've found all there is to find in the priest's chamber. I hope there's a key here to fit it."

The keys were a mixed assortment, most of them of fairly recent date, without a trace of ornament; but a few, and those not the smallest ones, betrayed some artistry: stems fluted and embossed, handles wrought in geometrical patterns or delicate snaky loops, and wards prettily but uselessly twisted into networks of crosses and diamond shapes.

"These are the ones to try," said Blakemore. "Locksmiths, like other craftsmen, had the time to create beautiful things when these were made."

Several of them fitted the lock, and at last they found one that would turn. Having shot the bolt, Blakemore undid the strap and handed Gardiner the key.

"Now for the other doors, and any more priests' holes or treasure chests." And he walked along the corridor to the first room.

The locks of all the rooms were similar. Selecting keys that resembled the one with which they had gained access to the corridor, they soon had the first door open. Inside the musty room a rickety oaken bureau which had lost its covering flap sprawled across the floor. Some of its drawers were missing; the rest gaped open to display a tumble of fishing tackle, dented powder flasks, broken clay pipes, an odd gaiter or two, a manuscript book of cookery recipes, a venerable road book, and a mass of string, old rags and paper. A saddle tree with but a few shreds of leather adhering to the skirts had been tossed into one corner, the barrel of a blunderbuss into another. Half a dozen coverless volumes of *Clarissa Harlowe* were scattered around, the torn and filthy leaves sheltering a few fish-hooks. Here and there lay the segments of old fishing rods, a fowling-piece with a broken stock, spurs with broken rowels, a fleam and a hoof-cutter, all witness to the sporting tastes of their long-dead owner. Everywhere was dust and rust, mildew and the ravages of moth, and over all the heavy, pervasive odour of decay.

"Not much to be discovered here, I think," said Blakemore. He tapped the walls. "Seem to be solid enough, but we may as well measure the dividing one."

Noting down the space between the door and wall, they went outside and measured off the corridor from that door to the next. Opening the second room with another key, they measured back to the dividing wall. Eighteen inches were unaccounted for. "Not enough to mean anything," Blakemore decided. "An ordinary partition wall."

The contents of the second room were as varied as those of the first, and equally mouldy. Yet they bore quite a distinct character. It seemed as if an attempt had been made to divide the articles between the rooms according to their uses, the outdoor items from the indoor, the stable from the drawing room. For whereas the first chamber had been crowded with the litter of the sportsman, there was an air almost of distinction about the poor decrepit objects that filled the present one.

Above the chimney-piece hung an upright Adams mirror, destitute of gilding, the glass shattered by a hole that led through into the wall behind, circular and clean-cut as the bullet that had caused it. Upon the mantel was a cracked, handleless mug bearing a portrait of General Wolfe, who leered at a headless porcelain shepherdess standing at the other end. One or two straight chairs with vestiges of velvet covering lay broken. A wing-shaped spinet, a mere stringless shell, rested against a wall. Above it hung a moth-eaten sampler in a broken frame, the work perhaps of the child who had earlier played with the now legless rocking-horse. The metal skeleton of an enormous hoop-petticoat reposed modestly in a corner. A scratch-wig with the rows of curls that marked the last effort of the eighteenth-century peruque-makers to extend the vogue of horsehair lay beneath the grate. A broken-ribbed fan and the cut-steel hilt of a dress sword completed the assemblage.

"We seem to be mounting higher in the social scale," Gardiner said, with a glance around. "First the stable, then the card-room and now my lady's chamber."

"Yes, but it is disappointing. Let's go back to the priest's room. It will take a great deal to convince me the treasure is far from there. However much of a hurry Sir Medway was in when he escaped, what was he doing with the inventory in there?"

"He may only have laid it down beside his gloves and forgotten it. Then, when he got safely away, he remembered leaving it there and so referred to the place as 'the tabernacle' in the cipher."

"But even so, where did he leave the treasure? He would never have taken all those pains to tell his son where to find a wretched bit of parchment."

Gardiner shrugged his shoulders helplessly. "I give it up," he said.

"So do I, in a way. But I should like to have another look at the place before it gets too dark."

As they passed into the corridor there was a loud knocking at the fallen partition.

"Mr. Gardiner! Are you there?" cried Mrs. Siton's voice. "There's a lad from Lawyer Hay to see you at once, please. I was to say he had some papers he's to take back with him very partic'lar."

tarnished candlestick of a pretty scalloped pattern, acutely bent by violent contact with the wall during some drunken brawl, lay below the mantel. As Gardiner picked up a tinder box, several pieces of bone fell out. They proved to be dice that had been fractured, doubtless to disprove some charge of leading, and providing a fair idea of the players' reputation. A Sheraton card-table with only two legs remaining, its inlay all flaked away, rested upside-down by the candlestick. And behind the door, with lids wrenched off and battered out of shape, was a pair of Sheffield tankards.

"Hullo, what have you got there?" Blakemore asked as Gardiner stooped and picked something up.

"Some sort of coin." Gardiner handed him a greenish little disc.

"My dear fellow, I congratulate you. Here is specie at last." Blakemore examined it with a pocket-lens. "Spanish? No, English, and quite modern—that is to say, seventeen-eighty-something. I can't read the last figure. A sixpence of George the Third, that's all. But it tells us something interesting. It must have been here at least a century, and that's just about the length of time these rooms have been cut off, I should say— since the place came into Siton's grandfather's hands. Now let's measure the wall and get on to the next room."

But here they experienced a check. Keys of the pattern they had been using were now exhausted, and none of the remaining ones would fit the lock.

"Well, we shall have to burst it open," Blakemore announced.

"Perhaps this is the treasure chamber," said Gardiner hopefully as he inserted the case-opener and forced the door.

By comparison this room was almost empty. Beneath a derelict sofa of richly striped satin peeped the end of a brass fender, cracked and battered almost flat. A spinning wheel lacking its treadle and connecting rod leaned in a corner. A

"Very well, Mrs. Siton, I'll come at once," Gardiner replied, and to Blakemore he murmured, "You had better come too. It will be the transfer of the mortgages and I may want you to witness my signature."

"Very well, and meanwhile I must do some serious thinking."

The business was brief: a signature in several places, duly witnessed by Blakemore, and it was over.

"I congratulate you for the second time today," said Blakemore, shaking his friend's hand. "Now you are lord of Embrook Manor."

"In fact if not yet in law, I suppose. At least, it beats a George-the-Third sixpence!"

They were interrupted by Mrs. Siton bearing the afternoon post. All of it was addressed to Blakemore, including an official envelope marked "Pressing."

"Hullo! Is this my recall?" Then, as he read it, "No, only a query about something. But I must answer it at once."

"I think I'll take a stroll, then, while you're doing it."

"To survey your new domain, eh?" was Blakemore's parting shot.

Gardiner took his way alone towards the farm. For the moment, matters other than the treasure occupied his thoughts, and even when he crossed the moat no recollection of the secret outlet sent his eye searching for the yew that hid it. Instead, he observed the rapidly changing face of the farm. The trees were now quite naked, the grass bunched in matted tufts, the paths all slippery with mire. Few birds except the raucous-voiced crows were in evidence, but as he looked up the starlings began to stream in countless flocks from their feeding places, summoned by the approaching darkness.

Now that winter had fully come, the barrenness and neglect was everywhere evident. The geese were nowhere to be seen, and as he neared the field where the goats had been tethered, he found it deserted. Puzzled, he looked around him. In the distance, he heard the tinkling of little bells, and across the hedge he saw the flock coming homeward; and shepherding them—surely not!

Could he believe his eyes? Only one woman had that particular gait and carriage. But what was she doing here? Time and again he had pictured her a fugitive, sharing the perils of her lover's flight, and now he saw her at her daily tasks as though nothing had arisen to disturb their round. And as he watched and waited in the thickening mist, he heard her singing!

Was it all fancy, then—that meeting on the road the night Sanders avoided the ambush? Had she refused at the last moment to go with him? The tie broken, had she returned to the old life, the old home, the old people? Or could it be—and the thought sent a surge of indignation over Gardiner—could it be that, with the ruins thoroughly explored, Sanders had heartlessly cast her aside?

While these reflections passed through his mind, the steps had slowed. Amy had recognised him and stood hesitant, while the sound of the little bells grew even louder. She need not fear that he wished to meet her again. He wheeled round abruptly, and not until trees, hedges and a gentle rise lay between them did he turn to make his way back to the house by a circuitous route.

He was walking up the carriage drive towards the garden entrance when a man converged on him from the darkness. It was Saxby!

"Good evening, Mr. Gardiner. I was just coming to see you. Could you spare me a few minutes?"

Gardiner hesitated. This meeting was hardly welcome. After his encounter with Amy he wished to be alone to sort out his thoughts. Saxby and his affairs no longer interested him. They must, after all, concern Sanders. Yet, though he shrank from

A MYSTERIOUS LETTER

any reference to Amy, it occurred to him that some word of the detective's might give a clue to her mysterious reappearance.

"Very well. Let's walk this way."

"You didn't stay long in town, sir?" Saxby began.

"No, some business called me back again."

"I see." He paused. "Well, sir, it's about that that I wanted to see you."

Gardiner stifled an exclamation. What did the man mean? Had some news of the treasure leaked out? Had Sanders been arrested? If so, had he revealed the secret? Or had Amy done so, and was the arrest the cause of her return?

"What do you mean?" he asked, as impassively as he could.

"I heard in Forbridge you had come down again to buy the estate."

Gardiner waited to hear more, and mistaking his silence, the other man made haste to apologise: "You know, sir, the police get to know a great deal, and in a place like this, one can't help hearing such an important thing as the estate's changing hands."

"Quite, quite." Gardiner brushed the apology away with a gesture.

"I want to search the place—that is, if you have no objection, sir."

"Indeed! What for?" As he spoke, all the items of the inventory flashed and gleamed before his inward eye.

"For Sanders," returned the other in low tones.

Gardiner stopped short and stared at the dim form of the speaker. "Sanders? I thought he was far away by now."

Saxby lowered his voice still further. "It's my opinion, sir, that he's still here."

"What on earth makes you say so?"

"This is in confidence . . ."

"Yes, yes. Go on."

"You know my man saw him with the girl?"

Gardiner nodded. He resented this allusion to Amy.

"Well, I shouldn't wonder if they saw that idiot watching them and talked about Southampton just to throw us off the scent!" Saxby pulled a wry face. "Oh, yes; he's very wide awake, not the least doubt about that! Though he did overlook those notes at Maidstone."

"Have any more been heard of?"

"Nowhere else, but they're still cropping up there. Well, after you went back to town I set every man I could lay my hands on making enquiries for miles around. I had every railway station—I was almost going to say every road—watched. But we never saw the ghost of a sign of him till the night before last."

"And then?"

"One of the best men down here was posted at Shindlestone two nights ago, and who should he see but the girl—"

"Miss Siton?" Gardiner's voice was sharp.

"Yes, Miss Siton. He knows her quite well, and he saw her drive up in the little mule-cart and go into the hotel. She was inside a little while, and then out she comes with the landlord after carrying a bag. He puts it in the cart and off she goes." Saxby became silent. They were nearing the high road, and he pointed to the hedges. "You never know who may be listening," he murmured.

"Let's walk back again," said Gardiner. "We can see if anyone is near us in the fields."

"Well, anyway, she drove off, and our man followed as well as he could on foot. But the mule went pretty fast, he says, and if he hadn't met a constable on a cycle he'd have lost her. He requisitioned the machine and went after her. She came back here, and he waited to make sure she put up the cart and didn't plan to come out again. Then he went back to interview the landlord. He told our man that the night before, at the time

A MYSTERIOUS LETTER 181

you and I were waiting in the ruins, a man came to the hotel and engaged a bed. He left his bag in the room, went for a stroll and never came back."

"And was it Sanders?"

"Not a doubt of it. I interviewed the landlord myself yesterday and he described him exactly."

"Then where can he have come from?"

"We found at the station that he came by rail and gave up a ticket from Chatham. He had had all day to get there, and most likely that's where he bought the bag, which was brand new. He was bound to get a new rig-out because he left all his clothes and things behind at Maidstone."

"Well, and what happened next?"

"Only that the bag remained there till the young lady came and fetched it away the next evening."

"And did she have to pay anything?"

"Trust the hotel for that! But she was all ready for them, made no fuss, gave them a sovereign, and left without waiting for her change."

"But surely they asked for an explanation?"

"They didn't get much out of her. She was as close as wax and said only that there had been some mistake. They didn't know her at the hotel and were glad enough to get the money."

"Most extraordinary!"

"It seems very simple to me, sir. Have you seen much of her since you came back?"

"I never set eyes on her till this evening. Her mother attends to us, you see. I thought she was with Sanders all the time."

"So she is, Mr. Gardiner! Else why did she fetch his bag? We know they were together nights ago, and I'm certain they're together now."

"Nonsense, inspector." Gardiner startled himself with his own vehemence. "That's absurd! My friend came down to advise me about the house and we've been all over it—all over it, I tell you!"

"Miss Siton's room as well?" Saxby looked at him askance.

Gardiner bit his lip till it bled. Must he tolerate this without protest? How dare he! But resent it how he would, there was nothing he could say. The man was arguing according to his lights, simply stating the hard unsentimental point of view.

"You see, sir," continued Saxby, rather nonplussed by the other's failure to respond, "I don't want to do anything unpleasant—I'm sure you'll give me credit for that. But I've got my duty to do. My prospects in the service depend upon my arresting him this time. All the information I've got points to a close connection between the two of them. I've the best of reasons for thinking that he's somewhere close at hand, and I ask you, sir, as a law-abiding man, to help me execute my warrant. I don't ask you to do anything more than just let me come and search the house—of course, with assistance. I suppose the man is no friend of yours, and if you'll let me remind you, he's caused you a great deal of unpleasantness. I can do nothing without your permission, but I put it to you: won't you be hindering the course of justice by refusing my request?"

It was fortunate that Saxby was so eloquent. Had his appeal been shorter or less earnest Gardiner might have done something regrettable. As it was he had time to think. Apart from Amy, apart even from the unwisdom of admitting the police to the house with the treasure still undiscovered, there was his own legal position to be remembered. He was but the mortgagee; Siton's position was still unaltered.

"I'm sorry, inspector, the answer is no. I have no power to give you permission to enter. It's not my house yet. You must ask Mr. Siton."

Saxby was obviously disconcerted. He thought a little, then asked, "Do you know if he's at home?"

"Yes, but I hear he's ill in bed. I'm sure you're mistaken, but if you insist on it, you had better come and see him tomorrow. Meanwhile, you must excuse me; I'm very tired. If you want me, you know where to find me." And with a curt nod of dismissal, he turned on his heel.

Blakemore in the interval had been doing some hard thinking. Difficulties and failures had only stimulated his imagination, and now he was full of new suggestions. As Gardiner sank wearily into a chair, Blakemore began talking eagerly. It was only when a question, thrice repeated, had provoked a quite irrelevant answer, that he started up and took his friend by the shoulders.

"Look here, old man! What's the matter with you? I asked you how long the Sitons have had this place, and you say 'about a fortnight'! What on earth's wrong? Have you seen a ghost?"

Gardiner summoned up a feeble smile. "Yes and no. At least, I've seen Amy—I mean, Miss Siton."

"Well," remarked Blakemore, subsiding again into his chair while Gardiner retailed the details, "I don't see why you need concern yourself. She has made her bed and must lie on it. If she parted from Sanders you have still less cause for worrying. All the same, I'm sorry, for your sake. I hoped you were beginning to forget her."

"But don't you see how it complicates things?"

"How?"

"I don't want to drive her out of the house, especially if she's separated from Sanders and has nowhere else to go."

"My dear Gardiner, your sentiments do you honour—I believe that is the correct expression—but I'm not going to let you be quixotic. I told you, but I suppose you weren't attending, that I've just got her mother's consent to examine the rooms on each side of Miss Siton's, which I understand are full of lumber. I don't propose interfering with her in any way, but if she doesn't like the proceedings, she can shut herself up in her room and sulk. You can't object to that. I've got the permission of her parents, and you have no *locus standi* at all."

"Very well. But that reminds me—I ran into Saxby outside. He tells me he's positive Sanders is still somewhere around here, and he wants to search the house for him."

Blakemore gave a low whistle. "Confound the fellow! We don't want anyone else searching about. And I can't believe what he says about Sanders."

"No, it's hard to believe, but he gave me some plausible reasons for his theory," and Gardiner repeated them. "Of course I referred him to Siton."

"Hmm! I'm sorry we didn't stick to it this afternoon and ransack the priest's chamber."

"Hullo, what's this?" Gardiner had begun to stroll aimlessly about the room, and his eye fell upon an envelope on the mantelpiece. Puzzled, he opened it and glanced at the signature. "Good heavens! Here, you read it."

Blakemore took the letter and read:

Dear Sir,

As I have something of the greatest importance to communicate with reference to a certain cipher, I write to ask you if you will favour me with an interview. Although my request may appear unusual, I can assure you that you will have no cause to regret acceding to it. I am close at hand, and venture to hope that both you and Mr. Blakemore will be good enough to accompany my representative, who will wait upon you tomorrow morning at nine.

Yours very faithfully,
W. Sanders.

J. Medway Gardiner Esq.

CHAPTER 16

A HARBOUR OF REFUGE

WHILE staying at Maidstone, Sanders had felt the need for caution more than ever. Naturally circumspect, he had avoided the fatal error of thinking his enemies less clever than himself. Indeed, he went to the opposite extreme and credited the police with an astuteness the Force is never likely to possess.

At the end of the Sittingbourne Road, on the very outskirts of the town, he settled himself in quiet lodgings. In the role of a literary man able to work only when all was quiet, he professed to spend the night writing and the morning, after an early walk, sleeping. In the afternoon he lay low with the newspaper and some volumes of Alison's *Europe* for company.

The widow who ran the house seemed to be accustomed to eccentric boarders. She had lodged actors and found Sanders an improvement on "the profession" in his not demanding supper in the middle of the night. She was glad enough to be able to get to bed early and asked no questions.

Although he had managed to infect Amy with a little of his interest in the treasure hunt, she was still restless and uneasy. She chafed at the delay and, hoping to get him away sooner, began to help him in his task. Each night they met for several hours of useless labour. Only once were they together during daylight—at the Registrar's Office, when they were married quietly by special licence.

After the brief ceremony they slipped out of the bare and forbidding room to make their way, hand in hand, by quiet byways to a hill outside the town. Only then, standing in the sunshine, did they exchange a long passionate kiss. They had reached Pennenden Heath, the ancient Saxon gathering place, and the town lay at their feet. Though largely hidden by trees, roofs peeped here and there through the thinning autumn foliage. An occasional wisp of blue smoke could be seen, and the distant chiming of All Saints reached them at regular intervals. Every now and again the faint hoot of a tug came from the river as it fussily marshalled its brood of barges.

"Let us rest here, darling," said Sanders. "We can talk without being overheard." After a long pause he went on. "It seems pretty certain now there's nothing to be found in the ruins."

"I'm afraid so, dear."

His hand sought hers again. "You've not seen Gardiner lately?"

"Yes, indeed, but I've not let him see me."

"Poor fellow! But you needn't fear him now."

"I never did."

"Does he ever go to the ruins?"

"I used to see him going there a good deal at first, but not lately."

"It's two days since we were there and we left rather a deep hole. I must at least go and fill it up. I don't want Gardiner to suspect I'm still anywhere about."

"But it'll be the last time, won't it?" she pleaded.

"All right, my love. Where shall we meet in future?"

"Why not the railway bridge? It's away from the house and it

A HARBOUR OF REFUGE

won't be so far for you to come. We can meet there at the same time each night."

"But it will be further for you."

"Oh, darling, as if I minded that! But I must be getting back now. They'll be wondering what on earth has become of me."

"There won't be many more partings, I hope! Till tonight, then."

Except for a final handclasp it had to be a trite and formal parting, for they were no longer alone. A waggoner with his team was ascending the hill towards them, and a cyclist was mending a puncture nearby.

That evening Sanders overslept; he did not rise until nearly midnight, and he had a walk of many miles ahead of him. When he finally reached the ruined chapel he found Amy crouching beside the remains of a buttress, and as he tried to raise her she trembled violently.

"Amy, dearest, what on earth is the matter?"

"The villain, the spy!" she sobbed.

"Who—who?" He looked around angrily, but he could see no one.

"Gardiner! He followed me here!"

"Oh, Gardiner." His voice betrayed relief.

"I heard a noise as I was working, so I put out the lantern. As he ran back across the field, I saw him distinctly in the moonlight."

"How long ago?"

"I don't know." She sobbed again. "It seemed so long before you came."

"Come on, old girl, buck up. You've come to no harm."

"Oh, Willie. Take warning! He's gone to fetch the police, I feel sure."

"I don't think so. Anyway, I've come to do some work and I intend to finish it. If Gardiner means mischief I run as much risk by going as staying. If he's in bed now, as I think he is, I shall have the whole night to finish the job. He hasn't seen much anyhow, and as we don't intend to come here again he won't be any the wiser."

Sanders walked into the ruins, lighted the lantern and set to work. Amy followed less resolutely. As she made to pick up a spade, Sanders gently took it from her.

"Now, now, darling! You're excited and nervous and I won't let you help me tonight."

"I'm staying, though."

"Well, then, you can keep watch." He looked around. "With this moon no one will be able to come near without your seeing him. I shall be done in an hour."

But the hour lengthened into two, and the two into three. The sky was already lightening in the east before he had finished. As he extinguished the lantern and collected the tools, Amy rose from the corner where for the last hour she had been dozing fitfully.

"Now, my sweet, we'll take these things back." And he shouldered the pick and shovel.

"Willie, this is madness! You mustn't come to the house."

"Nonsense! If anything was going to happen it would have happened here. I'm not going to let you carry these heavy things. Bring the lantern, if you like. Come on, there's still time for your beauty sleep."

For all his assurances and tender words on the way, it was with many an anxious glance around that Amy trudged beside him, worn out with the excitements of the day and the night. She could not share his confidence; even the knowledge that the search at the ruins was ended once and for all could not console her tonight. When they reached the farm she was again in a state of nervous agitation. Loath as he was to leave her, he dared not stay.

A HARBOUR OF REFUGE

No curious eyes watched their tender farewell now. As he kissed away her fears and assured her they would meet again that night, she choked back her sobs and summoned up a smile. Then, gently, he removed the clinging arms that sought to stay him and hurried away.

What should he do now? That was the subject of his anxious thoughts as he hastened back to his lodgings. Certainly, he must give up all thought of the treasure. Indeed, it was time to plan his escape. To hang on here was to court certain discovery. The apparent indifference of the police was ominous; he began to dread a strike that might be in preparation. Better to return to London at once, where the vast city might hide him safely.

But Amy? There was the difficulty. Should he take her with him? That, he knew, would be her own wish. Or should he let her remain here until all was ready and the ship due to sail? That seemed better, yet there was one flaw in it—the need of correspondence. His own letters he could trust her to destroy, but what of her replies? How could he conceal his address?

Sanders had not made up his mind by the time he reached Maidstone. As usual, he skirted the northern side of the town as far as a side street that led to the Sittingbourne Road. Halfway up that street, he breasted a rise and his lodgings came into view. In an instant he stopped dead! Outside the house he spied a man standing, alert and watchful. Sanders retreated a pace or two until he was hidden by laurel bushes. Besides the man on guard outside the house, two more were standing at the door, apparently talking to someone within. Had he returned just a few minutes sooner, had his evening's work been a degree less toilsome, he would have been taken. Sanders walked quietly back down the street. After he had turned the corner he ran his hardest until he was in the country again. Then, taking to the hill he had climbed with Amy, he regained the Sittingbourne Road and sped on through Detling. By the time he reached the summit of the Downs, he was exhausted. Turning into a wood, he lay down some fifty yards from the road and fell asleep almost at once.

He was roused by the sun striking full upon his face through a chink in the trees. As soon as he had collected his wits he pondered the question of what could have betrayed him. How had the police traced him? No answer to the puzzle occurred to him. But it was clear he must quit the district at once.

His watch said half-past one. Refreshed by his sleep, he stepped out manfully towards Sittingbourne. Halfway to Stockbury he reached a little inn, the sight of which reminded him of his long fast. He entered the bar and called for bread and cheese. The place was clear of other customers except for a garrulous van-driver who had been delivering mineral waters. From him Sanders secured a lift for the remaining five or six miles into Sittingbourne. He alighted just inside the town, announcing that he would walk the rest of the way to Canterbury; but as soon as the van was out of sight, he turned back to the station. There was an up-train due in half an hour, an interval he spent in the waiting room. Then, booking to Chatham, he boarded the train as it began to move from the platform.

Though his clothing was in Maidstone, he still carried all his money. Chatham swarms with outfitters of every description, and in less than two hours after his arrival he had replaced his wardrobe and was able to leave a well-filled portmanteau at the railway cloakroom. He dined at the "York and Sun" and wondered as he ate how his bride was faring.

That young lady began the day confidently enough with her husband's words of encouragement still ringing in her ears. With the passage of the hours she became a prey to nervousness again. Towards evening she escaped to her room, but there, alone, the suspense became harder to bear. At length she stole out of the house and was well on her way to the meeting place

A HARBOUR OF REFUGE

before ten had struck. Nearing the railway arch she turned into a plantation of stone-pine and, crouching on the carpet of cones and pine needles, counted the sluggish round of quarters by the chimes of Shindlestone church. In every passing step she fancied a detective, and at every light upon the road she shrank back into the shadows.

At length the hour of eleven struck, and she hastened to the rendezvous. A train thundered overhead; a voice, barely audible in the clamour, spoke to her, and she was seized and held tightly. With a shriek she struggled briefly until, the train having passed, she recognised Sanders.

"Oh, oh, Willie. I thought it was—"

"Gardiner?"

"Are you all right?"

"For the present."

In a few words he described his adventure. "So," he concluded, "my luck has held so far. But I must get away to Shindlestone tonight and then to London first thing tomorrow."

"You should have gone to London when you were at Chatham."

"What! And not met you?"

"You could have sent a telegram."

"I distrust the Post Office. I don't know how much information they may be allowed to give the police."

"Shindlestone is too close for comfort!"

Sanders smiled. "The police don't know I discovered them. They'll think I was kept away by accident because all my things are at the rooms. But let's not argue. I can't get to London tonight. Listen, there's quarter-past eleven striking. I can't even get back to Chatham now. Besides, I've left my bag at the Shindlestone Hotel."

"I'm sure you'll regret it," she persisted.

"Amy, dear girl, this is childishness! What earthly alternative is there?"

"A very simple one."

"Then tell me!"

"Come back to the farm."

"The farm!" he repeated in amazement. "With Gardiner there?"

"What did you tell me when you first went to Maidstone? The boldest course is the wisest. And anyway, Gardiner has gone."

"Really? When? What made him go?"

"I'll tell you that presently. But Willie, listen to me, please. Next to my room there are two we use for boxes and lumber. In one of them there's some old furniture, so you won't be so uncomfortable, and you could lock the door if you liked."

"And supposing your mother found it locked?"

"She never comes there, and if she did I should tell her that I had locked the door because it won't keep shut—the latch really is a bad one."

"Well, I should want some clothes and things, and I don't feel inclined to lose those I've just bought at Chatham. Besides, it wouldn't do to leave them at Shindlestone—the police would find out for a certainty."

"I'll go and fetch them tomorrow. I have to take the cart into Forbridge anyway, and no one knows me at Shindlestone."

"You're terribly persuasive, darling. You seem to have an answer for everything."

Just then they were startled by a beam of light that caught and held them, but it was only a cylist racing through the archway.

"Oh," she gasped, "that was a shock! Let's get away before we're recognised." Arm in arm they walked rapidly towards Embrook as she told him of her interview that morning with Gardiner and how he came to leave the farm.

"You're not jealous, are you, Willie?" she concluded.

"Jealous?" he laughed. "When you've given him his dismissal?"

"You don't think I encouraged him, I mean?"

"No one needs encouragement from you, darling. Discouragement is the normal requirement in your case. No, no; I'm not jealous at all. Poor Gardiner couldn't help it. Anyway, it shows his good taste. Now, here's a serious question for you. I see I'm going to be lodged all right, but how am I to be boarded?"

"I think I can manage that. Since they've worried me so much about Gardiner I've taken most of my meals alone, and I can easily help myself to enough for two."

"Well, I shan't want much, shut up in one room without exercise."

"Oh, that will never do. But I found a secret passage that will give you a way of escape when you need it." And she told him of how she had been moving an old easy chair from the room next to her own when objects stored beside it had fallen against the wall and knocked off some of the plaster, revealing the panelling behind. "There was a carved pillar in one corner that seemed loose," she continued, "and when I tried to push it back it came right open like a door."

"And was there anything behind?"

"I went in with a candle and found a long passage just wide enough to pass along, and, oh, so cold! Like a brick grave."

"How far did it go?"

"It seemed to go the whole length of the house. And then it turned a corner, and there was a flight of steps. I was wondering whether to go on or not when all sorts of noises seemed to come up towards me and the light went out, and then I felt so nervous I ran back. Don't laugh at me; it was all so lonesome and ghostly."

Sanders squeezed her arm affectionately. "Those noises— did they sound like people?"

"No, they might have been rats; but just as I got back to the room I heard a thud as if something had fallen. It quite shook the floor."

"Have you ever been there again?"

"No; a few days later I thought I would go right to the end and see all there was, but when I tried to open the pillar again it wouldn't move. I suppose when I'd got back I'd slammed it so hard it had locked in some way."

"Did you say anything about it?"

"No. It wouldn't have interested father, and mother would only have been frightened. I'm glad I didn't, now."

They walked on quietly while he pondered this new proof of Amy's resourcefulness. Though sometimes fearful, there was often an unexpected resoluteness about her that delighted him. The Shindlestone plan would have meant a certain risk that Amy's plan, in spite of its audacity, did not share. This plan, and the beginning of their new and thrilling relationship, cheered him. Maybe, he reflected, his ill luck was beginning to change.

CHAPTER 17

THE SECRET PASSAGE

"I SUPPOSE," said Sanders, "this is the place where you found the door." He gazed with interest at an area of the lumber room wall where a set of panels was exposed.

"That's the place," replied Amy proudly, "and here's the door." She tapped a projection in the corner that had also shed some of its covering to show an Ionic pilaster of the pattern seen elsewhere in the house.

"It's firm enough now," remarked Sanders as he attempted to shake it. "Did it open all the way up?"

"Yes, I think so. It certainly opened down to the floor."

"We ought to be able to see the crack in the plaster. You must have somehow pushed on a spring or catch. It would be a pity to force the door open." Patiently he explored the panelling with his fingers, and after a few minutes his patience was rewarded.

"Here it is!" he exclaimed, as an apparent knot in the panelling suddenly yielded to his pressure. There was a grating noise, and, with a jerk, the pilaster came towards him. Gripping the edge, he gave a pull, upon which it swung open on screaming hinges. A doorway two feet wide was now revealed.

"We shall need a light," said Amy, as Sanders peered into the dark and dusty passage.

"Yes, bring a candle and some matches, too," he called as she darted off.

Since his return two nights ago, Sanders had spent almost the whole time resting and enjoying his new-found security. Though his accommodation was anything but luxurious, his was the weariness which can snore upon the flint. But when he awoke this second morning, he had cursed the sloth that had kept him from examining the secret passage.

Though his new hiding place was secure enough for the moment, the police might turn their attention to the farm at any time. A secret exit would then become invaluable.

"Sorry, darling, I know I've been a long time." Amy's return broke into his reverie. "I had to wait until mother went out of the kitchen. I didn't want her to see me take all these."

Sanders kissed the tip of her nose. "I think, old girl," he observed, "that you've brought enough lights for us to explore the Roman Catacombs."

"One candle each to carry and one each in our pockets," she exclaimed gaily. "The rest we'll leave here." Handing him two from the packet, she lighted her own and made towards the doorway.

"Stop a minute!" exclaimed Sanders. "Let me get my bearings first. Does this passage go straight forwards?"

Amy thought a moment. "There *is* a turning, but it's a good way on. It goes quite straight at first."

Sanders crossed the window and looked into the court below. "I don't seem to recognise the place from here."

"Well, you've never been on this side of the house before," she explained. "My own room and these two lumber rooms are the only ones that look into the yard."

"But that window opposite—isn't that a room?"

"No; that's the staircase window, and the door below it is the one from the hall into the court. That's the way we have to go to get into the farmyard. But don't you remember you have to cross the court and go through a passage? That passage goes under my room; it used to be the carriage entrance, and the gate at the end that opens into the farmyard was the front door."

"This passage must be made in the thickness of the wall, then, as the courtyard is on one side of it. But what is there on its other side?"

"The bedroom corridor, I suppose."

"Of course, I see now. That corridor only has windows at each end and none at the side, so this passage is able to run inside a dead wall that has no windows. I wonder whether the house was built like that to provide for it? Well, now I've got an idea where we're going, let's go."

Although Sanders felt obliged to sidle as he entered the passage, its width was greater than appeared at first. It seemed narrow for its height—like a mere slit in the thickness of the courtyard wall. There was little space for anyone inclined to corpulence. The designer must have contemplated its use only by those of spare and lean physique, as indeed most Elizabethan men of action were.

So instinctively does everyone take more room in walking than is necessary, both Amy and Sanders held their lights at arm's length. At every step an elbow brushed the wall. But the brickwork, as true and well-laid as any on the outer walls, was smooth and clean. The floorboards, black with age but unwarped, offered excellent footing. Nowhere was there any sign of dampness, and though the air struck chill, yet it smelled surprisingly fresh.

As Sanders stood awhile, moving his light about to gather these details, there was a curious high-pitched twitter and something brushed his face. His candle went out. Ducking her head while shielding it with her arm, Amy dropped her light. It was several moments before they could strike a match and relight a candle, while the creature that had alarmed them continued to flit about in the dim twilight.

"Well, that's one mystery explained," remarked Sanders with a shaky laugh.

"A bat, was it?"

"Of course. And it was the cause of the noises that startled you so much before."

"Oh, no, they were very queer noises," retorted Amy with spirit. "Something made the floor shake—no bats could do that!"

"Come on, then, and perhaps we shall find out what it was." And off he started again as quickly as the narrow space permitted.

Amy, who had stopped to loop her skirts, was about to follow when there came a sudden exclamation and a scuffle, and the light ahead of her disappeared. A square mass seemed to rise from the floor, while only Sanders' head and shoulders were in view as he struggled to support himself upon the edge of an invisible chasm. With a cry of alarm, Amy rushed forward to the very brink of the pit. Desperately, Sanders was struggling to improve his grasp on the edge of the floor beyond, while his legs half-rested on the lower part of an inclined plane, a kind of see-saw that constituted a trap in the floor.

"Willie!" she cried. "What shall I do?"

"Is there a loose plank?" he gasped. "Or a ladder? Stretch it across quickly."

In an agony of horror she raced back to the lumber room, though she knew there was no plank or ladder anywhere at hand. Frantically she looked this way and that in search of something—anything—that might serve, and her eye fell on a hank of cord lying beneath some boxes. She grabbed it and rushed back to Sanders, whose arms could now be seen trembling with the strain.

THE SECRET PASSAGE

"Here's a rope," she gasped.

"Tie the end to something heavy," he groaned. "But hurry—hurry!"

Back to the room again like lightning. The old chair! Good! She dragged it out and saw behind it a pair of driving reins, rusty brown with age but still strong. Pulling the chair behind her, she wedged it in the doorway, rove the cord round it and passed the reins through the loop. Then along the passage once again. The plane now oscillated as Sanders, with declining strength, let his weight fall at intervals upon its treacherous support.

"Here, darling, dearest. Oh! Try to catch it as I throw," she sobbed. But the leather rattled uselessly on the slope behind him.

Again she threw. He was weakening rapidly and made but a feeble snatch. Once more! In a final bid he half-twisted round and caught the flying thong with one hand. As his fingers closed upon it, he released his grasp upon the edge of the floor and seized the rein with his other hand as well. Then, with his legs dangling into the pit, he drew himself painfully hand over hand along the plane. As fresh muscles were brought into action, some of his strength returned. The old chair groaned in the doorway and the panelling creaked as they bore his full weight. With each hand's grasp his task grew less, for the tilting plane was gradually returning to the horizontal.

But the strain upon his arms had been too great. When the upper end of the plane was only a foot above the true floor, he sank upon his face, his hands still grasping the reins.

Cursing her slow-wittedness, Amy pressed a foot upon the plane and then stood upon it. Her weight just made the balance. The false floor sank slowly to the level of the true, and as it settled flush upon a rebate beneath, the reins slipped from the fingers of the exhausted man. She stooped and, carefully keeping her feet in position, passed the thong beneath his arms.

By hauling on either side in turn, she was able to draw him inch by inch towards the safety of the solid floor. When his shoulders had slid across the junction she turned, and, with the reins across her shoulders, dragged him clear of the trap.

As she sank breathlessly on the floor he raised himself a trifle. "Safe?" he asked feebly.

"Yes, Willie—quite safe now."

"Oh, Amy! You saved me. What should I have done without you?"

She grasped his hand. "Do you think you can walk, dearest? Let's get out of this horrible place."

After the pair had rested for a few minutes in the lumber room, Amy rose to her feet. "Let me close the door," she said. "I never want to see that passage again."

"What! And not find out where it leads to?"

"No! It's just too horrible. If I hadn't been there you might have been killed."

"No doubt about that!" He shuddered. "But if I can only find how the trap works it will make me quite secure. No one would be able to follow me."

Amy grimaced. "How would you get across? It's too far to jump."

"Well, no, there has to be a way of fixing it, or the thing's useless. The last man who crossed it set it going and it's been waiting for the next one ever since."

"Perhaps you weren't the next one," she said, growing pale at the sudden thought.

"Perhaps not. We must have a good look below it, and before we start we'll get a long plank or ladder to throw across."

"And how are we going to manage that? I can easily get a ladder from the stable, but I can't bring it up here."

Sanders walked to the window. "I think I've got it. While the others are at dinner, find a ladder, not less than twenty rungs. Drag it, if you can, into the court and under this window. Then I'll draw it up with the rope. Bring a stable lantern, too, if you can, to let into the pit."

By dinner time Sanders had had a long rest and a meal of smuggled food, so that the dragging of a fifteen-foot ladder through the window gave him no difficulty. As for Amy, her curiosity almost made her forget the horror of the morning's adventure.

Sanders cautiously led the way along the passage, but so artfully was the trap concealed that he was within an ace of repeating his experience. Indeed, it was only by testing each foot of the way, advancing with the shortest steps, that he was able to retreat at the first movement of the trap. Even then it was hard to tell where the true floor ended and the false one began, for the boards throughout the passage were laid transversely, and the junction was almost invisible.

Throwing the ladder over, Sanders crossed and examined the trap from the far side. It was a section of floor about twelve feet long, poised on cylinders, like the trunnions of a gun, about a yard from the lumber room end. The short section was counter-weighted, but the balance was so delicate that the moment a foot passed beyond the trunnions the longer end began to sink, forming an inclined plane whose steepness increased with every step forward. When first built, and properly oiled and tended, it must have acted rapidly, shooting the victim into the pit without the slightest hope of salvation.

After reassuring himself that the ladder was safely placed, Sanders tried the action with his foot. The trap sank readily and rebounded with a thud that vibrated all along the passage.

"Why, that's what I heard when I came here the first time," called Amy from the other side. "Try it again. Yes, I remember the noise and the jar were just like that."

"But where are the steps you saw?" he asked, with a glance around.

"Oh, they were a long way on."

"Then you must have crossed the trap."

"Nonsense, darling. How could I?"

He thought deeply for a moment. "I think I see how," he explained. "The first time you walked over it the whole thing was stuck fast—hadn't moved for a century or two, perhaps. When you came back you ran—you were startled and nervous, weren't you?"

"Well—"

"Don't be cross. I mean that as you ran back you probably gave it a jolt, just enough to dislodge it, and that explains the thud you heard. When I came on to it, my heavier weight set it right off, but still slowly enough for me to grip the edge of the floor as I went down. It goes faster than that now—look at that! Nobody would have a chance!"

"Can you fix it so that I can come over?"

"No, darling. Don't move. Let me get the light and we'll see first what's down below."

He crossed by way of the ladder and coaxed the short end of the trap upwards. While he held it, Amy lowered the lantern on the end of the rope. They could see a narrow pit, bricked like the corridor, that went down and down almost the full length of the rope. Far below the level of the foundations, the bottom was of brownish sand, smooth and unruffled, as by the action of water.

"How deep it is!" said Amy.

"Not so deep as I expected. About thirty feet. Too deep for a man ever to get out even if he hadn't the luck to break his neck on the way. It probably communicated with the moat when it was full. A choice of drowning or starvation."

"Ugh! The whole place gives me the creeps!"

"At least there aren't any bones."

"There may be a body underneath the sand," she observed.

"If so, it's quite inoffensive by this time. But we must be moving. I want to fix this trap if I possibly can. You had better stay here in case I want anything when I've got over. If there's any fixing mechanism at all, it must be on the other side."

He crossed over with the lantern and carefully flashed the light along the walls, but their smoothness was unbroken. On his hands and knees he searched the floor. At first he found nothing, but when he ran his hand along the angle where the brick wall and the blackened boards of the floor met, he found two massive iron blocks that rattled loosely. Not an inch could they be drawn towards him, but when he pushed them towards the trap, they seemed to give just a little. Then, with a sudden jerk, they ran for several inches, and the trap vibrated as if it had been struck. He pressed his foot upon it, harder and harder still, but there was no sign of yielding.

Wrenching the blocks back again, he lay full length upon the floor and started the trap rocking. Seizing his moment, he forced the blocks towards it and watched two stout bolts jut across the pit. He let the trap adjust itself, reversed the blocks once more, then shot the bolts and stamped upon the wood above them. The trap was solid as the floor.

"Bravo, dearest," she called.

"You can come over now, Amy. It's firm enough for anything."

Just a little apprehensively she tripped across into his open arms and kissed him generously. The passage turned abruptly to the right, and the explorers found themselves at the head of a short flight of narrow steps.

"Is this as far as you've been?" asked Sanders, as he peered downwards into the gloom.

"Yes, and listen! Those are the noises I heard before."

From somewhere up above came a series of shrill pipings

which descended to low twitterings, and then died away in a murmur of little croaks. Overhead could be discerned pendant black masses clustered irregularly upon the drab wall. As Sanders raised the light the startled bats detached themselves and flitted off into the darkness.

"Nothing very formidable, after all," said Sanders. "I think we know the worst now."

"But there must be some way for the bats to get in and out. There's no food for them here!"

"Yes, and notice how fresh the air is here. There must be an opening somewhere above. You'd better keep well behind me, in case there are any more traps."

From the foot of the steps the passage went on again, and now the roof suddenly sloped downwards. After twenty feet of stooping they found the height increasing again, and they were glad to rest on a landing at the top of another flight of steps.

"What's the reason for that dip, I wonder?" mused Sanders, as he rubbed his aching back.

"Could it have to do with the staircase window?"

"Well, now, we came right along the wall on one side of the courtyard—that's where the trap is—then sharp to the right down these steps. You're right, darling! The steps took us below the level of the staircase window."

"Then there's the small door below it in the hall."

"And this passage has to go between the two? No wonder we had to bend ourselves double! It must be a tight fit; there can't be six feet between the bottom of the window and the top of the floor."

Thirty paces on they came to a second bend and another landing with a further set of steps. So far the passage had taken them round two sides of the courtyard; the long straight flight now before them was hidden in the dead and windowless wall

THE SECRET PASSAGE

on the third side. Down and still downward, step after step, short and steep, the monotonous tramp grew irksome to them both.

From the moment she first entered the passage, Amy had found it repulsive. The incident of the trap had been terrifying enough, but a deeper dread grew in her breast as her fatigue increased. The steady descent had carried them far below ground level, and with the lessened ventilation the atmosphere smelled more like a vault. The air struck their faces cold and damp. Lantern light was reflected in the moisture which everywhere bedewed the brickwork and ran in rivulets down the walls. In every crevice vegetable growths had attached themselves, and here and there livid fungi sprouted with a foul luxuriance. Greyish slime upon the steps caused them more than one anxious moment. At last Amy halted irresolutely. A step or two ahead, Sanders had reached a level surface. Ahead of him the passage widened and turned to the right. The air here was warmer and drier.

Hearing his bride's footsteps cease, he turned round to encourage her. "Come, Amy, we've reached the end at last!" he called, and, when she joined him, "We must hurry; this lantern may burn out before we're done."

They now stood in what, judging by the doorway at the end, was a high-roofed vestibule or lobby. The plain brick vaulting had ribs, very little raised from the surface, that sprang from the four corners to meet in a boss chiselled with the Gardiner device. At the far end, shallow steps led to a brick arch that enclosed a door with massive hinge straps terminating in the three heraldic lozenges.

Mounting the steps, Sanders thrust his hand into the enormous keyhole and tried the door, but the solid wood was firmly held.

"It seems strange they should have taken so much pains to make a secret staircase that doesn't lead outside the house.

Yet this door seems too large for a secret exit—there can't be much concealment on the other side." He stood the lantern on the step and tried to send its light beneath the door, but he could see nothing through the keyhole.

"We shall have to go back," he said. "We need tools."

"What time is it?" Amy's voice was anxious.

Sanders consulted his watch. "Good heavens! It's nearly five. We've been longer than I thought—and nothing done."

"Let's come back tomorrow, darling. At least we know all about the secret passage now. Mother will be anxious, and besides, I have to go to Forbridge tonight."

"And Shindlestone, too," Sanders reminded her as he led the way back.

CHAPTER 18

THE QUEEN'S TREASURE

NEXT morning found Sanders in a far from hopeful frame of mind. The arrival of Blakemore and Gardiner was disconcerting. Amy saw in it an excuse for all her fears, and a reason for instant flight.

It was useless for him to point out how foolish this would be when they were on the very point of a discovery, or to remind her of the increased danger of his arrest should he depart other than by the secret passage. Amy was torn between her fears for his safety and her dread of meeting Gardiner again.

Only when Sanders ceased to reason and appealed instead to her trust in him would she give way to the extent of consenting to just one more day's search. With this he had to content himself.

Impatient though he was to begin, the morning was well advanced before they could start. Amy smuggled into the courtyard the serviceable pickaxe and the largest hammer she could find—a four-pound monster with ball-peen—and, while Sanders hauled them up through the window, she disposed of her essential morning tasks. The way down the passage seemed shorter and easier this time, but the door, when they reached it, looked not a whit less formidable. As Sanders cast his eye over it, he saw the hinges presented the only chance. With Amy standing well to the side, he swung the pick and brought it down fiercely on the lower strap. The blow resounded like a pistol shot in the confined space.

"Good heavens! Can't you muffle it?" asked Amy, alarmed. "They'll hear us!"

"Oh, not at this depth, I don't think."

He struck again, and this time something dropped upon the floor. It was the head of one of the belts that had held the strap. Taking the hint, he changed the pick for the hammer and beat upon another belt until it snapped. Blow after rapid blow, the echoes mingled into a sustained booming. Suddenly the strap parted from the wood. With a stroke of the hammer, he forced it back and clear from the door. Now for the upper one! Rustier than its fellow, the strap broke quickly from the hinge, and the massive door was now supported only by the bolt.

Sanders paused a moment for breath before thrusting the cutting blade of the pick between the door and the frame and driving it well in with the hammer. With a mighty heave, he tried to lever the door outward, but there was no perceptible movement. Again and again he laboured, the sweat dripping from his chin. Suddenly the blade snapped off and clattered to the floor. Amy could not restrain a cry of disappointment.

"Never mind." Sanders summoned up a grim smile. "There's one blade left."

He drove the remaining blade into the narrow chink and heaved. This time there was a slight movement. With a second effort it yielded more. The bolt bent a hair's breadth, and the lock started. Bit by bit it gave, until he was able to get his hand behind the edge of the door. All at once the bolt dragged clear, and the door toppled towards him. Barely had he time to spring backwards out of the way before it collapsed upon

THE QUEEN'S TREASURE 209

the steps with a crash that echoed endlessly from wall to wall and up the stairs behind them.

Weary from his exertions, but eager still to press forward, he stepped through the empty portal. He found himself at the corner of a stone vault, measuring about twenty-five feet by ten. Its roof was more elaborately groined than that of the vestibule, the ribs springing from corbels halfway up the walls. In the recess opposite was a heavy table, with a sunken square upon the top for the consecrated slab, that told of its ancient use in the Mass. By the right-hand wall stood a chest, a deeper grey against the grey stone. There was no other furniture.

The chest was a large one, capacious enough to have served for a sarcophagus, deep and wide as any altar-tomb in an abbey. In panels on the front and sides, above the plain wood plinth, were carved effigies of the twelve apostles, while in the centre beneath the lock was a depiction of the Crucifixion. The lid, formed of a single oaken slab, was simply corniced with a deep-cut moulding. The hasp of the lock was as wide as a man's hand, and the keyhole must have owned a key of formidable bulk.

"Well, Amy, my dearest, what do you think?"

They had wandered round the vault and now stood by the door again.

She sighed. "It's nothing but a rat-trap." He nodded and after a moment's pause said in a low voice, "You can't feel more disappointed than I do. With all this labour I could have cut my own escape route. And the time we've wasted—"

"Then at least let's not waste any more." He hesitated. "Please!"

Absently, he walked over to the chest and struck it with a hammer. It sounded solid as a log. Into his mind crept a half-forgotten memory, and yet . . .

"Patience, darling." He grinned at his wife and squeezed

her waist. "Just one more minute, I promise you, and then we'll be off."

He whirled the hammer and brought it down on the hasp. A slight bending was the only result. Another blow, and in the wood behind a great crack appeared. He seized the pick and drove it in, upon which the lid split right across.

For all her protests Amy could not conceal her curiosity. Putting the lamp down, she helped Sanders lift the enormous lid and rest it against the wall.

After a first astonished glance at one another, neither stirred but gazed, arm in arm, at the wondrous sight. Half-hidden by a mouldering fold or two of velvet lay several curiously shaped yellow objects, most of them elaborately engraved, and all set with patterns of various colours. Packed in between them were little rolls and strips of decayed velvet that fell to pieces as Sanders at last began to remove them. A large cup was revealed, two-handled and at least a foot in height, its lid bearing a figure brandishing a sword. Its weight attested that it was of pure gold, and it was decked all about with large stones that, as Sanders rubbed them on his sleeve, flashed in the lantern light like the diamonds they were.

With murmurs of astonishment and delight the happy pair gently lifted out the treasures one by one and set them on the floor. First the large cup and then a smaller one, the cold gleam of its diamonds warmed by the glow of rubies. Next a jewelled bowl enamelled with an arabesque design, the handles bearing each a pearl as large as a filbert. Then came a pair of thuribles, each chain-link set with pearls; several chalices and cruets; a paten; and eight hand-bells, all of heavy gold richly bejewelled. Then two crucifixes, so beautiful that Sanders shrank from placing them on the grimy floor. He set them upright against the sloping lid of the chest, where their pearls, rubies and emeralds threw back rich gleams.

THE QUEEN'S TREASURE

As Sanders struggled to disengage a branched candlestick from the handle of an engraved ewer, he exposed a golden rod with a convex plate attached, unmistakably the mast and sail of a miniature ship.

"Is it a toy?" asked Amy, to whom all that was passing seemed like a dream.

It proved to be a fanciful craft with its single sail and unseaworthy lines, but the landsman who designed it had been more successful with the armoured figures that paced the deck and manned the crow's-nest. The golden candlestick was one of a pair, each almost too heavy to lift, the arms representing a grapevine without a single jewel to distract the eye from the restrained beauty of the design.

Below the gap left by the ship lay a barrel-shaped casket with a device of the Trinity in high relief, a dove entirely formed of pearls, rising with outstretched wings above the central figure. As Sanders turned it over, a lid flew open and a roll of velvet dropped out and crumbled, releasing a number of gold spoons and a small crucifix. This last had as its nimbus a nest of diamonds and as its base a large cornelian engraved as the matrix of a seal with a coat-of-arms of many quarterings and a triple crest above.

And now a large circular plate of gold, perforated and set upon a thick stem rising from a heavy foot, covered quite a third of the area of the chest. It lay upon its face, but when turned over showed a wheel of sun-like rays, glorious with jewels, and springing from a central globe of crystal.

"How beautiful! A sunflower?" asked Amy, as Sanders heaved out the massive disc.

"A monstrance—for the sacred Host. He was a strong man, the priest who elevated that."

With the chest almost emptied, a cluster of bracelets or something similar could be seen. Sanders tugged on the cord that held them together and hauled them out.

"What do you make of these, Amy?"

"I don't know. Bangles?"

"No, sword hilts! Twenty-two," as he told them off. "And every one of them worth a good round sum. See, this is where the blades have been snapped off," and he pointed to the fragments of the heels beyond the cross-guards. The collection must have been made haphazardly, for no two were of the same design or size, but all were of gold laboriously wrought with barrels gleaming with precious stones and pommels often mounted with large or especially fine jewels.

A letter-bag was found to contain fifty-two rings: large ones for the thumb, smaller ones for the fingers, others too huge for any but a giant's hand; some with double hoops, some with stones carved for a signet, and a few with knobs to serve the wearer for a rosary. Turquoise and ruby and diamond, sapphire and pearl, opal and emerald, set upon plain rings, and chased rings, and rings modelled with figures, often beautiful but sometimes grotesque, the whole worth as much as all the chest had yet yielded.

Sanders unpicked the fastening of another bag and drew out a handful of what seemed to be chips of dull glass.

"What are they?" asked the girl. "They look like lumps of soda."

"Only uncut diamonds, my darling. Many a man would sell his soul for such a handful as this! And see what a quantity is in the bag still."

A third bag was found to be replete with uncut rubies, others contained emeralds as the green hexagonal crystals of nature, topazes, amethysts and pearls.

The eighth and last bag was a leather sack, lighter than the rest. It contained a little pouncet-box with a cameo of the Virgin surrounded by diamonds; a gold brooch in the shape of an escalloped shell holding an enormous pearl; another clasp of gold filagree and enamel inlaid with diamonds; earrings, each with two large pearls; a pendant of a pear-shaped pearl surrounded by smaller ones; another of a gigantic emerald within a chased gold circlet; and a golden filagree belt with alternate plates of single pearls and rubies of great size and beauty. At the bottom were a dozen shoe-buckles shimmering with diamonds.

A layer of coarsest canvas had been laid across the chest at this level, hiding any objects stored in the lower half. Like the velvet it had been rotted by age, and when Sanders raised it, it tore across.

Twelve small sacks were now exposed. The first tore open as it was lifted out, and a shower of golden coins strewed the sacks on either side. These coins were large and rather thin, but not with wear and use, for the busts of a king and queen, rudely fashioned and grotesquely face-to-face, were sharp and clear on every one, as was the many-quartered shield supported by an eagle on the reverse.

Sanders tried to shift the other sacks, but they all ripped, to leave a great heap of gold coins. Beneath the coins were sixteen more sacks, neatly packed and smaller than the others. Their canvas also split, releasing more gold coins, of a size with the others but thicker and with a single head, that of a bearded king in clear relief on each one.

Sanders at last stood up, rubbed his aching back and smiled at his wife. "What are you thinking of all this time?" he asked her.

Amy had stood by, holding the lantern with scarce a word, only catching her breath as each marvel was displayed. "I'm wondering what is to be done with all this."

"We'll think of that when we've finished. There's more to come yet." And he bent to his task again.

Raking the loose coins to one side, he exposed several short stout bars, lying side by side on the bottom of the chest. When he scraped at the grey-black coating with his knife, they could be seen to be pure silver. Behind them were three wedge-shaped lumps that in shape and colour resembled sections of cheese. They were so tightly packed together that Sanders had to force the point of the pick between them and even then was only able to dislodge one of them slightly. It fell back into place with a shock that made not only the chest vibrate but the entire vault resound.

"What are they?" Amy asked. "Weights?"

He smiled. "Yes, but not of lead or iron. Gold, solid gold! They must be worth—" He opened his arms descriptively.

"Well, so this is the treasure," said Amy.

"This is the treasure."

"And to think it's useless, after all!"

"What? What do you mean?"

"What can you do with it? You can't take it away, the way things are."

"Only let me find a way out of here—"

"Willie! Be reasonable! We've been searching for days and found nothing but this miserable treasure."

"Are you sure there's no other way out?"

"Are you serious?"

"Yes. Look at the chest. It's over three feet wide at its narrowest. How did it get here?"

"The table over there is just as large."

"Exactly! Neither of them could be brought in by the way we came. The stairs are too narrow and the corners far too sharp to get them through." Taking the lantern, Sanders made a circuit of the vault, tapping with the hammer as he went. At the door he stopped. "This lobby is wide enough to take them—it must be somewhere here." Passing through, he began to tap the walls again.

"Look here," said Amy. "Surely this is wood."

While Sanders was tapping on each side of the entrance she had gone on and now stood pointing to the opposite wall which had sounded hollow when she struck it with her hand.

He gave it a hammer-blow. What had seemed a solid brick wall echoed dully, and an obvious dent now showed upon the surface.

"Bright girl! But if this is a door, how does it open?"

"Look! Isn't this a keyhole?"

A foot out from the angle of the lobby was a slit, about an inch and a half long, in what at first appeared to be the bonding of the bricks. The whole wall at this end of the lobby was a sham, artfully painted to match the brickwork.

"Yes, and the chest must have come in here," he said.

He drew the pick along the lower border of the door, a good inch above the floor. Then, forcing the blade below, he gave a wrench. Although the door had been a stout one, it stood at a lower level than the vault and had received all the moisture from the steps and walls. At the first wrench, a crack ran sharply from the rotten lower edge to the top; at the next, the crack became a split and the greater portion broke away, leaving only a strip that contained the lock. With a to-and-fro motion Sanders worked the hinges till at last they opened and a passage running right and left could be seen behind.

In a moment Amy had rushed into the passage, clapping her hands in unrestrained delight. "Come, Willie! Don't lose a second. This is what we've been looking for."

"Here, wait a minute. Which way do we go?"

He shone the light first one way, then the other. To the right the passage ran further than they could see, but on the left it ceased abruptly after a yard or two, where a small door, nail-studded and rickety, stood in the opposite wall. As he hesitated, a steady "tramp, tramp" could be heard, growing rapidly more distinct. They both looked back involuntarily, so real seemed the sound of footsteps on the stair. But all was still upon the long flight behind, and when they turned again the noise came unmistakably from the crazy door in front. Dragging Amy by the arm, Sanders retreated and, beckoning to the girl to help him, pulled the door from before the steps. As the tramping ceased and voices sounded through the little door, they were jamming the false wall back into position.

"Listen!" whispered Sanders.

From out in the passage came a muffled conversation, and a moment later the footsteps moved away, the sound at last dying out in the distance.

"Gardiner and Blakemore!" he said. "I recognised both the voices. What can they be doing here? If that's really a way out of the house, I don't relish their knowing it."

"Never mind, dear. It's something to have found it. Let's get back; we can do nothing more while they're about."

"There's no hurry. We're safe here; they can't have noticed this door. If they've found a way out I mean to follow. We'll give them an hour. Would you stand here and listen while I get the treasure packed away?"

It was a weary hour for Amy and a laborious one for her husband, but at length the chest was full and with a little persuasion the lid was closed. They got the wall-door open and Sanders, with a sign to Amy to remain behind, stole noiselessly along the passage.

In the utter silence the girl could hear the beating of her own heart. As minute after minute passed without a sound, she found the suspense hard to bear. She was on the point of following her husband when she heard an approaching footstep. For a moment her resolution failed her and she pressed herself against the wall.

"Hello, darling. It's only me, not Gardiner!" He kissed her as he took the lantern from her hand, and she saw that he was smiling broadly. "It's better than I thought. It opens into the orchard by quite a little rabbit-hole. So small I can't think how Blakemore got through. But a bigger puzzle is how they managed to find their way down here."

"Let's go now, dearest," she pleaded. "When I get back I'll find out what they've been up to."

Waiting that afternoon in the room, which despite all Amy's labours was barely comfortable, his thoughts oscillated strangely from elation at finding the treasure to despair at his inability to profit by it. Amy's remarks were nothing but the truth. The chest might as well hold so much dirt and pebbles if he could not escape. With wealth enough to make them both rich half a dozen times over, he was still a prisoner. He resembled a shipwrecked sailor who, having found a gold mine, had neither tools to work it nor a boat to escape in. True, he had found the secret exit, but since Gardiner and Blakemore knew it also, what hope could he have that the police had not been told?

So the weary afternoon passed until Amy came. Her smile of greeting soon gave way to a troubled expression as she told him how Gardiner and Blakemore had broken open a wing of the house. This was a clear indication of their eagerness to find the treasure. But to Amy's mind the really bad news was that a messenger from Hay, the lawyer, was waiting to take back signed papers. What could this mean if not that Gardiner had bought the farm?

"And do you see what that means, Willie?" she went on. "Have you forgotten what you said that day when you told me—told me all about yourself?"

"Do you mean about the law of treasure-trove?"

"Yes. It belongs to the landowner, you said. I've been thinking of it all the afternoon. That treasure has been nothing but a curse to you. But for that you could have been in safety long ago. And now it is Gardiner's. And Willie, I don't care two pins for anything you may have done before we met. I mean that!"

He gave her a smile and a grateful caress. Then, after several minutes of thoughtful pacing of the room, his frown disappeared and he bent and kissed her upturned face.

"You're right, old girl. Just keep me on the straight and narrow."

CHAPTER 19

THE TRAP

FEW surprises have sufficient vitality to survive a night's rest, but the piquancy of Sanders' message seemed as great as ever at breakfast. The whole evening spent in discussing it and a restless night being kept awake by it had left Gardiner and Blakemore still puzzled.

Punctually at nine came a knock at the door, and Gardiner opened it to admit Sanders' representative. As the two men rose and bowed to her, she enquired of Gardiner in tones as cool as though they had never met before, "Will you see Mr. Sanders now?"

Her self-possession was admirable. Gardiner replied in the affirmative with equal composure and added, "My friend Mr. Blakemore would like to come with me."

With a mere inclination of the head, Amy withdrew. The others silently followed her but, as she opened the door of the lumber room, they exchanged a meaningful glance.

Entering the room ahead of Blakemore, Gardiner was aware that his overnight reflections had failed to solve the delicate problem of just how to greet Sanders, but that gentleman settled the matter by his opening announcement. Taking Amy's hand, Sanders said, "First, gentlemen, let me introduce my wife!"

The ice being thus thoroughly broken and, despite some remaining resentment, relieved to find Amy's position assured, Gardiner without hesitation took the hand that Sanders offered. Blakemore followed suit in more boisterous fashion, voicing the congratulations that Gardiner did not trust himself to utter.

"And now," Sanders said, "if you'll be good enough to sit down, I'll tell you why I asked you to come here." He wasted no time in preliminaries but told the gist of his story in a few terse sentences.

"Well, I'm dashed!" said Blakemore. "We were nearer to the treasure yesterday than we thought."

"You were indeed," said Sanders with a grin. "Of course you know," he added frankly, "my position here is a difficult one. I owe it to my dear wife that I have escaped arrest so far. She brought me here the night before you arrived, but I must now get away. The moment I've handed the treasure over to you I must disappear, and I want you to forget you have seen me here."

"You need have no fears on that score," Gardiner said, glancing towards Blakemore for confirmation. "But let me be equally candid. The position is even graver than you think." And he related his meeting with Saxby.

"Then don't let us waste time now," said Blakemore, rising and ushering them through the pilaster door.

Sanders led the way with the lantern, Gardiner followed with Blakemore close upon his heels, and Amy came last with the cycle lamp. The trap called a halt, for it was too interesting for even the impatient Blakemore to ignore. But a minute or two later the passage echoed with their footfalls again.

Once the chest had been reopened Blakemore was in his element. As the golden vessels were taken out one by one and set upon the floor, he handled them lovingly and explained the function of each. The barrel-shaped casket which held the spoons was, he explained, a reliquary; the hand-bells, chalices and other furniture were spoils from countless churches, as were the larger rings—too huge for any but the fingers of a statue.

"What is the money?" Sanders asked when the heap of coins was reached.

Blakemore took one of the thinner ones with the twin busts upon it. "This seems to be a coin of Ferdinand and Isabella—twenty escudos, worth about two pounds sterling; and this," as he exchanged it for one of the thicker kind, "is a pistole, a double one, I think, of Phillip II. They are all in fine condition, newly minted by the look of them, and probably taken from some galleon on its way to the Spanish colonies."

"Have you counted them?" asked Gardiner.

Sanders shook his head. "Hopeless to try unless you're willing to spend several days over it. Better take a bushel measure to them for the present!" He stooped to tug at the three heavy gold wedges, and managed with difficulty to drag one of them out.

"See that roughened surface?" said Blakemore. "That means the molten metal was run into sand moulds. They must weigh about half a hundredweight at least. In other words—let's see—yes, over three thousand pounds each! There's probably ten thousand pounds in gold bullion alone."

"What do you put the total value at?" Gardiner asked him.

"Of the whole chest?" Blakemore repeated. "Of the treasure as we see it? I don't suppose I should lose much if I were to offer you fifty thousand pounds for the lot. The stones are certainly worth that, and the rest of the things, as works of art, perhaps as much more, but I was only placing a melting-pot value on them." He paused. "Well, here's the 'Queen's Treasure,' just as the inventory described it. It would be interesting to know how much blood was spilt and how many Spanish ships were sunk before Drake collected it all. This is only a small part of what he got—only the cream of it, skimmed off for Elizabeth. Perhaps it's as well we don't know all the murder and brutality it represents."

A long and thoughtful silence fell, broken when Gardiner turned to Sanders. "Would you be satisfied to take the gold wedges?"

Sanders looked from him to Amy and back again. The gold wedges? Ten thousand pounds? As settlement for a treasure to which he had absolutely no claim? He was struck speechless. In his wildest dreams he had not imagined anything approaching such wealth. After his treachery and fraud, he would have settled for his liberty.

Gardiner spoke again. "Ten thousand pounds represents only a fifth to a tenth of the whole. Don't hesitate to say so if you don't think it a fair offer."

"Fair!" exclaimed Sanders at last. "It's more than fair! Amy, you tell him."

"It's too generous, Mr. Gardiner," said Amy. "He cannot take it." She looked frankly into Gardiner's face, and he dropped his eyes.

"Nonsense!" Blakemore interrupted. "This is no time for sentiment. We're talking business now. Gardiner is indebted to you for finding the treasure, and any fair-minded man would say you were entitled to part of it. We've got an idea what the value of the gold is, but as to the other things, it may take years to value them exactly. It would never do to flood the market with all those stones at once, to say nothing of the awkward enquiries that might follow."

Sanders and his bride stood silent in the lamplight, not fully convinced by Blakemore's arguments.

"Then," exclaimed Gardiner, seeing Sanders and Amy hesitate, "if you won't take it for yourself I must ask Mrs.

THE TRAP 223

Sanders to accept it as a wedding present."

Before Amy could protest, Sanders interposed. "All right, then, but on one condition: that you, Mr. Gardiner, reserve a thousand pounds of it to send out to Lewis in Sekondi, in my name."

"That I will, and gladly," said Gardiner heartily.

"But he can't carry a hundredweight and a half of gold about with him," objected Blakemore, always practical. "You must give him value in cash."

"Yes, I can have a letter of credit sent to any firm you name."

Sanders looked from Amy to Gardiner. "My plan is to get to Buenos Aires or Rosario, and then on to Paraguay. I can give you no address at present."

Blakemore pointed out a difficulty. "To reach even Buenos Aires, he must get away from here first!"

Even Amy, for all her anxiousness, joined in the laughter that followed. There was no constraint among them now; they chatted familiarly together like old acquaintances.

"We must hold a council of war presently," Blakemore continued. "But the thing to do now is to remove all these things to a place of safety."

"Surely this is safe enough," said Gardiner.

"Not if Saxby found his way down here!" Sanders warned.

"How about the disused wing, then?" Gardiner suggested. "We can lock them up there, and if they are seen we can pass them off as just more rubbish."

"Yes, for some things," Blakemore agreed. "At any rate the cups and the bulky things could be mixed up with the furniture and the odds and ends, but the bullion and the stones had better be put in our trunks." He turned to Sanders. "Where is this door you spoke of?"

Sanders opened the moat passage, and Blakemore carefully examined the door. "All for the benefit of the priest," he observed. "He would come down from his hiding place through the little door over there. Afterwards, when he had celebrated Mass in the vault, he could go back the same way. Even if he were surprised, which isn't likely, he had plenty of escape routes, either through the moat passage or up the stairs the way we came, or into the priest's chamber itself. Sir Medway evidently could hear Mass as often as he liked."

"We shall need some lights to get up through the priest's room," Gardiner observed.

While Amy went off with the cycle lamp to fetch candles, the three men collected all the plate by the false door. From that point Sanders and Gardiner, with many a journey up and down the ladders, carried it to the rooms above. Blakemore worked hard to clear the chest, and Amy produced a dozen little meal-sacks for the coins, rings and uncut stones. The silver bars and sword hilts engaged the four for but a single journey, but the gold wedges were another matter. After many ideas had been tried and rejected, Sanders took them in separate journeys in a small leather suitcase of Blakemore's. This was slung by a stout strap across his shoulders, and Gardiner, behind him, supported some of the weight.

At last the chest was empty and the lid back in place, but it was nearing one o'clock before Blakemore and Gardiner had cleared out their trunks and stowed the treasure safely in them, and joined the other two in the lumber room.

"Now, Sanders, have you any plans for getting away from here?" Gardiner asked.

"I had thought of taking the mule-cart into Strood tonight, putting it up there and taking the train to London. But from what you say about Saxby, I fear that won't do."

"It certainly won't," said Blakemore. "Even if you got the cart out without being seen, you'd be stopped before you cleared the district."

THE TRAP

After some discussion, animated at times, it was decided that Sanders should escape on Gardiner's bicycle, which Amy would leave ahead of time at an abandoned shepherd's hut nearly a mile away.

At that point, Blakemore was ready with another objection. "I don't think it is at all a good plan," he said, "to take the train at Strood. The station might be watched. Why go to London at all? My advice is to have nothing to do with the railway. Tell me, if you were going to Strood, is there anywhere you could turn off beforehand?"

"Only at Cuxton," said Amy, "and that is the Cobham Road."

"Better still!" cried Blakemore. "This is what I propose—lend us your notebook, Gardiner. See here, now." He sketched a rough plan. "This is the river: go along the west bank through—what's the name of the place?"

"Snodland?" Amy suggested.

"That's it! Snodland and some other villages—heaven-forsaken places all of them, with their factories and filth. On to Cuxton, then turn sharp off to Cobham, and from there it's only five miles into Gravesend. Put up there, cross to Tilbury by the ferry in the morning, and board the steamer to Ostend—they sail nearly every day. Once at Ostend you'll be pretty safe, but I shouldn't stay there long. Go overland to Lisbon. No one will look for you there, and the connections to Buenos Aires are excellent."

"Could we—should we go together?" Amy coloured as she asked the question.

"By all means!" said Blakemore emphatically. "If you went later, unless it were a very long while after, you would be watched and followed."

"I hope you don't think me ungrateful, either of you," said Sanders, looking from one to the other of the two men, "but I don't know how to thank you for all your kindness.

And as to you especially, Gardiner, I don't know what to say at all!"

"Then say nothing." Gardiner smiled. "But we must try and keep Mr. Siton at home at all hazards. Saxby is on his mettle, he told me as much, and he'll stop at nothing to get into the house. We'd better stay in and rest this afternoon, Blakemore. Then we'll be on the spot to deal with Saxby if he does manage to get in. Anyhow, Sanders, we'll see you again before we go."

It was with a light heart that Sanders awaited the coming of the night. The gain of two valuable friends, the prospect of beginning a new life with Amy in financial security, the amends he had been able to make: all these coming at once had revolutionised his life. There was even the minor dividend of now being able to smoke a pipe for the first time since his imprisonment here, for if Mrs. Siton smelt it, she would no doubt credit it to Gardiner or Blakemore.

At dusk Amy paid him a flying visit and reported all quiet. She was on her way to get the cycles out and had come for Blakemore's lamp.

As the time drew near, Sanders lost some of his equanimity. He changed his clothes, then walked nervously about the room, fidgeted with the pilaster spring, and looked repeatedly at his watch. He was smoking a final pipe by lantern light when footsteps sounded outside and someone knocked at the door. He jumped to his feet and tiptoed to the door.

"Can he have gone already?" said a voice—Gardiner's!

"I haven't had a smoke for four days," Sanders grinned, as he let in the two visitors. "Pardon the fug."

They were talking together in low voices when Amy suddenly appeared, ill at ease.

"What's the matter?" enquired Sanders. "The cycles?"

"They're all right—at the shed. But I saw father walking through the yard!"

THE TRAP

"You must be off at once!" said Blakemore.

"Better both go this way." Gardiner pointed to the secret door.

"Come on, Gardiner," cried Blakemore. "Let's find Siton and keep him occupied!"

A rapid handshake and the two hurried off. As Sanders seized the lantern, it toppled over and the light went out.

"The matches, Amy? Where did you put them?"

In the darkness and confusion several moments went by before the matches could be found. Just as Sanders was striking one, a hand fumbled at the door.

"Why Amy, what ye doing here?"

Amy rushed forward. "One minute, father, I'm changing my dress." She pushed the door closed.

"Don't light the lantern," whispered the girl. "There was someone else there!"

"Quick, then!" He felt for the pilaster and held it open for her.

"No, no! They've seen me! I must stay here."

"Then I stay too!"

"For God's sake, go!" she whispered urgently. "I can get out the other way. Go now, and set the trap behind you." With all her strength she shoved him in, but before her trembling hands could close the door behind him, her father entered.

"Now then, Amy! Ain't ye done? What to goodness d'ye want to change in here for, in the dark, when ye've got your own room?"

Close behind came Saxby and another, larger man.

"Is there not a lady's maid here?" said the detective, with a quick, suspicious glance around. "I thought I heard voices."

His partner sniffed the air. A moment more, and he had picked up the pipe.

"Hot," he remarked.

"Does your daughter smoke, Mr. Siton?" Saxby asked, shooting a strange look at Amy standing before the pilaster.

The large man crossed the room and Amy sprang forward, but she was too late to move the bag which lay open at the detective's feet.

Saxby took her place at the half-shut door. Suddenly he bent forward, listening, and made a sharp exclamation. The large man ceased to turn the trunk over.

"This way, Jones!" cried Saxby. "I can hear him!" He seized the light from Siton and, tearing the door open, rushed through, followed by Jones. Amy and her father heard the sound of a fall, and Amy rushed from the room and collided with a man in the corridor.

"Have they got him?" It was Gardiner.

"No, they've fallen into the trap. Please let me go."

"You can't go by the back door. The house is surrounded. We were too late to stop your father."

"Oh, poor, poor Willie."

"Don't give up hope yet. But you must go the other way, through the priest's room."

He took her by the arm and hustled her round the corridor and along the gallery to the other side of the house.

"Will they see him outside?" she panted, as he helped her through the fallen partition.

"They're only on this side of the moat. Follow close."

"Where are we? I can't see!" She stumbled blindly through the false cupboard.

"Here, sit on this chair! I shan't be a minute. I'm going for one of those candles." He struck another match and raised the creaking lid of the chest.

She heard his footsteps on the ladder and was tempted to run back. The chamber, cramped and narrow with the sinister-looking chest at one end, filled her with renewed apprehension,

THE TRAP

and she bit her lip. Her old dread of Gardiner sprang up afresh. What was this gloomy place? Why had he brought her there? She rose and felt her way along the wall, but as she reached the cupboard a rattling sound came from the chest. A gentle light began to shine, and Gardiner reappeared.

"Not there!" he said. "Come over here. Can you climb down this ladder?"

Doubtfully, she walked towards him and peered into the chest.

"It's awkward, but the ladder is short and the steps are wide," he said encouragingly.

"But where does it go to?"

"To the moat passage. There's another ladder, and then some steps further on. I'll follow you as soon as you're down this one."

She took his hand and gamely tackled the ladder. He joined her at the bottom, raised the trap door and followed her again. At the winding stairs he went first. A few minutes more, and they stood together in the passage.

"See! He's got through all right." He pointed to the false door that stood open.

"Are they following?"

They listened. Not a breath broke the stillness. "The trap has delayed them. But come, we've still a little way to go."

At the moat exit he scrambled through the yew tree first and then turned to help her, but she was already by his side.

"Well," he said, and hesitated. "I'll go back now," he added at last.

Her face was turned away from him.

"Goodbye," he said huskily. "And God bless you."

Slowly she turned towards him. In the dim light he could see tears streaming down her cheeks. Touched, he bent over her.

"Amy," he whispered, for the last time.

With a sob, she reached up and drew down his head. A second more and she was gone, leaving on his lips the indelible sensation of her swift impassioned kiss.

CHAPTER 20

THE RIVER ROAD

SANDERS had no sooner passed into the secret passage than he repented of his stupidity. Why, he asked himself, had he let Amy persuade him to go alone? What matter that she had been seen? With the trap once set behind them, they would have been secure against pursuit. As it was, he was prey to all kinds of vague presentiments. So happy had he been with Amy during the last few days, he might have known it could not last. Now they were separated, a score of chances might part them indefinitely. But, as he hesitated, Siton's voice sounded through the pilaster, and he hurried to the trap. He stooped and felt along the floor for the blocks. Confound it! He could not budge them. The traffic of the morning had jammed them, and he was obliged to sit down and tug with all his might before they would slide back. But once free, the trap worked easily; the merest touch of his heel made it sink at once.

The sound of voices in the lumber room suddenly ceased. Before he could rise, Saxby and his partner had burst into the passage. He scrambled to his feet and faced them.

"Stand where you are," he cried, "unless you wish to die!"

Saxby stopped. He had no wish to be shot at point-blank

range, and in the dim light it was hard to see whether Sanders held a gun.

"I hold a warrant for your arrest," he said. "You can't escape; the whole house is surrounded."

"We shall see! Remember that I warned you not to follow me." And Sanders moved a step or two backwards.

"You're only making the case worse for yourself if you resist," said Saxby. "I tell you the game's up."

"Let's rush him," whispered Jones, just behind. He laid his hands on Saxby's shoulders and they rushed together, but at their first step the floor tilted beneath their feet, and Saxby fell with Jones on his back. Under their double weight the trap dropped instantaneously, and Saxby disappeared. Jones, higher up the plane, fell a little more slowly. For a moment or two he floundered, vainly clutching; then, with a groan that rang in Sanders' ears, he too slid swiftly down. The trap righted itself with a heavy thud, repeated at intervals as it continued to oscillate.

Cautiously, Sanders approached the trap and listened. No sound came from below. The lumber room was also silent. Amy must have got away. Had Saxby and Jones been alone in the house? Had they both been killed? He hoped not.

He lighted the lamp and pushed down the margin of the trap. Silence! He lay down and put his ear to the opening. Now he could detect a low murmur; they were talking! So both were alive and probably unhurt. Though the pit was deep, the sandy bottom was evidently soft. Serious injury would be likely only if the victim struck the wall on the way down.

He set the trap rocking and shot the bolts out. The gap that resulted allowed their voices to echo upward. Their cries would be heard when a search was made. The way had never seemed so long, the steps so endless as now. In his haste he took them in pairs, only to have his feet shoot off the slimy stone and the lantern pitch from his hand. He slid to the bottom in darkness. Badly bruised, with scratched and bleeding hands, he hunted for the lantern, but it had rolled into some far corner, and he gave up at last. Groping his way to the false door, he shook it open and limped along the further passage until the softer ground told him he was near the end. Here was his greatest danger! Crawling up the slope to the exit, he peered through the branches of the yew. No one was in sight. He crept out and swiftly glided between the trees in the moat. The further slope rose bare and coverless before him. He was about to climb when a slight sound made him pause. The silhouette of a man appeared above. Sanders dropped on his face and lay motionless for a full minute. When he looked up again, the man had passed on.

To linger here was foolish. He must risk the presence of other sentinels. He crawled up to the edge of the moat and glanced about. The man he had seen was at a distance, moving away. In front of Sanders lay a hedge. Stooping low, he ran and ducked beside it. It had been the right moment, for the lookout had just turned and was retracing his steps. Sanders waited till he had passed on, then, bent double, he ran behind the hedge and turned into the field beyond. One more and yet a third he traversed with a limping run, always in the cover of a hedge, and at last gained the hut.

It was only a tiny place, useless as a hideout. Within were two bicycles, Gardiner's spick-and-span from its recent cleaning. But Amy—where was she? Having regained his breath he wandered impatiently round and round the hut, scanning the distant prospect for any hint of her approach. His imagination travelled with her every step of the way: along the corridor, down the stairs by the hall door to the court, and then across it to the farm. The garden front was less direct but might save her from being challenged by the sentinel on this side. But that was useless, he remembered. Saxby had boasted that the house was surrounded. Could they indeed have stopped her? Nothing else could account for the delay. Or was she being followed? If so, did she know it, and was she leading them on, perhaps all round the farm, until she saw a chance to slip away? How could he help her? To return was suicidal: to go without her unthinkable. He could only wait.

A distant murmur came from the house. He walked back towards it. Voices—one of them a woman's! In frantic haste to help, he forsook the hedge and ran on recklessly. Abruptly the voices ceased. A figure skimmed across the field, nearer and nearer. Amy, trembling with excitement, flung herself into his arms and hugged him tight.

"Darling, darling," she panted.

"Are you all right? What went wrong?"

"It was Gardiner—"

"Gardiner!"

"Yes, he helped me escape. The whole place is watched! He took me through the priest's chamber and down the ladders to the moat."

"Those voices just now?"

"I was stopped by a man above the moat."

"I dodged him."

"Well, I ran right into him. He asked me who I was and where I was going. I told him someone was ill, and I was going to cycle into Shindlestone for a doctor."

"Did he believe you?"

"He wanted to know all about it, and then I remembered the trap. I told him one of the police had had a fall and was injured."

"Good girl! And . . . ?"

"He made off towards the house, and I ran on as fast as I could."

While they talked, they hurried back to the shed. Soon they had wheeled the cycles along the muddy paths to the road.

"Now, Amy, ride on. I'll overtake you in a minute."

"Come with me, Willie! They may be just behind us."

"No. There may be another patrol about. If you're alone, you'll have no trouble. Never fear. I'll catch you up before the first village."

She obeyed reluctantly. He stood and watched until her lamp had ceased to gleam upon the hedges, turning every few moments to look for pursuers. A mist had begun to gather, the hedges were being blotted out, and even the shed was being hidden fast. He mounted the machine and followed Amy's path. As he rode, it was clear something was wrong with the bicycle. It ran stiffly and, for all his efforts, he seemed to be slowing every minute. He got down and turned the cranks. They revolved stiffly, with a distinct grating sound. The bearings were dry; Gardiner must have forgotten to oil them after cleaning. Sanders felt in the tool-bag but found no oil-can. His luck was giving out. He must ride on at a snail's pace and trust to Amy's carrying some oil.

He pedalled on slowly as the machine squeaked in protest. Though he strained every muscle in his body he was going at little more than walking speed. He would be exhausted soon! He had just resolved to walk when a light shone full upon him out of the mist.

"Where's your light?" cried the other rider.

Sanders made no answer. To his dismay the other dismounted. "I want to speak to you," he called.

Whether this was another of Saxby's patrols or not, he was evidently a member of the Force. There was a gap in the hedge beside Sanders and another some dozen yards further on. He got down and ran behind the hedge with the squeaking machine. At the gap he stopped and, raising the cycle above his head, threw it with all his strength. It fell with a prodigious crash in the middle of the road and lay wrecked as the pursuing lamp approached. Sanders floundered through the hedge with as much rustling of the branches as possible, then doubled back quietly and entered the road again at the lower gap.

A cycle leaned against the hedge beside the remains of Gardiner's machine. A man in partial uniform stood in the gap, peering into the mist for any sign of Sanders. Clearly he did not think he could be far away after such a catastrophe.

Sanders hesitated. Should he tackle the policeman from behind? The man was of athletic build, and the outcome of a tussle on that slippery ground was by no means certain. As Sanders weighed the odds, the policeman solved the question by stepping further into the field. Now the hedge separated them. Springing to the machine, Sanders wheeled it into the road. His foot on the step, he was rising to the saddle when the policeman scrambled through the gap. He made a rush for his machine as Sanders desperately drove the pedals, but his foot caught in the wreckage of the other cycle and, as he fell into it with an oath, Sanders was already fading into the mist.

About a mile further on, he overtook Amy wheeling her machine.

"What a long time you were, darling! I was afraid I might get too far ahead."

It was a happy reunion. He laughed as he described his adventures and his borrowing of a new bicycle.

"We had better ride again now," she said presently. "I can see the lights of Snodland ahead."

"Then let me go in front."

"No, Willie, don't let's separate again."

"I only want to keep ahead of you until we get to Cuxton. We may be followed this time by someone who knows you."

THE RIVER ROAD

"Then let me keep you in sight," she insisted.

"Of course! But hang back when you see me talking to anyone. I want to ask the way to Strood more than once so as to leave a false trail. I'll wait for you beyond Cuxton."

Twice in Snodland Sanders asked the way to Strood. Near Halling a carter gave him the direction which he took in ostentatious haste. Outside Cuxton he stopped another cart, telling the driver he had to catch a train.

"At last, dearest!" Amy cried, as she joined him at the turning.

He put out the lamps. "Let's wait here under the hedge," he said.

Pressed close against the hedge and against each other with only an occasional whisper, they stood for several minutes. A gentle purr arose behind, lights flashed along the high road, and as a pair of cycles swiftly passed the turning, one rider spoke: "He can't be far ahead. We'll soon—"

"If they find me at Strood, they're welcome to me," he whispered as he hugged her. "Let's go."

He took the two machines and wheeled them past the few cottages dotted along the road. The friendly mist was beginning to thin. Moonlight struck molten silver from a pond beside the way. One after the other he slid the bicycles into the water.

That done, he turned to Amy with a smile. "We're safer so. Safe as we can ever be in England. Come, let's step out, two hours will see us there."

* * * * *

Night had fallen; the Southern Cross floated high above the horizon. The ship was silent, save when the saloon doors opened and a hum of talk ascended to the upper deck. There a solitary couple sat watching the phosphorescent wake. Far behind it stretched—so far it seemed it must reach to that land both were thinking of, the land they had left behind.

"Like a moonlit path," she said.

"Would you wish to travel back along it, if it were?" he asked.

Her hand sought his. "Someday, darling. With you."

THE END